AT THE WOLF'S DOOR

©2019 Chaz Osburn. All rights reserved. No part of this publication may be reproduced or used in any form or by any means, graphic, electronic or mechanical, including photocopying, recording, taping, or information and retrieval systems without written permission of the publisher. This is a work of fiction. Names, characters, businesses, places, events and incidents are either the products of the author's imagination or used in a fictitious manner. Any resemblance to actual persons, living or dead, or actual events is purely coincidental.

Published by Hellgate Press
(An imprint of L&R Publishing, LLC)
Hellgate Press
PO Box 3531
Ashland, OR 97520
email: info@hellgatepress.com

Interior & Cover Design: L. Redding

Cataloging In Publication Data is available from the publisher upon request.
ISBN: 978-1-55571-941-8 (paperback); 978-1-55571-942-5 (e-book)

Printed and bound in the United States of America
First edition 10 9 8 7 6 5 4 3 2 1

AT THE WOLF'S DOOR

CHAZ OSBURN

To Raj — Thanks for your friendship!

Hellgate Press Ashland, Oregon

To Anna

FIRST ENCOUNTER
....

August 31, 1939
Canadian Rockies

IT WAS FIVE-thirty in the morning when the left front tire blew on Colin Williams' old Ford. He was angry, but he had no one to blame but himself. He'd been meaning to stop by the gas station near the lodge where he was staying to replace the tire in the trunk—the one that went flat last weekend—but just kept putting it off. There are always other priorities during a vacation.

Colin was not like the other tourists who came to the Canadian Rockies—not the rich ones, at least. He had driven his seven-year-old Model A from Halifax, Nova Scotia, to Jasper, Alberta—a distance of 2,300 miles—because it was cheaper than taking the train. It had taken five days, but money was tight. Already eighteen days into his twenty-eight-day military leave, the thought of spending even an hour on a routine task like waiting for a tire repair was depressing.

Colin shifted into first gear and nudged the old sedan as far off the rutted dirt lane that led to Patricia Lake as possible. He knew that his friend Daniel would be along in an hour or so and that he could wait—they had agreed to meet at the lake to fish at seven o'clock—but it was already light enough to see, so he decided to walk the two and a half miles to the lake. It didn't make sense to walk to Jasper, the nearest town, even though it was closer, because the only service station didn't open until eight.

Reaching into the back seat, Colin retrieved the container of coffee he had made on the hotplate in his room at the lodge. He placed it and a bottle of whiskey in a small canvas rucksack, put on his fishing vest, and picked up his fly rod. He was especially careful handling the rod. It was a gift from his father, given to him when he graduated from the Royal Military College of Canada six years ago.

Colin had few possessions—as a lieutenant in the Royal Canadian Navy who moved from base to base, he did not have the luxury of accumulating things—or the room to store them. But the Wright & McGill fly rod and matching case was prized, and did not take up much space. Light as a feather, with a gently swelled bamboo butt and lightly colored cane, the rod fit his hands perfectly. Each time he used it he had success. And each time he used it, he was reminded of the times he'd spent fishing with his father on Bras d'Or Lake near Baddeck, Nova Scotia, where he grew up.

Remember what Dad would say, he told himself. "*The worst day fishing is better than the best day working.*" Flat tire or not, he was determined to have a good day.

Colin did not bother locking the car. There was nothing of value inside, and it was unlikely that anyone but Daniel would venture up the lane for hours. He was much more likely to run into a moose, big horn sheep or an elk than another human being. Which was perfectly fine. He had not come here to be with people—other than Daniel, his best friend since childhood.

The road to Patricia Lake is breathtakingly beautiful in late August, just as the aspens between the pines change from green to bright gold to signal the end of what are always amazingly short summers. While Colin had spent all twenty-eight years of his life in Canada and was used to cold and snow and short seasons, he found springtime and fall in the part provinces most delightful. Each season was like watching a film using time-lapse photography. In the spring it was possible to actually *see* a flower sprout from the ground and grow an inch or two in a day. In the autumn a tree could have green leaves one morning and yellow leaves the next.

Overhead, an eagle appeared from above the pines and headed in the direction of Patricia Lake. Colin stopped, pulled a pack of cigarettes from his shirt pocket, lit one, and took a long draw as he watched the bird catch the upwind. Then, putting his head down, he began a brisk walk up the twisty mountain road. With any luck he would be at the lake by six-fifteen. That would give him time to build a fire on the beach, assemble his fly rod and reel, and have a snack. There might even be time for a whiskey and coffee before Daniel arrived.

As he made his way along the road, a fawn and its mother appeared from the woods and stopped when they saw Colin. Colin guessed that the fawn was probably only a few days old, and likely had never before seen a human. He marveled at how tiny it was and how the animal's spots were so large and pronounced.

The adult deer lifted her nose and turned her head to the right. A moment later she was off, her baby close behind.

The morning grew lighter as Colin trudged along, until it became so bright from the sun overhead that he stopped again, this time to retrieve a pair of sunglasses from his pack.

It was then, kneeling in the gravel, Colin had the sensation that he was being watched.

What a ridiculous notion. There are no people around.

Still, he could not ignore the sensation. *I'm definitely being watched.*

Removing the cigarette from his lips, he let out a slow exhale and scanned the surroundings. It was hard to make out what was in the woods. He initially dismissed the shape under a large fir tree about thirty feet away, but something in his brain told him to look at the object again. This time more closely.

A lump arose in Colin's throat when he realized that what he had seen was a wolf—and its gaze was fixed firmly on him!

Colin did not move. Judging from the wolf's size, he guessed it was a year to a year-and-a-half old. The way it laid on the ground, with its front paws together, reminded Colin more of a dog than a wolf.

What a magnificent beast!

Colin continued to remain motionless, not because he was frightened—he could not explain why, but he did not fear the animal—but because he knew that a sudden move might provoke an attack. While on the small side, the wolf could inflict damage. An adult wolf may weigh as much as one hundred twenty-five pounds. This one looked as though it weighed about sixty-five.

Even that small, I could be in a world of hurt if it attacks.

Colin wished he had not left his pistol back at the lodge. The only thing even close to a weapon was a jackknife in the pocket of his fishing vest, but it was not large enough to inflict any damage, assuming the beast lunged at him and he managed to stab it through its thick coat.

Before he had died, Colin's father had taught him about wolves. He had learned, for example, that wolves have two layers of fur. The layer closest to the skin is thick and soft, and designed to trap air and insulate a wolf from the elements. The outer layer, the guard layer, is made up of long, coarse hairs that can shed water, ice, and snow. This is the layer that gives the wolf its color, which usually consists of a combination of white, gray, and brown. Such layering allows a wolf to remain relatively cool in the heat of summer—though in this part of Alberta, the temperature rarely rose above eighty degrees Fahrenheit, even on the hottest summer day.

Colin had seen wolves in the wild before and knew that, for the most part, they don't bother you if you don't bother them. For the most part.

The best thing for me is wait. Wait and not show fear.

Colin tried to remember all he knew about the animals. He was curious as to why this particular creature was alone. Wolves are generally social. They hunt together, eat together, sleep together, and travel together. It was rare to see one, especially a young one, by itself—even here, in the solitude of the Rockies.

There was no denying this particular wolf was one of the most beautiful animals Colin had seen in the wild. Gray and white, it was trim and sleek, but not skinny. In fact, from where Colin was kneeling, the white patch on the wolf's neck, shoulders, and back reminded him of a cross.

After waiting about five minutes, Colin was getting restless.

This is stupid. I'm not going to stay here all morning. I came here to fish. It's time to show this wolf who's boss.

With that he pulled his lighter from his pocket, lit another cigarette, and picked up a dead tree limb about the length of his arm from the ground. The wolf, whose eyes were still fixed on Colin, watched as Colin held the tip of the branch above the lighter.

Within seconds the branch smoldered before, with a soft pop, it caught fire. An orange flame appeared.

The wolf raised its front legs and shifted to a sitting position. As the dry branch popped and crackled and the flame grew, the animal cocked its head to the right and to the left.

Is it trying to figure out what I'm doing? Are wolves that intelligent?

"Ah, what's the matter, Mr. Wolf, don't you like fire?" Colin said aloud as he got off his knees.

The wolf cocked its head again.

"Oh, you know, don't you? You know about fire."

Though he was at a loss to explain why, Colin was convinced that the wolf now realized it was at a disadvantage. Colin considered flinging the burning stick in the wolf's direction but stopped himself at the last moment. The dry pine needles on the floor of the forest would catch fire quickly—to Colin's knowledge, it had not rained once during August—and there was a good chance he would not be able to put out the fire by himself before the forest went up in flames. His mind went to the worst-case scenario.

With my luck I'll probably start a forest fire and then the wind will shift direction and take the town of Jasper along with it. No thanks.

Colin had an idea. He set the stick down in the gravel.

"Hey, Mr. Wolf, you hungry?" he asked, kneeling again to peer inside his pack. The wolf opened its mouth, as though yawning, and started to pant.

"I know I brought it; it was in here yesterday," Colin continued. "Ah, here we go. *Ta dah!*"

He held up half a stick of salami that he had purchased two days before at the market in Jasper. After cutting a slice about an inch thick with his jackknife, he held it at arm's length.

The wolf stopped panting.

"Would you like this, Mr. Wolf?" Colin tossed the piece in the wolf's direction. It landed about six inches in front of the animal.

Initially the wolf did not seem interested. But then it rose and leaned forward to sniff the object. It looked at the meat, then Colin, then the meat.

"It's okay," Colin said, cutting a piece for himself. He took a bite. "See, Mr. Wolf. It's delicious; genuine Italian Genoa salami. Imported from Calgary."

Again, the wolf looked at Colin. Then the meat. It took a step and, in one quick gulp, the piece of salami was gone.

The wolf licked the outside of its mouth and yawned.

"Are we friends now, Mr. Wolf?" Colin asked. He cut another piece of salami and threw it in the wolf's direction. It landed about five feet short of the first spot, though that was not his original intention.

The wolf came forward and ate the meat. Colin was pleased. Any negative thoughts of what the wolf might do were gone.

"So what do you do for fun around here, Mr. Wolf? And where's the rest of your pack?"

The wolf sat on its haunches and looked at Colin, cocking its head. And then it did something Colin had not expected. It raised its nose into the air, closed its eyes, and howled.

Colin had heard wolf howls before, but only at night, and usually far, far away. "Incredible!" he exclaimed.

Colin suddenly felt a connection to the animal that he could not explain. He wondered whether he could coax the wolf to come even closer. He wanted the creature to know that not only did he not mean it harm, but that he also respected the wolf's place in nature, and appreciated having this encounter.

Colin cut an extra thick piece of salami and threw it deliberately short so the animal would have to rise and get it.

It did!

"Make sure you chew it this time," Colin said. "That's a fairly big piece. I don't want you choking."

The animal picked up the piece of salami in its teeth, chewed, and swallowed. Colin clapped his hands and said, "*Very* good!"

He was about to cut another piece of meat when, off in the distance, he heard the sound of a vehicle shifting. The wolf must have heard it as well, for in an instant, it bounded into the forest and turned to look in Colin's direction just as a black coupe rounded the curve in a cloud of dust. Then it disappeared.

Seeing Colin crouching in the middle of the road, the driver honked his horn and slowed the car to a crawl before bringing it to a stop beside him. With the engine still running, a door opened and a tall man in khaki pants and khaki shirt got out. He was wearing aviator sunglasses.

"Whatcha doing, building a fire so the rescue planes will find you?"

It was Colin's friend, Daniel Masters. A pilot in the Royal Canadian Air Force, he, too, had arranged for a four-week leave from his base in Kingston, Ontario, to come to Alberta to fish.

"No...long story, I'll tell you on the way to the lake," Colin said, as he carefully doused the fire with gravel.

"I saw your car back there with the flat tire. Don't tell me—you never took the first one in to get fixed?"

"Okay, I won't tell you," Colin chuckled, rising to put the sack back on his shoulder.

"Good thing I happened along," Daniel said. "Now come on, let's get going. We've got some fishing to do. When we're done we'll take off the flat and drop it off at the Imperial station. It'll still be open."

Colin complied, putting his gear in the now-open trunk of the car, and climbed in the front seat alongside his friend.

From the darkness of the trees, the wolf watched the two men. When the car was out of sight, the creature walked from the shadows and across the dirt road, then down the side of the mountain. It stopped when it reached a small plateau that was bathed in sunlight, looked around, and resumed walking until it came to the lifeless body of another, larger wolf. A truck had struck the larger wolf while it was crossing the

Yellowhead Highway at the base of the mountain the previous evening.

Seeing that its mother was dead, the smaller wolf sat down on its hind legs. A train whistle sounded in the distance. The wolf raised its head and howled.

PATRICIA LAKE
....

THE SMALLER OF the two lakes along Pyramid Lake Road, Patricia Lake is a boomerang-shaped body of water in Jasper National Park. Named for Princess Patricia of Connaught, a granddaughter of Queen Victoria, it was often ignored by the tourists because of its small size. They gravitated toward Maligne Lake because of its boat cruises and breathtaking hiking trails and the chance to marvel at nearby Medicine Lake, which is fed by the waters of Maligne. When the snow in the mountains melts, Medicine Lake fills with water, only to disappear in the fall and winter. The native people said it was because spirits controlled the lake. They had no concept of a natural underground drainage system.

None of that mattered to Colin or Daniel. They had been coming to the park for nearly a decade and a half, and had never been disappointed with the quality of the trout and mountain whitefish at Patricia Lake. That Patricia Lake was off the beaten path with the tourists was just fine.

Colin and Daniel first visited the lake during the summer of 1925, when Colin's father took both boys on their first train trip outside of Nova Scotia. Colin Williams Sr. had worked as a maintenance/handyman for Alexander Graham Bell. Bell died at his estate in Beinn Bhreagh (pronounced *Ban Vreeah*) in 1922, forcing the elder Williams to find employment elsewhere.

He landed a job at a forestry products company, which sent him to northern Alberta each year to secure supplies of wood to produce pulp for its North American paper customers. Because Colin Sr. was a man who liked to fish, he usually added a week of vacation to his trips to fish in the mountains. He had come to Patricia Lake on the recommendation of a local fishing guide in 1923 and was hooked on the lake ever since.

Colin Sr. had intended to take his son the following year, but the boy fell ill just before the start of the trip. The next year, however, with the permission of Daniel's father (Daniel's mother had died when he was young), the three made the trip from Halifax to Jasper aboard a magnificent Canadian National Railroad train.

The fishing did not disappoint the boys, who were almost fifteen at the time. Colin's father surmised that the fishing was fantastic because the fish in Patricia Lake had never seen an artificial fly before, much less a human being. He bragged that he could catch a fish using anything, and to make his point, he cut off a piece of an old hockey stick he had found and wrapped a lock of Colin's hair around it with yellow string. Within five minutes of casting he landed a one-and-a-half-pound rainbow trout.

But it was not fish Colin talked about on the way to the lake that August morning.

It was wolves.

"Do you actually think it was a good idea to feed that wolf?" Daniel asked, as he brought his car to a stop at the lake. "The last thing we need is a wolf hanging around."

"He won't be back," Colin said. He opened his car door, stepped outside, and stretched. "Wolves aren't like bears. It was a chance encounter—one I'm happy to say I had."

Daniel opened the trunk and unpacked his gear as Colin walked to an old wooden boat leaning against a tree and brought it to the ground.

"Animals are animals," Daniel continued. "You start feeding them and they get used to you. Then when they show up and you don't have food—*kchet*!" He ran his finger in a quick, straight line across his neck.

"I don't think you need to worry about that," Colin said. "If I were you, I'd worry more about getting out-fished today. Again."

"Pardon me—*out-fished*? Said the man who only caught, what was it, six yesterday? Seems I ended up with two more."

"Minnows don't count."

By now, Daniel had moved to help his friend push the heavy wooden boat to the water's edge. Though desperately in need of a paint job and new oars—part of the bottom of one of the oars was missing—the boat would allow them to get to the part of the lake where the fish would be at this time of day. It was in terrible shape, but well worth the two dollars and fifty cents Colin spent at the estate sale before leaving Halifax with it tied to the roof of his Ford.

Colin gazed north toward Pyramid Mountain, its peak capped with snow. "Just look at that blue sky," he said. The copper and gray colors of the mountain shone spectacularly in the sunlight.

Daniel stopped what he was doing. "Beautiful, isn't it?" he said. "I can't think of a place I'd rather be right now. It makes you forget about all the things that're happening in the world."

Colin said, "You know, if we could get Hitler, Stalin, Chamberlain, and Mussolini here, and give each of them a fishing pole, we'd have peace in the world."

"Yeah, that's going to happen," Daniel said. "You know as well as I do that it's only a matter of time…"

He did not finish. He did not have to. Both men were aware of the situation in Europe.

But on that day and at that time—seven o'clock in the morning on August 31, 1939—things could not have been more peaceful for the two men who stood alongside the calm waters of Patricia Lake.

What they did not know—what the world did not know—was that in just a matter of hours the Nazis would begin the invasion of Poland and set into motion the events that would thrust Great Britain and its Canadian ally into the Second World War.

* * * *

After six hours on the lake, Colin and Daniel each had caught nine trout. They also consumed all the coffee, the last of the salami, two packs of crackers, and more than half a bottle of rye whiskey.

They would later blame the whiskey for failing to notice that it was turning cold.

The weather in the Canadian Rockies in the latter part of summer can change rapidly. One moment the temperature can be in the seventies and the sun can be shining. Fifteen minutes later, a front of arctic air can swoop in from the northwest over the mountains and the thermometer can plunge to the forties as the wind kicks in and the sun disappears. It's one reason many of the tourist shops in the mountain towns of Jasper and Banff leave their sweater displays up year-round.

For Colin and Daniel, what had begun as a day with just the hint of a gentle breeze turned into one with a wind so stiff it produced greenish-brown whitecaps on the small lake—whitecaps that were almost a foot high.

Colin failed to notice the change until he realized that he had to keep rowing to keep the boat from drifting.

"We've got a front coming in," he said, as he worked to position the rowboat so the wind was at their backs. No luck. He knew he would have to work hard to get the boat closer to shore.

At a little over five feet nine inches tall and weighing one hundred sixty-five pounds, Colin appeared of average build in the baggy clothes that were the style of the day. But he had always been athletic and muscular and, after six years in the Royal Canadian Navy, was anything but weak. Still, after ten minutes of hard rowing, the boat had made little progress. Within a few minutes, Colin's shirt was drenched in sweat.

"Daniel, come up here and take the right side," he said, wiping his forehead with his arm. There was a tone of anxiousness to his voice. "Maybe between the two of us we can make more headway. We need to get closer to shore as quickly as we can."

Colin had been on a small boat on a lake when a storm had struck once before. He would never forget the experience. He was nine, and he and his father were on Bras d'Or Lake in Nova Scotia. He remembered how his father struggled with the oars that day, the water sloshing into the boat as the thunder crashed around them and lightning filled the sky. Colin was at the bottom of the boat, shivering in the wet and the cold. He was sure they would die, but somehow his father managed to reach the shore.

"It was the Heavenly Father, not me," Colin recalled his father saying afterwards. "God always answers prayer."

The image of that day was fresh in Colin's mind as he struggled with the oars.

Please, God, help us! he prayed. *Please don't let us die out here.*

With Daniel at his side, the two rowed in unison toward one of the lake's peninsulas. Though it meant turning the boat perpendicular to the wind, Colin figured that having to deal with a shorter distance was the better of two bad options. But the question was: could they reach it?

It was a bad choice. The boat capsized a little less than halfway to their target, sending both men into the frigid water.

"Oh my God, that's freezing!" Daniel yelled, coughing up water as he clung to an oar.

The shock of suddenly being in the water made Colin forget everything he knew about how to handle such a situation. Instead, he thought about the irony of the circumstances.

I can see the headlines now: "*Navy officers drown in boating accident.*"

Daniel's voice brought him back to reality. His friend was in trouble.

"Colin! Help!"

Colin was about four feet away but it may as well have been forty. The waves were relentless. Somehow he reached out with his left arm and grabbed the oar Daniel clung to. He pulled hard until Daniel was at his side.

"Kick with me, buddy!" Colin commanded, setting off in the direction of the boat, which was drifting away.

"It's bloody freezing!" Daniel coughed.

His friend was right. The water was cold. Ice-cold. Deadly cold. He knew they would not be able to last more than a few minutes, and that they had to reach the boat and pull themselves up onto it if they hoped to survive. He also knew that they had to keep calm if they wished to live; they could not give in to panic.

"This is why I picked the air force," Daniel said. "I can't stand the thought of drowning."

Colin tried to laugh at the joke. "You're not going to drown," Colin said between the waves. "Just keep kicking. Just keep kicking. Just keep kicking."

He knew that concentrating on one goal at a time would help them survive.

When they finally reached the boat, Colin and Daniel's fingers were so numb they could hardly bend them. Each man tried to find something to grasp onto in order to pull himself up, but their attempts only made them more tired. To make matters worse, every now and then a wave would lift the boat slightly and the boat would crash into the side of Colin's head.

Oh, God, please don't let us die, Colin prayed again. *Not today. Not like this. I'll do anything you want me to do. But please don't let either of us die. Please!*

At that, a strange sensation overtook Colin. Suddenly he was sleepy and imagined himself snuggling under the blankets of a warm, cozy bed on a cold night.

Just then there was the crack of thunder. Colin shook his head. He had to think clearly.

I can't give up. I just can't end this way.

"Danny,"—he had not called his friend that since they were kids—"come over here and climb on my back!" Colin was so exhausted he was not sure how much longer he could tread water. If they were going to save themselves, they had to act now.

Daniel made his way as best he could along the side of the boat until he was at Colin's side. His lips were blue and his teeth were chattering. Spitting a mouthful of water, he placed his boot on Colin's left hip and raised himself about eight inches. As he did so, the weight of his body pushed Colin under the water.

Resurfacing, he saw Daniel at the side of the boat.

"I...I...there's nothing to grab hold of," Daniel said. "The bottom of the boat's too slippery."

That's it then, Colin thought. *This is the end. We'll be dead in a few minutes.*

Reason returned. *The hell this is the end—I am not giving up!*

"Try again!" Colin commanded, reaching the side of the boat. With both hands he grasped the side of the boat again and yelled, "This time get right on my shoulders. As...as high up as you can get!"

Colin felt one boot and then another. Again, the weight pushed him under and again, he was forced to let go. But then something strange happened. He became aware of something underneath the surface—something not there the last time.

He pushed down with his left knee first, then his right. Then he did something quite remarkable. It was the last thing either man expected.

He stood up!

Daniel did the same. "What the...? How is this possible?"

Colin ran the toe of his sock—he had kicked off both shoes as soon as he had been thrown into the water—and said, "It's slippery. Ice!"

They laughed. And laughed.

By now the wind was subsiding, and rays of sunlight streamed from the sky as though it were a screen. A noticeable change in the temperature followed. It was getting warmer. As quickly as the cold front had blown in, a warm front was taking its place.

"Come on, help me flip the boat," said Colin, using his fingers to comb back the thick mop of brown hair that had fallen past his eyes.

Neither man had any idea how large the sheet of ice floating just below the surface was. Though a bit mushy in places—the ice was weak and broke apart when heavy pressure was applied—it was stable enough to allow them to flip the boat over, though it took some effort.

"Where do you suppose this piece of ice came from?" Daniel asked, climbing into the half-swamped boat.

Colin thought back to what his father had said about prayer, though that was not what he told Daniel.

"Remember the guy we bought the bait from a couple weeks ago—the one who said the ice wasn't off the lake until, what, the first of June?" he said. "You gotta figure that in a lot of these lakes, some of the ice never totally melts. It just starts sinking. It's probably been like that on this lake for years.

Centuries. I don't think the lake ever really thaws. Summer is just too short and the water's too cold."

Daniel shivered. Still standing knee-deep in water, Colin unbuttoned his jacket and reached inside.

"I was saving this till later," he said, handing Daniel a flask. "Take a sip. You'll feel better."

Daniel obeyed and, when finished, smacked his lips. "Canadian Club?" he asked. "Not that swill we were drinking earlier," Colin said.

Colin flopped into the boat and handed his friend the one oar he could find.

Motioning Daniel toward the middle of the boat, he said, "You row with that, and I'll paddle with my free hand. We're about two hundred yards from the shore. If we both put our backs into it we can be there in twenty minutes."

As it was, it took a little more than that. The boat was heavy from all the water and therefore difficult to row. But at least the men were no longer shivering.

"Oh no!" Colin said, a look of disgust on his face as the boat reached the shore. "What?" said Daniel, who was gathering twigs to build a fire so they could warm themselves.

"Our fishing poles..."

THE SINKING OF THE *ANKA*
....

September 1, 1939, 4:30 a.m.
Baltic Sea, off the coast of Poland

CAPTAIN WOLFGANG EICHER looked through the periscope of his U-boat, codenamed UX-1, and studied the black shape of what he knew to be the Polish cargo ship *Anka*.

"Range?" he asked, resting his wrists on the arms of the periscope.

"Three hundred fifty meters, sir."

"Any sign of detection?"

"No, Captain."

"Slow to seven knots and prepare to surface. I want to come up right off her starboard bow. Position her at precisely one hundred meters."

Eicher backed away from the eyepiece and caught his reflection in the glass.

God, I look old—like my father. He was only forty-two when he died. Back then he seemed so...ancient.

Eicher was forty-four, though most of his hair had turned from blond to gray, and deep lines crisscrossed his face. Even his blue eyes, so intense with energy when he was young, seemed duller. It was understandable. The last two years had been emotionally draining. Losing his beloved Heidi after twenty-two years of marriage had been devastating. Cancer. He knew it would take years before that pain subsided.

That he'd had little sleep the past few months had not helped. The days he had spent at the shipyard at Kiel, working on the UX-1, had been long ones. No wonder he felt so old.

But Eicher would not have it any other way for the work had taken his mind off Heidi. And there was no denying that the UX-1 was an incredible boat. He knew he was fortunate to have been chosen to be its commander. He could not—would not—let the Fatherland down, pain or no pain.

Under the Treaty of Versailles, Germany was forbidden to have submarines. But Hitler had gambled correctly after coming to power that he could rearm and that no nation would stop him. As a result, the navy built dozens of smaller coastal service subs. German naval command surmised that other countries looked the other way because they knew such vessels had limited range and firepower.

While Hitler was pleased with the buildup, he wanted more. If Germany was to resume its rightful place as a global military power, Hitler had once told a gathering of admirals, it needed a larger, faster vessel with greater range and weaponry. Thus, the UX-1, the navy's best-kept secret, came to be.

Eicher embraced the vision. And today he could take solace in knowing that his work to create the world's first submarine capable of running—and attacking—for sustained periods underwater was a reality.

Yes, he could feel the days and months of loneliness and weariness in his bones, but being at sea again was good therapy. It had been too long. Far too long.

The captain pushed both handles up on the periscope and felt the boat rise gently, purposefully. Today marked exactly thirty days since the UX-1 had left Kiel, and he was grateful that the U-boat had experienced only a few problems during its shakedown cruise. The UX-1 was an excellent addition to the navy.

Eicher did not doubt that Germany would need weapons like the UX-1 if Hitler was to fulfill his quest for dominance. But there were others in command positions who were much more cautious, advocating instead for the construction of additional Type VIIs and Type IXs, the conventional submarines that would eventually become the workhorses of the Nazi U-boat fleet. Hitler was taking a gamble with the UX-1—but it was a gamble that Eicher knew would work in Germany's favor.

Eicher's years of submarining experience were critical to the UX-1's development. It was his idea for the U-boat's innovative snorkel system—another German first. The snorkel brought air to the boat's twin Daimler Benz diesel engines, each capable of producing twenty-two hundred horsepower, which, in conjunction with the sub's sleek design, allowed for a top speed of nineteen knots on the surface and an amazing twenty-one knots while submerged. And because she carried three times the batteries that were on a conventional submarine, the UX-1 could stay underwater for days at a time, providing power for pretty much anything. Other submarines—British, French, American, Italian, Soviet, and Japanese—spent most of their time running on the surface, submerging only when threatened. And then only for two to four hours.

Eicher was also proud of another technological advantage he'd helped develop—again, a German first. The UX-1 could communicate via radio while underwater. This was possible because of a buoyant wire antenna system, which was built into the snorkel.

Now it was time for the UX-1's next and final test. Eicher's orders were to sink the *Anka*.

The captain had proposed that the first test should be conducted against a military target—"she is, after all, a military vessel," he had argued—but he was turned down by

Karl Donitz, the head of the German U-boat Command, who also happened to be one of his closest friends. No, it had to be a merchant ship, Donitz argued. One that could not fire back in case something went wrong. Donitz assured Eicher he would get the chance to engage a military vessel soon, but not this time.

"Remember, my dear Wolf, the UX-1 is a prototype," Donitz had reminded him. "Things can go wrong."

Eicher's ears popped as the submarine's angle increased. He brushed his beard with his fingers and reached inside the pocket of his coat for a cigarette.

"Prepare to surface!" he said.

Okay, it's time for the next test. I know you won't let me down, Heidi. (He had named the boat after his first great love.)

A tall, thin figure with a gaunt face that had been standing beside Eicher turned and said in a low voice, "I don't understand, Captain. Why are we surfacing?"

Eicher looked at his first officer, Lieutenant Ernest Schopter, and smiled. "Did you not see the women and children on the deck yesterday?"

"Yah," said Schopter. "*So?*"

"So, we are the German Navy, Lieutenant. We are not barbarians. We do not kill women and children."

Schopter looked at the captain and tilted his head to the right. Eicher could tell by his expression that the officer was confused.

"We will still send that vessel to the bottom of the sea, Lieutenant," Eicher assured him. "But not with women and children aboard."

"Yes, Captain," the lieutenant acknowledged.

"Thirty-five meters!" a crewman called out. "Thirty meters. Twenty meters..." Eicher said, "Load torpedo bays one and two."

"Fifteen meters. Ten meters. Five meters."

"Torpedo bays loaded!"

The submarine listed sharply to the left for a moment, causing a few of the men to lose their balance and fall to their knees. But the boat quickly righted itself.

"Surfacing."

"Lieutenant," Eicher said. "Make a note to have the chief engineer look at the port diving plane again. It still sticks. And has any progress been made on the rat?"

A rat had been onboard since they'd left Kiel. Eicher was irritated because the animal had gotten into his private supply of smoked sausages, which hung in Battery Room No. 3.

"We have put some traps out but as yet no luck," the first officer said, moving to the ladder leading to the conning tower.

Eicher had seen the rat only once on the cruise, seven days previously. It darted out a doorway one night as he was making his way to his cabin. He wished he had been carrying his Luger with him, for he could have killed it then and there.

"Let the men know there is a week's leave to the crewman who brings me the carcass of that rat," Eicher said.

"Now surfacing!" a crewman called out.

Lieutenant Schopter pointed at three men in the control room and said, "You're with me. You there, Seaman Grubka—man the cannon."

The three gave the Nazi salute and began making their way up the ladder, along with Lieutenant Schopter. Eicher reached into his gun holster and checked to make sure there were bullets in his pistol. Grinding his cigarette out in an ashtray, he pulled his binoculars from a hook, put the strap over his head, and climbed the ladder.

The sky was orange when he emerged from the hatch and took the commander's position at the conning tower. The sea was calm.

He pointed at the freighter on his left. "Signal her to stop," he said.

A seaman at the signal lamp obeyed and sent the command. He waited a moment and repeated the message.

"No response, sir," Lieutenant Schopter said. "I believe they're ignoring us."

"Is that so?" Eicher said. Amused, he lit another cigarette. "Have Mr. Grubka fire a warning shot across the ship's bow," he said.

The first officer raised his arm over his head and brought it down quickly.

Seaman Grubka, who had been looking up at the conning tower from his position on the deck just below, turned and fired one round from the eighty-eight millimeter cannon.

"I would imagine that will get their attention, don't you agree, Lieutenant?"

"It got mine, sir."

"The vessel is slowing, Captain," said another crewman, who had been watching the *Anka* through binoculars. "Seven knots. Six knots."

"We can see, Seaman."

"Signal the captain of our intention to board," Eicher said.

At that, several men with rifles on their backs emerged from the aft deck hatch and unrolled and inflated an inflatable boat, which they placed in the water, and secured to the side of the sub with ropes. The sea was calm.

Eicher instructed Lieutenant Schopter to bring the UX-1 alongside the *Anka* once the boarding party was aboard. He climbed down from the conning tower, got into the boat, and finished his cigarette as the men rowed to a set of boarding stairs that the crew of the *Anka* had lowered. Off in the distance—perhaps fifteen miles away—Eicher could see the lights of the village of Karwia on the northern strip of Polish territory known as the Danzig Corridor. He knew from the intelligence reports that Gdynia, just south of Karwia in Danzig Bay, was to be the vessel's final destination.

He also knew that the *Anka* would never reach the port.

The group of Germans reached the ship and climbed the boarding stairs to the *Anka's* deck. Two of the German crewman located the room with the radio and disappeared to disable it. A short man with a bald head and red cheeks emerged from the doorway the crewmen had entered.

"*Sprechen sie Deutsch?*" Eicher asked.

"*Nein,*" the man said. He pointed at a flag fluttering in the gentle breeze above the bridge. "Polish."

I know you're Polish, asshole, Eicher thought. *I'm trying to figure out what language you do speak.*

"*Parla l'Italiano?*" Eicher asked in Italian. Again, the Polish captain pointed toward the flag. "English? Do you speak English?" Eicher said.

"Oh, yah!" came the reply. "I speak English good."

"*Gut,*" Eicher said. "Now we are getting somewhere. I take it you are the captain of this vessel?"

"Oh yah!" the man said. He smiled. "Captain Lech Kowalski. This is *Anka*. And who do I have the pleasure of addressing?"

"Captain Wolfgang Eicher of the *Kriegsmarine,*" he said, using the German term for German Navy. "My friends call me Wolf."

"Welcome aboard, Wolf," Kowalski said, stepping forward to shake Eicher's hand.

Eicher folded his arms. He said, "I'm sorry, you and I are not friends." He looked at his watch. It was five-fifteen.

"In fact," he continued, "as of zero four thirty, you and your country are enemies of the German Reich. I therefore must inform you that I am here to confiscate a portion of your shipment of diesel fuel in order to refill my own vessel. And then I'm afraid I must destroy yours."

"What?" Kowalski exclaimed. His chin almost dropped to his chest. He could not believe what he was hearing.

"How do you know what we are carrying?"

"My dear captain," said Eicher, not bothering to tell him that German intelligence had relayed a manifest of the *Anka's* cargo two days earlier, "it is my business to know such things."

Eicher turned to his crewmates. "Men, shoot anyone on their crew who refuses to aid in the refueling of our ship."

"Captain, I must protest!" the Polish captain said.

Eicher ignored him and nodded to one of the four men with rifles near him. The seaman lifted his gun and pointed it at members of the *Anka's* crew. His crewmates did the same.

"You heard the captain!" one sailor said.

"Captain Eicher, again...I must protest," said the Polish captain, who had begun to tremble. "I don't understand what you are doing. Are you trying to start a war?"

Eicher turned and stared at his counterpart with eyes that were no longer dim, but full of life. He spoke in a sharp, calculated tone.

"I am not starting a war. I am simply finishing one—one that has remained unresolved for the past twenty-one years."

* * * *

As the U-boat came alongside the *Anka*, additional German sailors emerged from the hatches. Those at the front of the ship stood and smoked as those at the rear helped pump fuel from the *Anka*.

Meanwhile, more people aboard the *Anka* began streaming from below decks as well. They included an assortment of men—some crewmembers, and others passengers—and women and children. Most stared in disbelief at the German sub that had come alongside.

Eicher listened. "What are they doing? Why are they here?" said one man. Said another: "I guess they just need some fuel."

* * * *

Some men are meant to be poets, some woodworkers, and some businessmen.

Eicher was meant to be a submariner.

The son of a fisherman, he was born at sea—on a fishing vessel off the coast of Cuxhaven, Germany, on the North Sea. His mother delivered two weeks early. She would joke that nothing would stop her son from going to sea.

Even before Eicher could walk, he would accompany his father on his fishing boat. As he grew older, and when not in school or on the family fishing boat, young Wolfgang could be found building ships. At first he made toy boats from walnuts, but his abilities grew. When he became a teenager, he built beautiful scale replicas of the famous German P-Liners, the *Palmyra* and *Parma*, from scratch.

Eicher's parents were not surprised when, at age eighteen, he enlisted in the navy. Shortly afterward, the Great War began, and he discovered the submarine corps. That is when he found his purpose in life.

As his men refueled the UX-1, Eicher scanned the faces of the women and children gathered on the *Anka's* deck. Suddenly he was drawn to a young woman. She had long blond hair, cheeks that reminded him of two pink roses in a snow bank, and beautiful blue eyes—just like Heidi when she was young. He guessed her to be about eighteen or nineteen years old, his age when he met Heidi. There was a heavy feeling inside his chest, so much so that he had to turn away. Pulling another cigarette from his pocket, he lit it and turned back toward the woman. She was watching him.

"What is your name?" he finally asked.

"Dorota," she said in a voice just above a whisper. Eicher could tell she was frightened. He did not want her to be scared. Not of him.

Glancing down at her midsection, he asked, "When is your baby due?"

"February."

Eicher said nothing else. He turned and walked down the boarding stairs along the side of the *Anka* to the waiting submarine. Moments later a seaman crawled out of the conning tower hatch and handed the captain a message, which he wadded up and tossed into the sea when he was done reading it.

It was forty-five minutes before the UX-1's fuel tanks were full and the other German sailors returned to the sub.

"We are ready, Captain," said Schopter, handing Eicher a megaphone. "Attention passengers and crew of the enemy vessel *Anka*," Eicher called out from his spot on the conning tower. "Today is a glorious day for the Führer and the Fatherland—a day that will be remembered for a thousand years. Today a grievous wrong is being righted."

He waited for his words to sink in.

"Less than an hour ago I received a message that the German battleship *Schleswig-Holstein* has commenced shelling the Polish garrison of Westerplatte Fort in the Danzig Corridor, an area that has effectively divided the German nation for the past two decades. Today that changes. You have thirty minutes to get to your lifeboats before I destroy this vessel."

Eicher could hear murmuring from the people gathered along the rail of the ship.

"I want you to tell your children and have them tell your children's children's children the great compassion the German Navy has shown you today," he continued. "For rather than losing your life, you have been given the chance to live. We have shown you mercy—true mercy. Not the mercy of the Treaty of Versailles."

He waited again.

Patting the side of the conning tower, Eicher added, "You have my beloved Heidi to thank for this mercy. It is Heidi who lets you live. Remember that."

He motioned his crew to go below. The crowd on the deck above him was scrambling for lifeboats. He tried to find the young blond woman he had spoken to. He could not.

Eicher made his way to the hatch and climbed down the passage, pulling the hatch closed as he did so. A few moments later, the UX-1 disappeared into the brackish depths of the Baltic.

Thirty-nine people—everyone but the captain—had made it safely to the lifeboats when the two torpedoes streaked from the depths of the sea and slammed into the side of the *Anka*, scattering the ship and its cargo of diesel fuel drums and tractor parts across the bottom of the ocean.

"The captain stays with the ship—always," the captain had told his pregnant daughter-in-law as he helped her into the lifeboat.

"It is the way of the sea."

KILLING HITLER

That evening
Jasper, Alberta

"HELL OF A DAY, Colin."

"That it was, laddie," Colin said to Daniel, as the two sat in a bar hours after returning from Patricia Lake. "That it was."

Colin smiled. *I sound just like my dad*, he thought. *He always said "laddie."*

Colin was proud of his Scottish roots. His father came to Nova Scotia in 1885 at age fifteen with four dollars and one suitcase of clothes.

"You get a flat tire," Daniel said, "you come upon a wolf; you almost get us killed."

Colin turned his mug of beer so the handle faced outward, took a sip, and wiped his mouth.

"I almost get us killed?" he said. "I? If memory serves me right, it was I who saved us."

Daniel's smile disappeared as he leaned forward and pushed his mug of beer toward Colin's.

"You think you-know-who was looking out for us today, my friend?" Daniel asked.

Colin did not answer immediately. It was approaching midnight, and he and Daniel had spent the last three hours drinking. Sometimes when Daniel was drunk he would try to bait Colin into debates about God's existence—something he did not want to do tonight.

"Who are you talking about?" Colin said.

"God, that's who."

"Could be."

Lifting his mug, Daniel shouted, "Then God save the king!"

Colin lifted his glass and took a drink, as did the other three bar patrons, before adding, "Where did that come from?"

"I dunno."

Colin looked at his friend. He could see that Daniel's brown eyes were bloodshot from the smoky haze that permeated the inside of the tavern.

"I think you're drunk," he said.

"I think *you're* drunk," Daniel repeated. And then, "I honestly thought that, when I joined the air force, I'd never see combat. I mean, even though that's all I've trained for. Now I'm convinced that it's only a matter of time."

Colin did not know what his friend was getting at. "Time for what?"

"Before we have a war. A goddamned, bloody, full-fledged war, that's what."

"Are you okay with that?"

Daniel sat upright in his chair and considered Colin's question. "Yeah, I guess I am. How about you?"

"I never really thought about it until the last few months, but yeah. I think it's about time someone put that little prick in his place."

"Hitler?" Daniel said, drawing closer.

"*Ya voult*. Nobody's had the guts to stand up to the guy."

Daniel leaned forward even more. "You should have killed him when you could. Saved us a lot of trouble."

Yes, I should have, Colin thought. *I had the chance—three years ago, during the summer of 1936. After the Olympic Games in Berlin. There was Hitler, standing in the back of his Mercedes, saluting the masses—not more than eight or ten feet away. Everyone around me was enthralled, hypnotized. No one would have noticed me pulling out my pistol. I could have easily shot him—killed him. And the weird thing is that's what the voice inside my head was saying, "Take your pistol out and kill him." It seemed so real, but it made absolutely no sense. At least not then. Was that some sort of message from above? Did I miss it? Was I was brought into this life only to miss what I was really supposed to do—kill Hitler?*

"Hey, are you listening?"

"What?" Colin said.

"I thought so," said Daniel, finishing his beer. "I said I'm going to go up to the bar and get us a couple more. You in?"

"I'm in," said Colin, draining his mug.

They stayed at the tavern until closing time at midnight, unaware that on the other side of the globe the Second World War was just beginning.

RENDEZVOUS AT SEA

The Baltic Sea

NEARLY TWELVE HOURS after the sinking of the *Anka*, the UX-1 surfaced at its prescribed rendezvous point eighty-five miles south of Gotland off the coast of Sweden, and pulled alongside a smaller U-boat flying the flag of Nazi Germany from its stern. The sea was calm, with just a gentle rhythm of waves, and the water reflected the fading sun of late summer.

Captain Eicher was the first of three men to emerge from the UX-1's conning tower hatchway. He stopped to inhale the warm salt air, which tasted wonderful. There was something about the scent of the sea that he had always found appealing, and he was grateful for moments like this, drinking in the natural air after hours underwater.

Despite its remarkable technology and ample space, conditions aboard the submarine were not always perfect. Things often did not work as they were designed. There were leaks, and occasional electrical failures, and the re-circulated compressed air the crew was forced to breathe always contained just a hint of a stale odor the chief engineer had been unable to track down. Eicher believed the rat that had been eating his sausages was the cause. The chief engineer, however, was convinced that there was a faulty relay in the ventilation system.

Eicher searched the conning tower of the other sub and spotted the man he was to meet: his friend, the commander of the German U-boat service, Karl Donitz. It had been weeks since they had last seen each other.

"*Heil Hitler!*" Donitz shouted, his arm extended in the Nazi salute.

"*Heil Hitler, Fuhrer der Unterseeboote!*" Eicher shouted in return, adding Donitz's formal military title—leader of the U-boats—to his greeting. "It is a glorious day for the German Navy."

"I take it your mission was successful, Captain?"

"Quite," replied Eicher, reaching over the conning tower to pat its side as though it were a pet. "She is a fine boat. A fine boat indeed."

"Good, good. So come aboard and join me in a glass of bitters to celebrate."

"I will be right there, sir. But first, I have a gift for you."

Eicher disappeared down the hatch. It took several minutes to reach Battery Room No. 3, at the lowest level of the sub. It was in this room that Eicher kept several large sticks of venison sausage that he had made just before coming aboard.

Like ham, venison sausage tastes better if allowed aging time, and the dark, dry battery room provided the perfect conditions. The sausages were each about a foot long and three inches in diameter. Eicher felt one—he wanted to make sure it was nice and firm—and then another, before making his selection. He took out his jackknife and cut the casing where two of the sausages joined, then tied off the end of the one still hanging before heading back. He knew Donitz loved his homemade sausage.

Donitz was alone when Eicher returned topside and boarded the smaller sub. "Is that what I think it is?" Donitz asked as Eicher climbed the ladder to the conning tower where he was positioned. Eicher used one hand to climb; the other held the sausage.

Donitz didn't wait for an answer. "*Wunderbar!*" he exclaimed as his friend drew closer. "*Wunderbar!*"

It was not Donitz's nature to laugh. He almost always appeared serious, as though he were concentrating on solving a complex problem—which many times he was.

Extremely intelligent, with eyes that penetrated from his round head, he also had a very high forehead—almost freakishly high—which he was particularly conscious about. So much so that he preferred to wear his naval cap whenever possible, to make it seem less noticeable.

The two men shook hands, then embraced and patted each other's back before going below to Donitz's cabin, where the commander shut the door and pulled out one of two chairs for Eicher to sit on. He produced two crystal glasses, a bottle of bitters, and a knife and cutting board from an overhead cabinet. As he took the cap off the bitters and filled the glasses, he motioned for Eicher to cut the sausage, which he did.

Donitz raised his glass and said, "To the Fuhrer."

Eicher rose and bowed his head. "The Fuhrer."

They each drained their glass and ate a piece of sausage. "Your best batch yet," Donitz said between bites.

They sat in silence until Donitz said, "So my friend, it is only a matter of time now..."

He did not have to finish. Eicher understood what he meant. The Germans had unleashed their *blitzkrieg*—lightning war—on Poland. The English and the French would certainly come to the aid of their ally. That meant within days, perhaps hours, the two countries were almost certain to be at war with Germany—if they weren't already.

"It's too bad, really," Donitz continued. "The timing does not work in our favor. But the Fuhrer is not one who likes to wait."

Again, Eicher knew what the commander meant. U-boat command needed more time—a year or two at minimum—to build up its fleet so it could overwhelm the British and French and, at some point, the Americans, all at the same time. The German Navy possessed only fifty-seven submarines, the majority being Type IIs and Type IXs. Those would be okay for coastal warfare, but were not designed for prolonged use in the Atlantic, where both Donitz and Eicher knew the war at sea would have to be waged.

There were only twenty-two Type VII U-boats, the kind Eicher was aboard now, dispatched to the Atlantic fleet. And while more were being built each week, both Donitz and Eicher knew that what the navy really needed were a couple dozen of the new electroboats like the UX-1, assuming the boat continued to perform well. It would be years before that were possible, however.

"I understand you surfaced before sinking the Polish freighter," Donitz said, pouring two more glasses of bitters.

How could he know that? Eicher wondered. *Unless...of course, the Gestapo has seen to it that I have a spy aboard. Who could it be? Schopter?*

"There were women and children aboard, Karl."

"I was not informed of that."

"I didn't know either until I saw them on deck Thursday. I gave them time to disembark before I sank her. But I must point out that we were submerged at the time we fired our torpedoes. As far as I am concerned, I carried out my orders. The test was successful."

"And how has the boat functioned thus far?"

"Extremely well," Eicher said. "I am already working on a list of design changes. For example, if we mount a turret gun in the conning tower rather than on deck, I am sure we can improve the hydrodynamics and pick up one or two knots while submerged."

Donitz listened intently. Eicher was his protégé. No one understood submarine design or submarine warfare better—with the exception of himself, of course. That Eicher had already found a way to improve on the design of one of Germany's most advanced weapons did not surprise him. His grasp of submarining was exceptional, if not a gift. It was an awareness that Donitz had first recognized during World War I as the commander of UB-68, and Eicher was a fresh recruit. In those days, U-boat commanders had few rules to guide them. They were at the mercy of the weather, the operating range, and limitations of their vessels—and the luck of being in the right place at the right time.

The navies of the world—notably the German, French, British, and to some extent, the Americans—learned what a powerful weapon a submarine was during World War I. So, they adapted their defenses to accommodate the threat. The British were the first to use airplanes with torpedoes to combat U-boats. Because German U-boats, like any submarine of the time, attacked from the surface and needed time to submerge, a quick-witted pilot could drop a torpedo and destroy a sub before it could get deep underwater. Even if the sub could submerge in time, its range was limited, and it was nearly impossible to maneuver away from depth charges.

It was a depth charge that so heavily damaged the UB-68 that he, Eicher, and eleven other survivors of the crew were on when they were taken prisoner by the British in 1918. They spent the remainder of the war in a prisoner of war camp.

With no war to fight, Donitz and Eicher did not waste their time. They talked constantly of ways to improve submarine performance and worked out a variety of offensive and defensive maneuvers, including a radical new tactic that Donitz called *rudeltaktik*.

Donitz came up with the idea after Eicher shared a story about hunting with his father when he was a boy. The two were in a forest during the wintertime; there was heavy snow on the ground. Coming up a rise to a clearing, they watched as a pair of wolves worked in unison for several minutes to lead a large doe to a clearing where the remainder of a wolf pack waited and pounced on their prey.

Rather than having each submarine fight on its own, Donitz reasoned that a coordinated attack using radio would enable just a few subs to sink a large number of ships—even those with military escort.

Eicher's new boat would make *rudeltaktik* even more effective because it did not have to surface or come close to the surface to fire, or even to radio orders. And the UX-1 could quickly maneuver away underwater and remain there for days if necessary should any enemy surface ships try to attack with depth charges.

After Eicher had given Donitz a rundown on how the sub had operated during its shakedown, he asked, "Has the Fuhrer given any more thought to making the electroboats a priority?"

"No, I'm afraid not," Donitz said. "The *Bismarck* and the *Tirpitz* are at the top of his list right now."

The *Bismarck* and the *Tirpitz* were battleships, the largest vessels of their kind. They, too, were forbidden under the Treaty of Versailles; but again, the Fuhrer did not give a damn about what was allowed and not allowed under the treaty, and had calculated that he could build them and the world would do nothing to stop him. Launched in February 1939, it would be several more months before the Bismarck was battle-ready. The *Tirpitz* was not scheduled for launch until 1941.

"Do you think the Fuhrer is right about this?" Eicher asked. He already knew the answer before he asked the question, but he wanted Donitz's verification. For Hitler, perception and power went hand in hand. Possessing two of the largest, most technologically advanced behemoths prowling the oceans could not help but send a shiver down the spine of anyone—even though he and Donitz knew submarines like the UX-1 were the way of the future.

"Is the Fuhrer *right?*" said Donitz disbelievingly. "Is the Fuhrer right? If there is one thing I have learned after five years of knowing the man, it's that in comparison, we are all pipsqueaks to Adolf Hitler. You know I don't believe in God. But I do believe in the Fuhrer. He has once again made Germany great."

He's absolutely correct, of course, Eicher thought. *The Fatherland owes Hitler its gratitude—its very lives. The Fuhrer has done so much, while others have done so little but talk. The German people were beaten down emotionally and financially after the war—and unjustly. Germany did not lose the war; at best, it was a stalemate. But the world humiliated Germany afterwards, stripping it of its rights, its assets, its dignity. Yes, that's what Hitler had done, restored the dignity of the German people. He was right; we are a people born to lead, and the German way not only is the right way, it is the ONLY way. The rest of the world will pay for humiliating the German people. France, England and all its allies, even the United States if it goes that way, must be brought to their knees for this injustice.*

"Heil Hitler," said Eicher, rising.

"Heil Hitler," Donitz said. He poured two more glasses of bitters, lifted his glass and said, "The next time we see each other, Germany will officially be at war. We must strike quickly and we must strike often. It is the only way to compensate." He waited a moment before adding, "Here's to good hunting."

"To good hunting," Eicher said. "It's time to set the wolves loose."

ORDERS FROM OTTAWA
....

September 1, 1939
Jasper, Alberta

THE KNOCK AT the door came just a few minutes before noon.

Almost twelve hours had passed since Colin and Daniel stumbled out of the bar in downtown Jasper and drove back to the bungalow they shared at the mountain lodge just off the Yellowhead Highway that links Alberta to British Columbia. But only six hours since they had stopped drinking and finally gone to bed.

While Colin had made it to his bedroom, Daniel passed out on the floor of the living room.

"Mr. Williams...Mr. Williams, are you in there?" said a female voice at the screen door.

Colin opened his eyes and, seeing the sun outside his window, instantly shut them.

"*Argh,*" he groaned, grabbing both sides of his hair with his hands once he realized how bad his hangover felt.

He pressed his temples gently with the palms of his hand.

What did I end up drinking last night? He counted six beers at the tavern. Then almost another bottle of rye Daniel had purchased before leaving, which they had mixed with warm Coca-Cola.

Colin's mouth was dry.

I need water. I should have downed a couple glasses before I went to sleep. Then I wouldn't feel this way.

Still rubbing his temples, Colin turned on his side. Perhaps if he found the correct position he could fall back asleep and forget about his pain.

There was another knock. "Mr. Williams?"

There was that voice again.

"Mr. Williams, please open the door. A telegram just arrived for you from Ottawa. It's marked urgent. I was told to give it to you immediately."

"For Christ's sake, get up and get the bloody door!" Daniel yelled. "Hurry up before my head falls off!"

Colin pulled back the sheet and sat up. He was nauseous.

"Where are my pants?" he muttered. Seeing them in a ball on the floor, he put them on, as well as a crumpled military-issued tee shirt at the foot of his bed. He stumbled toward the door, almost stepping on Daniel, who was lying on the floor under a blanket.

"Yes, what is it?" Colin said, pushing the screen door open.

On the other side was a pretty teenage girl in a khaki skirt, khaki shirt, and green apron. Colin had seen her before. She normally worked the front desk or in the lounge of the main hall.

"Telegram, Mr. Williams," she said. There was an amused smile on her face. "Late night?"

Colin considered the intent of the question. *What does that mean? Could she be flirting with me? Or do I just look like I've just fallen off a train, 'cause that's what I feel like?*

"Something like that," he answered, fishing in his pocket for a dime to tip her. He took the telegram and went inside.

"Who the hell is sending you telegrams?" Daniel asked.

"I'll tell you in a sec," he said. "First I've gotta get some water. God, I feel horrible. I hope I still have aspirin."

"I need some too," Daniel said. He rolled onto his side and said, "How much did we drink last night?"

"Too much," said Colin, who by now had reached the bathroom and poured himself a glass of water from the sink. He drank it quickly, like a man who had been in the desert, followed by two more. Looking inside his shaving kit atop the toilet tank, he found a bottle of Bayer aspirin and swallowed three tablets. He filled another glass with water, took two more aspirin, and walked over to Daniel.

"Here, get up and take these," he said, gently nudging his friend with his foot. He reached out an arm to touch the wall so he would not fall down. The room was spinning.

Daniel sat up, took the aspirin, dropped them into the glass of water and drank it quickly. As he was doing so, Colin tore open the telegram.

"*Holy*...!" he said.

"What?" said Daniel.

"It's from the Office of the Chief of the Naval Staff," Colin said, letting the telegram fall to the floor. "My leave is over. I'm to report to Halifax as soon as possible. I'm being assigned to a ship."

Halifax, on the other side of the country, was the home of the Royal Canadian Navy's Atlantic Fleet.

"Why now?" asked Daniel. "Couldn't they have waited until your leave ended to tell you?"

"Germany's invaded Poland."

Forgetting his hangover, Daniel rose to his feet. "Are we at war?"

Colin did not—could not—answer. His head was spinning. He turned suddenly and ran to the bathroom, where he fell to his knees and began throwing up in the toilet.

I will never drink again, he said to himself. *I swear.*

"Oh, nice," he heard Daniel say.

This was all happening way too fast. How am I going to get to Halifax? Could I get a train from Jasper to Edmonton or Calgary today? Or maybe a plane? Wait, first I have to get the tires fixed on my car, which is still parked alongside the lane on the way to Patricia Lake. Aw hell, maybe I should just leave it there. No, I'll just drive it into the lake and be done with it.

"Hey," said Colin, rising from his knees and rinsing a washcloth in the sink to clean himself. "Didn't you tell me the RCAF has a training base in Edmonton?"

"Yes," said Daniel, who was putting on his pants.

"That may be my best bet. I gotta get there and figure out if the boys there can get me to Halifax. Actually, you should come with me. If we're going to war, they'll be wanting you to report to your unit."

"So, this is it...this is really it. We're going to get some Jerries."

Before he could respond Colin was on his knees—throwing up again.

WAR
....

Three days later
Halifax, Nova Scotia

GETTING TO HALIFAX turned out to be an ordeal. Because of Canada's size geographically, and because commercial air travel was almost non-existent in many areas, the quickest—most times, the only—means of travel was by train. Colin's journey had been long and exhausting. He had not eaten much and had slept little. And most of it had been in a boxcar.

He forgot all about that when he reached the city.

"Extra! Extra!" yelled a newsboy roaming the platform, a newspaper held high. "Great Britain declares war on Germany!"

Quickly digging into his pocket for two pennies, Colin bought a paper and found a bench to sit down and read the main story. But halfway through the article on the front page his eye went to another headline, not as bold but very prominent: "Churchill To Lead Admiralty." Colin read the story quickly. British Prime Minister Neville Chamberlain had named Winston Churchill First Lord of the Admiralty. To the layman, that might not seem like such a big deal, but Halifax was a naval town and the story, by a Halifax-based reporter, explained how Churchill's oversight of the Royal Navy would affect the branch Colin served under, the Royal Canadian Navy.

As a member of the Commonwealth, Canada was also expected to enter the war within a matter of days.

Navy men like Colin knew that Churchill had been a vocal critic of Hitler's power grab for years, and had urged the use of force to contain the Nazi leader. But no one had listened. Colin was also familiar with the fact that Churchill was no stranger to the admiralty, holding the post from 1911 to 1915, and gaining the respect of officers and sailors alike for his efforts to modernize the British fleet—a respect that was prevalent today in many of the officers near retirement. There was no doubt in Colin's mind that Churchill would follow a similar tactic again.

The pre-war situation unfolded quickly for Colin.

Within forty-eight hours of his arrival, he was appointed first officer aboard His Majesty's Canadian Ship (HMCS) *Hancock*. That the RCN had roughly three hundred officers, and around one in ten were assigned to administrative positions in Halifax and Ottawa, Canada's capital, worked in Colin's favor. That Colin was intelligent, personable, tenacious, and had a reputation for integrity also helped.

It was difficult to forget Colin once you met him—something his superiors took note of. There were few others in their late twenties in the RCN who rose to the rank of first officer.

On September 10, one week after Chamberlain's declaration of war, the remaining members of the British Commonwealth, including Canada, declared war on Germany and its Axis partners. One week after that, the Soviet Union invaded Poland's eastern front.

This would be no isolated skirmish, Colin realized. It was turning into a bona fide world war.

The British had hoped the Americans would join the fight against what Chamberlain called "the evil things that we shall be fighting against: brute force, bad faith, injustice, oppression, and persecution." Instead, to the disappointment of many Canadians, their hoped-for allies declared themselves neutral.

Colin took the news hard. His mother, who had died when he was three, was born in America. Colin found it hard to believe that the Americans could not see that Hitler was a madman bent on world domination. But then again, why had it taken an invasion before Great Britain and Canada had decided to stand against the German leader?

Such questions could be debated later, Colin decided. Canada was at war, and as a naval officer, he had a duty to do whatever he could to stop what he referred to as "the Nazi disease" from spreading and infecting all mankind. It would prove to be a difficult task. Every officer and sailor in the Atlantic Fleet was aware that the German war machine was big and powerful.

Germany was a lion. They were little more than rabbits. And if the truth were to be told, shivering rabbits at that.

As war began, Canada's navy was comprised of just eleven vessels. Most of the ships were older, coal-powered vessels of the early Twentieth Century, and the German and Italian navies outmatched almost every class of vessel.

The HMCS *Hancock* was termed a Pelican Class frigate. Built in 1927 and one of just a handful of Canadian ships powered by oil, she was armed with two four-inch guns and six twenty-millimeter guns. But she had her plusses. A sleek-looking vessel—Colin proudly proclaimed that she had the best design in the Royal Canadian Navy—she was much larger than the HMCS *Badger*, the minesweeper Colin served aboard for a year following his graduation from the Royal Military College. And she was faster, too, with a top speed of nearly nineteen knots.

Though he was not immediately informed of the *Hancock's* orders—probably because the Atlantic Fleet office was in chaos as the war began, and no one was certain which vessel would perform what task—Colin correctly surmised that the ship would conduct anti-submarine escorts for trans-Atlantic convoys. Great Britain was relying heavily on its close ties with Canada for critical resources to help the war effort.

Colin's first order was to oversee a quick retrofit to make the *Hancock* ready for battle. This included a new paint job, from a slate-gray finish to a camouflage scheme so she would be difficult to detect at sea. As well, she needed the addition of two depth charge racks, eight depth charge projectors, and four additional twenty-millimeter guns to give her as much firepower as possible.

There was so much confusion in those early days it was a wonder the *Hancock* ever made it out of Halifax Harbour, Colin would realize later. But in early November she finally left port to rendezvous with four other ships of the Atlantic Fleet for three weeks of training drills. Then it was back to Halifax to pick up and transfer crewmen, then back out into the Atlantic for more training, then back to Halifax to await orders.

"At the rate we're going, I expect we'll enter the fray about 1942," Colin wrote in a letter in late November to Daniel, who had been ordered to England to train on the new Spitfire fighter aircraft.

As all of this was going on, Karl Donitz and the German U-boat forces under his commander was finding great success with his limited number of submarines. In September alone, the Germans sank fifty British and French ships, with two more damaged.

The next month it was thirty-four sunk and three damaged. In November the count was twenty-nine sunk and one damaged, and December's total rose to forty-three sunk and four damaged. What's more, the Nazi U-boat captains were being much more selective in their attacks. The bigger the ship or the lower a ship sat in the water, meaning it was laden with war material, the better.

Two developments toward the end of 1939 exasperated the Allies' situation.

The first was something called Order 154. Personally issued by Donitz a few weeks before Christmas, Order 154 was a call to his U-boat captains for unrestricted submarine warfare. The only caveat was that the vessel had to be from a country at war with Germany. That meant no American vessels; Germany was not yet in a position to take on the United States. But whether it was a British destroyer or a French cargo ship with refugees aboard made no matter.

Because British and French intelligence at the time was so spotty and unsophisticated, the Allies were not aware of the significance of Order 154—despite learning of it just a few weeks after Donitz issued it. It took almost a month, until the last week of January 1940, to figure out the order's significance.

The second, and perhaps even more significant development that brought pain to the Allies was the enemy application of *rudeltaktik*—Donitz's wolf pack tactic. The attacks by groups of U-boats were becoming extremely effective. Of the one hundred fifty-six ships sunk between September 1 and December 31, *rudeltaktik* accounted for nearly one-quarter of the kills. Of that, Captain Eicher's submarine logged a remarkable eighteen sinkings.

In a relatively short time span, the UX-1 earned an almost mythical reputation on the seas, both in the German Navy as well as in the Allied shipping world. Like the legendary *Flying Dutchman*, the ghost sailing ship purportedly seen by sailors over centuries, survivors of ships sunk by the UX-1 began telling stories of a mysterious "ghost submarine" that attacked from nowhere.

"It was a beautiful, sunny, cloudless day," one sailor testified at a government inquest after one of the first sinkings in the fall of 1939. "We could clearly see the silhouettes of three German U-boats off our starboard side. But then, as best we could determine, two torpedoes came from out of nowhere and hit us portside. Our lookout's got the eyes of a hawk. He didn't see nothing but the two torpedo trails comin' up outta the deep before we were hit."

There was a simple reason the wolf pack tactic was so effective. As a new approach, it was unexpected.

Once war was declared, merchant marine ship captains knew their best means—in some cases, their only means—of survival meant traveling in a convoy, preferably with a British, French, or Canadian warship (or warships, depending on the convoy's size) serving as an escort.

The strategy of deploying ships in a convoy to protect them from enemy sub attacks was first used toward the end of World War I. A number of ships would travel in a group, like a herd of sheep, protected by several warships stationed strategically around the perimeter, like shepherds. In a short period, merchant losses decreased dramatically, while enemy losses increased.

With *rudeltaktik*, the reverse occurred. A pack of four to eight U-boats would converge and wait to attack in an organized fashion, throwing the convoy defense into confusion by the number of attacking submarines. As one Allied warship peeled off from the convoy to pursue a sub, the remaining subs would move in and fire their torpedoes—sometimes at near point-blank range—at their unarmed merchant targets before submerging.

In the first few months, the wolf packs attacked only at night, using the cover of darkness for added defense. But as their tactic proved effective, they began attacking during daylight hours as well.

The addition of the UX-1 to any wolf pack made that particular pack that much more effective. Donitz and Eicher dreamed of the day when an entire wolf pack would consist of the new electroboats. Between electroboats and the battleships *Bismarck* and *Tirpitz*, any country would think twice before sending a ship out onto the ocean. And that, they hoped, would include the American Navy, which they realized was sure to aid the British at some point. Hopefully later rather than sooner. Much later.

It was Donitz who informed Eicher of the UX-1's reputation.

Eicher would never forget the time or date: three o'clock in the afternoon of December 31, 1939. Each officer's U-boat had surfaced and rendezvoused at predetermined coordinates in the North Sea, about twenty-five miles east of Aberdeen in northern Scotland.

"Welcome, *Geist* Captain," Donitz said when Eicher came aboard.

Eicher laughed at being referred to as the "ghost" captain. He laughed hard, something he had rarely done since his wife died.

"*Geist* Captain—I like that," he said. "The UX-1 is indeed a *geist*. No one sees us. No one knows we are there."

"Fear can be a very effective emotion," Donitz said, slapping Eicher on the shoulder. "We need to employ every weapon we have."

He backed away and stared Eicher in the eyes. "Wolf, you have admirably demonstrated what you and I both knew: that *rudeltaktik* will be central to our winning the battle for the ocean. The Fuhrer himself has taken notice. He asked me to give you a gift. Call it a belated Christmas present."

Donitz reached into his pocket and produced a small box. "Open it."

Eicher was unable to take the box in his friend's hand. He could not move. He was stunned.

The Fuhrer is giving me a gift? The Fuhrer? I am unworthy

to untie the Fuhrer's shoes—we are all unworthy to untie the Fuhrer's shoes—yet he is giving me something?

"Wolf, open it," Donitz repeated. He smiled.

This time Eicher complied. Inside was an Iron Cross, the highest and most coveted decoration a soldier in the Third Reich could receive. He had secretly longed for one—what German officer didn't?—but, truth be told, he never believed he would measure up.

Eicher's right hand trembled as he lifted the object from the box and brought it to eye level. It was the most gorgeous object he had ever seen. The cross itself was black with a gold outline, and the center contained a small gold swastika. As he studied every detail of the metal and felt the coldness and heaviness of the medal against his flesh, he became aware that tears were coming from his eyes.

I am such a little boy. Crying as though I am leaving my mother for the first time. I am a rock when the enemy is unloading depth charges and my boat is shaking around me, but here I am, bawling like a baby. Because the Fuhrer gave me a gift.

"Turn it over and look at the back," Donitz said.

"I'm sorry to be so emotional, Karl." Eicher wiped his eyes and turned the Iron Cross over. On the back he saw two capital letters: *A* and *H*.

"He does not give the personalized crosses to just anyone, my friend," said Donitz, not waiting for the question he knew was on Eicher's mind. "This is a special cross. You must wear it often. It will give you protection—the Fuhrer's divine protection."

More tears streamed down Eicher's cheeks. "I am not worthy," he said between sobs.

"None of us are. Turn around and I will put it on you. Wear it with pride, *Geist* Captain. It will be your shield."

SETTING THE TRAP
....

February 16, 1940
North Atlantic Ocean

COLIN WILLIAMS STOOD atop the bridge of HMCS *Hancock* and looked through his binoculars at the surface of the ocean that stretched before him. It was just after lunchtime, and it was unseasonably warm, approaching sixty degrees in the direct sun. Except for the hum of the *Hancock's* engines and the slight vibration of the deck, all was quiet. The war seemed a million miles away.

This was just the third convoy the *Hancock* had accompanied since it went into active duty. The retrofit had taken much longer than anticipated—it was surprising how few spare parts there were and how unprepared the Royal Canadian Navy was for war—and the training runs seemed to go on forever. It was not until mid-December that the *Hancock* was able to join the first convoy of sixteen ships, laden with mostly wheat from Saskatchewan and clothing from Manitoba and northern Ontario, on a voyage to the port at Brest, France.

That first crossing was a tense one for Colin and the others aboard the *Hancock*—everyone, that is, except Captain Noah Andrews, Colin's commanding officer and a career RCN officer who first saw service during the First World War.

Captain Andrews was in his early fifties, tall and slender, with broad shoulders, a bald head, and dark, weathered skin, almost like leather, from years at sea. His knowledge of Royal Canadian naval strategy was impressive, as was his understanding of British naval history. But what impressed Colin most was Andrews' ability to get the most out of his men and his boat, and the way he remained so calm, even under great pressure. He exuded confidence that his men took comfort in.

There was one other thing about the captain. Whenever Andrews found something favorable, particularly if it was a good performance from a sailor or even his ship, he would say, "Good show." Colin liked that. The men always knew where they stood with the captain.

As it turned out, there were no U-boat sightings during the *Hancock's* first crossing. Or the second. But all of that was about to change.

The lookout on a ship following the French battle cruiser *Clermont*, which accompanied the *Hancock*, reported seeing what may have been a submarine conning tower just before dusk the day the convoy departed Sydney, Nova Scotia.

After consulting with Captain Andrews, the captain of the *Clermont*, who was the senior convoy officer, decided it would be best to steam northwards toward the coast of Greenland rather than to continue on the Great Circle Route, Allied Command's codename for the most direct route across the Atlantic to England. The French captain's reasoning made sense. If the convoy were being shadowed, it was likely that other U-boats could be waiting further along the route. Although none of the men on any of the ships in the convoy had any experience defending against a wolf pack, they were familiar enough with the German strategy by this time to know there was no use taking any chances. Suddenly turning north may throw other subs off their trail. And it was unlikely the other subs would follow because they would be hampered by fuel constraints.

Had those aboard the convoy had the benefit of being able to look years into the future and apply the knowledge and experience that would be gained fighting wolf packs, the plan might have worked. But what none aboard the convoy realized was that the Germans now had additional Type IX submarines in their fleet. These Type IXs were specifically designed for longer ocean-going missions, having much greater range then the Type VIIs. And while not as technologically sophisticated as Eicher's electroboat, Type IX U-boats carried plenty of firepower—twenty-two torpedoes each—meaning they could make multiple strikes multiple times.

The other thing that worked against Colin's convoy was the misconception on the part of the *Clermont's* captain that his decision was a defensive action. In reality, he was doing exactly what the wolf pack commander wanted him to do. Eicher had deliberately surfaced close enough to the convoy that first day to be spotted. Call it instinct, but he knew the convoy would turn north. His wolf pack would be waiting— just outside the ice field south of Greenland.

Eicher's plan was to wait until the ships in the convoy slowed and broke formation to negotiate the automobile-sized chunks of ice in the southern region of Baffin Bay, between Greenland and Canada. As the convoy came out of the ice field off the southern tip of Greenland toward Iceland, the wolf pack would be waiting, and could pick the ships off one by one. As far as Eicher was concerned, it was a perfect plan. The convoy would be out of range for air cover, and the ships would be unable to retreat quickly because of the ice, leaving them helpless. With luck, the pack could sink the entire convoy.

Feeling the afternoon sun against his face, Colin unbuttoned his naval overcoat and the chinstrap on his battle helmet. He lit a cigarette and took a long draw before turning to Captain Andrews.

"We should be through the ice by sixteen hundred hours, sir," he said.

"Good show, Lieutenant," Andrews replied. "We're losing at least six knots an hour and we are at our most vulnerable right now. I would very much like to pick up the pace."

The eight-ship convoy was traveling in a line, with the *Clermont* in the lead, the six merchant ships following, and the *Hancock* in the rear.

Unbeknownst to the men on the *Hancock*, Eicher had been watching the convoy's progress through the ice field through the UX-1's periscope. The submerged U-boat had been trailing the convoy for nearly twenty hours now.

"Time to point of contact?" Eicher called out to his first officer.

"Twenty-eight minutes at current speed," Lieutenant Schopter responded.

Eicher stepped back from the eyepiece, lowered the periscope, walked to the galley in the front of the sub, and poured a cup of coffee. Even wearing a thick wool turtleneck and officer's jacket, he was cold. Being underwater this long this far north made the U-boat cool. The thermometer read fifteen degrees Centigrade, or about fifty-nine degrees Fahrenheit. He finished the coffee, smoked a cigarette, and made his way back to his previous position on the bridge—jumping once along the way when a rat ran out in front of him.

"We can sink a destroyer but we cannot kill one rat!" Eicher exclaimed. *I really must start carrying my Luger*, he told himself.

Looking at his watch, he raised the periscope. He could

clearly see the stern of the *Hancock*, which was about three hundred meters in front of the UX-1. "Torpedo bays one and two loaded?" he asked Schopter.

"*Jawohl.*"

Eicher looked at his watch one last time before giving the command: "Fire torpedoes." And then he added, "And Lieutenant…"

"Yes, my Captain?"

"Let's do something about that rat, shall we? Perhaps you can set a trap."

INTO THE SEA
....

THE FIRST TORPEDO struck the *Hancock's* starboard twin rudder.

The vessel shook briefly, followed by an almost imperceptible rocking motion, leading Colin and the others on the bridge to conclude that the ship had come up against a large chunk of ice. There was no sound other than the growl of the *Hancock's* engine, and the fainter hum of the engines of the other ships in the line ahead. Captain Andrews and Colin looked at each other for a moment before Andrews, his brow furrowed, leaned over the mouthpiece of the ship's intercom system and said, "Engine Room, report! Did we just throw a piston?"

This was a captain who knew his ship. He had spent enough time aboard the *Hancock* to know that something sounded—felt—different.

The answer would come to haunt Colin's dreams for weeks afterwards. It came from the ship's engineer, his voice barely audible over the sound of what Colin later learned was rushing water.

"We took a hit, Captain!" the out-of-breath voice said. "A torpedo just tore a hole through the stern. It looks bad. We're taking on water."

"Torpedo?" the captain asked in a voice so calm he may

have been asking for a refill on his coffee at a restaurant. He turned to Colin. "How is that possible? I see no submarine."

Andrews had no way of knowing that the Germans had a U-boat that did not need to surface to fire.

There were no other words, just a series of screams before the intercom to the Engine Room went dead. The reason was quickly apparent. Two more torpedoes had struck in rapid succession, triggering a fireball just below one of the *Hancock*'s main gun turrets.

"Battle stations!" Captain Andrews ordered.

With a heavy jerk that sent anything not secured flying, the *Hancock* listed to the right.

"Not good," Andrews said in his ever-calm voice. Once again he was at the intercom, this time to the navigator.

"Signal the *Clermont* that we've been struck," he instructed. "Have them contact Newfoundland for rescue planes; I believe Gander's the closest base. Pronto." He turned and pointed to Colin. In a low voice he said, "Lieutenant, go below and get me a damage report. If I'm correct, we won't have much time."

"Time for what, sir?" Colin asked.

"To abandon ship. Waste no time!"

Is it possible we're sinking? Colin wondered as he ran for the stairs.

Upon reaching the main deck, Colin realized the captain's suspicions were correct. The reports from those below deck were that the ship was filling with water.

"Seaman, get the crew to the lifeboats!" Colin yelled as the *Hancock* shifted again. "We've signaled Gander for rescue planes but we need the crew to get to safety."

As he ran back to the bridge, Colin quickly analyzed the situation. It would be hours before any planes could reach them, but he knew it could have been worse. Had the convey been struck the following day it would have been in a part of the ocean known as The Pit—the point where military planes could not fly because they would not have enough fuel to return to base. Had that been the case, they would have had to wait to be rescued by another ship—something that could take days.

When Colin returned to the bridge, the captain pulled him aside. "She's going to the bottom," Andrews said in an almost-whisper. "I've given the order to abandon ship. We've got less than thirty minutes. It is imperative we get the crew off the ship. I do not want to lose one man."

Before the captain could continue, the torpedoes from the U-boats ahead of the *Hancock* hit their targets. A freighter two ship lengths ahead of the *Hancock* sustained a direct hit, exploding with such force that it was later determined all aboard were likely killed immediately. Fiery chunks of the ship rained down on the *Hancock's* deck.

As Colin assisted with the evacuation, he witnessed two German submarines surface almost simultaneously and fire their torpedoes at the other ships in the convoy. He could also see that the *Clermont* had been hit as well, and was burning.

The next few minutes unfolded so quickly that Colin would later have a hard time remembering the chain of events. In the sea below and ahead of the *Hancock* were about a dozen lifeboats, all trying to make their way away from the burning hulks of freighters and warships. He could hear men screaming. Swearing. Praying.

Colin was helping to deploy one of the *Hancock's* last lifeboats when the ship let out what sounded like a death scream, and lifted its bow at least ten feet out of the water. One of the davits holding the lifeboat bent at a ninety-degree angle as the ship shifted, causing a rope to break, propelling the lifeboat and its dozen or so occupants into the icy sea. Colin managed to cling to the davit as all this was happening—he was about to step in the boat when the *Hancock* raised itself—but could not hold onto the cold metal. The next thing he knew, he too was falling.

He hit the water with such force that he was certain he would have been knocked unconscious had it not been for the shock of the ice-cold water. For an instant he imagined himself alongside Daniel clinging to the capsized rowboat on Patricia Lake the previous September.

Colin surmised that he could not stay long in the water. Although he had on a life vest that would keep him from drowning, the immediate danger was freezing to death due to the low water temperature. He looked around for something to cling to—a piece of wreckage. Anything.

A chunk of ice, about the size of his old Ford, floated about a hundred feet to his left.

I've got to get there and pull myself up. Then one of the lifeboats can come around and get me.

He swam as hard as he could.

Realizing that the cold was sapping him of strength—he seemed no closer to the ice than when he started—he tried to keep his mind focused.

Stroke, stroke, stroke, he said to himself, trying to match his arm movements.

Stroke...stroke...stroke. He was slowing. *Must keep moving. Must keep moving. Must...*

He stopped.

It's no use. Must think of something else.

As he floated, Colin was aware of nothing but the sound of his breathing. He was cold, but it did not matter. It made no sense to struggle. He was at peace—a peace he was at a loss to explain but one that enveloped him in contentment.

As the waves gently lapped against him, Colin had the sensation of being lifted into the air. He could not feel his arms or his legs, but smiled as he looked into the sky above. It was so blue. There were no clouds. It reminded him of the way the sky looked in the Canadian Rockies. He closed his eyes.

And then he heard a voice—a voice he was not familiar with. He opened his eyes to see a tall man with a gray beard in a gray wool turtleneck sweater looking down at him. One of the man's black boots was against his left arm. The man smiled.

Thinking he was dreaming, Colin again closed his eyes.

There was the voice again. This time it was accompanied by the sensation of being kicked in the arm. His left arm.

Colin opened his eyes a second time. At this, the figure bent down and stared him in the eyes. Colin jerked backwards when he realized the man wore a German naval cap and an Iron Cross around his neck!

"*Guten tag*," the man said, touching an index finger to the bill of his cap.

Colin raised himself on his elbows and said the only thing he could think of at the time.

"Canadian."

"Ah, Canadian," said the figure. "I speak English." The man snapped his fingers, and a German sailor wrapped a wool blanket around Colin's shoulders. He could not help notice that a red swastika was stitched to the center.

"Tha-thanks," Colin said. He was shivering.

"I could not watch you die such a death," the tall man continued. "When I was a young lad fishing with my poppa and opa I fell overboard. It was so cold. It was the closest I have come to drowning. That is not a way for a warrior to die. That is not a way for anyone to die."

What Colin did not—could not—know at the time was that Eicher had seen him through his periscope and ordered the sub to surface directly below Colin as he floated in the water.

"We are coming alongside one of your lifeboats now, so I must ask you to leave," Eicher said, helping Colin to his feet.

His teeth chattering even more than before, Colin stood and tightened the blanket around his body. It was then he saw that he was on the deck of a very large submarine—he was not familiar with its design—and that a group of men in a lifeboat from one of the merchant vessels was motioning for him to come aboard, which he eventually did.

Once aboard the lifeboat, Colin removed the blanket from around his shoulders and held it out to Eicher, who was now standing above him on the deck of the U-boat.

"No, you keep it," he said, turning to make his way back to the conning tower. "Compliments of the *Kriegsmarine*."

With that, the crew and its captain entered the sub and with a whoosh, the UX-1 slipped beneath the surface of the sea and was gone.

Colin could not explain why, but he was certain that this would not be his last run-in with this U-boat.

DESK DUTY
....

Spring 1940
Halifax, Nova Scotia

THE ATTACK ON Convoy SC-235 marked the first time in the war that Germany's new wolf pack tactic led to the destruction of an entire convoy. It unfolded so quickly and in such an unforgiving area that neither the *Hancock* nor the *Clermont* had time to fire.

Losing two warships was devastating to convoy coordinators in London because they were in such short supply, and it was becoming clear that many of the German vessels outmatched the Allied ships in firepower and maneuverability. Merchant ships needed protection during their runs across the Atlantic, and the owners of shipping companies did not want to see their assets jeopardized. And while the factories and naval construction yards throughout the Commonwealth had been running full-out since war began the previous September, Allied strategists knew it would be months before additional warships could be launched, which meant future convoys were that much more vulnerable.

With the Americans still refusing to join the fight, the outlook was as dark as the winter days were long. For Great Britain and its allies, 1940 was shaping up to be a miserable year.

The situation worsened in the spring.

On May 10, the Germans invaded France, Belgium, and the Netherlands. The Third Reich next set its sights on the British Expeditionary Force, which had been sent to the mainland in late 1939 to help defend France after the invasion of Poland. At the port of Dunkirk on the French coast on May 26, 1940, the British faced one of the toughest decisions in its history. It could stand against the German Army and face certain decimation. Or it could retreat.

It chose the latter.

The decision was bittersweet. On the one hand, more than three hundred thousand soldiers escaped death or capture. On the other, morale throughout the Commonwealth plummeted.

Perhaps it was providence, or perhaps it was simply that he was in the right place at the right time, but one figure had emerged during that dark time to give the Allies hope: First Lord of the Admiralty Winston Churchill, who was appointed prime minister.

The news was greeted with cheers and a round of "For He's A Jolly Good Fellow" by Colin, Captain Andrews, and others at the officer's club at the naval base in Halifax.

"Finally, someone who gives a damn about the navy," Colin said as he pushed his glass to the edge of the bar for a refill.

Colin had been spending a lot of his free time at the officer's club since returning to Halifax. Part of the reason was that he was bored. But he was also trying to forget.

Colin was one of fourteen hundred thirty-seven survivors of Convoy SC-235—six hundred and eighty men lost their lives. After nearly twenty-two hours in freezing conditions on the lifeboat, he spent the first two weeks after his rescue in a hospital in St. John's, Newfoundland. There he was treated for frostbite and shock.

The frostbite had been bad. So bad, in fact, the medical staff was forced to remove most of the big toe on his left foot. Colin was surprised at how important the big toe was to balance; try as he might, he walked with a limp from that day on.

The injury did not make Colin bitter. He realized that he could have been casualty number six hundred eighty-one had it not been for the German U-boat captain.

What he had the most difficult time dealing with was why he was spared. It was not that he had wanted to die—though in retrospect he was at peace with the notion when he thought about floating in the ice-cold waters of the North Atlantic—but why did he get to live? What made him so special? Or was it just the luck of the draw?

Those thoughts kept bringing him back to the U-boat captain. Try as he might, he could not get the image of the tall man in the turtleneck and beard, that Iron Cross dangling from his neck, staring down at him. He would have dreams—nightmares that would wake him from his sleep—of the German, his blue eyes blazing, looking at him and raising his shiny black boot to press against his neck. And as the blackness of the boot descended it was replaced with the image of a wolf bearing down on him, its mouth open to reveal a set of sharp fangs.

Why did the German captain save me? And would I have done the same? What does it all mean?

Throughout his stay in the hospital, Colin would not part with the blanket he had received from the U-boat captain. Cognizant of the red swastika in its center, he kept the blanket balled up beneath the sheets during his recovery so as not to draw attention to it. He did not want to tell people his story. More than once the nurses had tried to take it away but he would not let them. He was not sure why it was so important, but he knew he had to keep it. At least for now.

Following his discharge from the hospital, Colin participated in a two-day hearing with Captain Andrews before an Atlantic Fleet panel of inquiry, which was standard operating procedure and was held to ensure that proper convoy procedures had been adhered to. When that was over and the panel cleared the crew of negligence, Colin was handed a desk job in a nondescript Royal Canadian Navy administrative office at the Halifax base, overseeing fuel orders for ships scheduled for future convoy runs.

"I'll sum up the job in two words," Colin told Captain Andrews shortly after he received his orders. "*Bore. Ing.*"

Colin was frustrated that he did not have a sea assignment. His frustration grew as spring turned into summer.

On June 22, 1940, the French government signed an armistice with Germany.

That night, at the officer's club, Colin's irritation with his circumstance spilled out onto Captain Andrews. "How the hell long are we supposed to sit here and do nothing? Now that the Nazis have France, what's to stop them from invading England? Hell, Captain, we've got to do *something*. Who the hell is running this war?"

"We are doing something, Lieutenant," Andrews told him. His voice was calm, steady.

"Determining how much bunker oil a Class One or Class Two freighter on a convoy run needs while burning seventeen hundred gallons an hour at eleven knots is hardly my idea of serving my country," Colin complained.

Captain Andrews rose from his chair, folded his arms, and looked at Colin.

"You are a naval officer, Lieutenant Williams. Your quote-unquote idea of "serving my country" is irrelevant at this time. What is relevant is that you are performing a duty for the king and for the Commonwealth, a duty that the Atlantic Fleet believes is correct for you at this moment in time. Perhaps it's time for you to stop thinking about yourself and consider the larger picture. If a ship were available, we would have it. But it's not. The next Canadian-built warship is not due to launch until October, and there's no guarantee we'll be assigned to her. Whether you like it or not, you're just going to have to wait and perform the duties to which you've been assigned to the best of your ability. And not for you, but for your country."

When he was finished, the captain picked up his hat from the table, put a dollar down to pay for his drinks, and left.

Alone, Colin pushed away his drink.

I'm an arsehole.

* * * *

It was not until late August 1940 that Colin and Captain Andrews received new orders and were transferred to ACNCASO—Allied Central Naval Command's Anti- Submarine Office—in Portsmouth, England. As veterans—and victims—of a convoy sinking, command believed both men could contribute insight to a small group tasked with finding creative ways to battle the U-boat menace.

The group included a former French submarine commander who managed to get his boat out of the country before the Nazis were able to seize it, a British sub captain whose experience went back to the First World War, and three professors from the University of Portsmouth. One specialized in British naval strategy while the other two were experts in the physical sciences and mathematics.

For the next six weeks, the seven men shared everything they knew about naval tactics. They studied convoy configurations, routes, and defensive maneuvers. They looked at weaponry, frequency, and location of attacks and limitations in such areas as air power. They pored over and dissected eyewitness accounts of how the German U-boats were moving away from sole attacks to organized ones like the one that had decimated Convoy SC-235. They even took into account fuel consumption and ship speeds, which, it turned out, would not have been considered had Colin not been there.

After looking at reams of data, coupled with some very blurry photos sailors had taken, the group was able to conclude that the Germans were employing a new type of U-boat that was technologically superior to anything the Allies had seen before. The stories they had heard of the "ghost sub" were credible, they decided.

But this new submarine was only a small part of a much larger problem. For it was this group that dissected the wolf pack tactic and formulated the first strategies to defend against such attacks.

Two challenges faced the group. First, was there a way to find the one sub in a wolf pack serving as the command sub, directing the others? If so, a convoy might have the ability to cripple a wolf pack's communication system and give the Allied warships time to lay down depth charges.

But there was an even greater challenge. The data showed that convoys with air protection had a ninety percent plus chance of survival versus those without. But then there was The Pit. Running several hundred miles in length, ships in The Pit were especially vulnerable to U-boat attacks because they were unreachable by aircraft. It was painfully apparent to the group that the Germans had grasped this fact before they had, which was why the majority of their successful attacks in The Pit.

Colin's group determined that the best way to close the gap was to have the British deploy one of its aircraft carriers to patrol The Pit. That would give some of the convoys a fighting chance. With evidence pointing out that an average of twenty percent of a convoy's merchant ships were sunk on each crossing, with almost all the attacks occurring in The Pit, the group was certain its suggestion would be approved.

It was not.

The group was informed that only one carrier, the HMS *Illustrious*, which had been commissioned just three months before, was capable of patrolling the area, and it was needed elsewhere.

During his assignment in Portsmouth, Colin's dreams about the German U-boat captain returned after a hiatus of several weeks. But this time, as the captain raised his boot to press against Colin's neck, a plane would appear overhead and the captain would turn, look up at the sky, and run away.

In early October, three events occurred within days of each other that would change the course of Colin's military career—and his life.

The first was that American President Franklin Roosevelt signed an order that gave Britain fifty outdated and obsolete U.S. destroyers in return for ninety-nine-year leases to land in Newfoundland and the Caribbean for military bases.

The second was that the Canadian Atlantic Fleet Command ordered Colin to return to Halifax and report to his new ship, the HMCS *Penticton*, which was to be under the command of Captain Andrews. Colin's first task as first officer would be to oversee the retrofit of the *Penticton*, the former USS *Arnold Caldwell*, a coal-powered destroyer that had been mothballed since 1936; it needed to be ready for convoy duty in three months.

The third event was that Colin received a week's leave. It would be the first time since the war began that he would have time off. And Colin was determined to make the most of each day.

LEAVE
....

October 1940
London, England

RATHER THAN RETURN to Canada, Colin decided to spend his days off in London. He had always wanted to visit the city. That Daniel could be on leave at the same time was an added bonus.

Daniel was stationed at Biggin Hill Airfield, a Royal Air Force base southeast of the city. He had been given the opportunity to go to England to train on the Spitfire the previous spring, and proved to be a quick learner on the single-seat fighter—so much so that he was assigned his own plane. He scored his first kill on May 28, flying air cover for the British during the Dunkirk evacuation.

From July through September, Daniel took part in the Battle of Britain, engaging with the German Luftwaffe over the skies of central and southern England. Because of men like Daniel, the Allies thwarted Hitler's plans to establish air supremacy in advance of a planned land invasion. There were some days Daniel flew back-to-back-to-back missions for as long as eighteen hours. But he was not alone.

The Germans began their campaign by targeting the important coastal cities like Portsmouth. The British defense, however, proved to be surprisingly strong, so within a month the Nazis changed strategy and moved inland in an effort to destroy RAF airfields and installations.

Dogfights were a daily occurrence. The stakes were enormous, but so was the casualty rate. More than twenty-three hundred pilots from Allied countries joined to fight. About a quarter of them were killed.

During a sixty-day period beginning in mid-June, Daniel shot down seventeen German fighters and bombers, and in doing so became something of a hero—at least back in Nova Scotia. But his luck ran out on August 22. A German Focke-Wulf 190 fighter came up behind his Spitfire over the English Channel and the next thing he knew, his wing was on fire, forcing him to bail out over southern England. Worse yet, the German pilot continued to shoot at him as he parachuted to the ground. Though he was not struck, his parachute sustained multiple bullet holes, and Daniel ended up with two broken ribs and a broken collarbone from a landing the doctor informed him he should not have survived. He was told it would be December at the minimum before he could fly again.

Daniel was waiting for his friend on the platform at the station in central London when Colin's train pulled in. Colin spotted him from the window of his car. Tall, square-jawed, blonde, and handsome in his leather flying jacket and boots, Daniel looked like a pilot. Even with the cast he wore on one arm to lessen the pressure on his collarbone.

"Well, look what's washed ashore," Daniel grinned as he grasped his friend's free hand and pulled Colin close to hug him.

It was an obvious dig, but Colin did not mind.

"I guess we're both fortunate to be here today," Colin said. "Remind me, how many planes is it you've crashed since you arrived in England?"

"Arsehole," Daniel growled.

They laughed as they walked to their hotel. Colin was struck at how silent and dark the city was at seven o'clock at night. He did not say anything. He did not need to. He knew all about the Blitz—the bombing campaign of London by the Luftwaffe.

Daniel sensed that Colin was uneasy.

"It's been this way ever since the Krauts started targeting London," he said. "You get used to it rather quickly. Just keep away from the falling bombs and you'll be fine."

As the Battle of Britain was winding down, Hitler sent bombers to London to hit military targets. But on August 24, several German bombers went off course and struck homes in London by mistake. Hundreds of civilians were killed.

Churchill and the British people were outraged, believing the act was deliberate.

So, Churchill ordered British planes to bomb Berlin. This infuriated Hitler, who reciprocated. And so it went.

"Really, you *do* get used to it," Daniel repeated. "The Germans come, they bomb, we clean up, go about our business, and the next day the entire process is repeated." He looked up at the sky.

"Damn, I wish I could do something."

Colin thought back to his time in Halifax calculating fuel loads for ships and remembered the dressing down from Captain Andrews.

"You'll get your chance," Colin assured him. "Your job right now is to make sure you heal."

I sound like Captain Andrews.

The air raid sirens sounded just as the two men entered the lobby of their hotel. "Downstairs everyone!" the concierge yelled at the small crowd in the lobby.

"Come with me," Daniel said, taking Colin by the elbow as they climbed the main stairs.

They walked up six flights, sometimes brushing against people rushing in the opposite direction, until they reached Daniel's floor and, eventually, his room. He unlocked the door and motioned to Colin which of the two beds would be his. By this time they could hear the muffled sounds of bomb blasts in the distance.

Colin set his bag on his bed and removed his jacket and tie. "How long will it last?" he said.

Daniel was at the window. He looked up into the sky as he pulled the thick black curtain shut to shield the light from the outside.

"Hard to say," he said. "Could be two hours. Could be all night."

"So are we going to go downstairs?"

"Nah, I got a better idea."

Daniel went to the dresser, opened a drawer, and pulled out a full bottle of Canadian Club, which he tossed to his friend.

"I've been saving that especially for you," he said.

Taking the two coffee cups atop the dresser, he walked to the door and motioned for Colin to follow. Then it was back to the stairwell. But Daniel did not turn to go down the stairs. He went up.

Where the hell is he going? Colin wondered.

All the lights in the stairwell were out by this time, so each man lit a cigarette and relied on the faint glow to help them negotiate their way. Colin counted one hundred and fourteen steps before he heard Daniel say that they had reached their objective. Daniel dropped his cigarette to the floor, snuffed it out, and clicked his cigarette lighter.

"There it is," he said, reaching for a rung on a ladder. They were headed for the roof.

"Once I get the hatch open you'll be able to see," Daniel said.

For the next few moments there was darkness. Colin could hear Daniel climbing and the clinking of coffee cups, followed by a long, high-pitched squeak. He saw his friend's shadow against a much brighter night sky than he had expected.

"Be careful with that bottle as you come up," Daniel said. "It's hard to get CC here."

There's no other way but to be careful, Colin told himself as he climbed the ladder.

"What do you think?" asked Daniel, his free arm stretched wide as Colin emerged from the roof hatch. "You and I now have front row seats to history. This is better than any newsreel you'll ever see. It's all in living color."

Colin did not know what to say. It was as though he were looking at a gigantic movie screen. Everything beside and behind them was black. But the scene in front was filled with spectacular oranges, yellows, reds, and pinks—the aftermath of the bombs dropped by Luftwaffe bombers in the distance. Occasionally the sky was punctuated by streams of white light from the searchlights and explosions of silver and blue-green from London's flak guns, which were trying to bring down the planes. From time to time Colin was able to spot the silhouettes of barrage balloons—the giant blimps that could be raised or lowered to prevent enemy planes from descending, thus throwing off the accuracy of the German pilots' bombing runs.

"It's like a Saturday afternoon matinee at the cinema," Colin agreed.

"It is somewhat unique, isn't it?" Daniel said, dragging two empty vegetable crates together.

"Did you bring these up here?"

"Hell no," Daniel said, seating himself and motioning for Colin to do the same. "I think the hotel staff used to come up here to smoke. Before the Blitz, that is. Now everybody goes down into the Tube or the basement."

He held both coffee cups out. Colin filled each about a quarter of the way with Canadian Club.

"God save the king," Daniel said.

The booms of anti-aircraft guns and bombs filled the air. Colin flinched. Daniel did not seem to notice.

"The Jerries seem to be concentrating on Battersea tonight," Daniel said. "That's five, maybe six miles from where we are."

"You do this a lot, Daniel?"

"This is only the second time on this roof. I've done it a couple other times on other roofs. Why, you *scared*?"

The truth was, Colin wasn't sure. Daniel had always been the daredevil. Colin, on the other hand, was the cautious one. His first response was to assess whether his initial emotional reaction was valid.

"No, I'm not scared," he finally said. "I haven't been scared in quite a while. Not even after the *Hancock* was torpedoed."

That was true.

Daniel, who had finished his drink, held out his cup for a refill. "Tell me about that."

Colin had written Daniel about the attack and sinking after his release from the hospital. As the bombs fell, he shared the details about being in the water, and how it had reminded him of their near drowning on Patricia Lake. And he told him about being rescued by the Nazi U-boat. And about the recurring dream.

"How about you?" Colin asked when he had finished. "Were you scared when you were shot down?"

Daniel shook his head.

"There wasn't bloody time to be scared. I don't know how that Jerry got on my tail but the next thing I know my plane's burning up around me. Intuition took over. I knew I didn't want to bail out over the Channel so I flew with the wing on fire until I had reached land. Then I just jumped out. I knew I'd be safe because I was in England. No, I wasn't scared at all."

The two spent the next hour and a half drinking, talking

about the fights they were in, about the war, and about their hopes when the war was over, all the time watching the bombing in the distance.

It turned out that Daniel had dated a waitress who worked at a pub in Wembley "but there wasn't anything there worth continuing."

Passing the bottle to Colin, he asked, "How 'bout you—you getting any?"

"Took a nurse out after I got out of hospital," he answered. "A pretty one. Nicest smile. But—how did you say it—there wasn't anything there."

"Not Barbara Bealowski, huh?"

Colin began to laugh. That was a name he had not heard in years. Before he realized it, he was lost in a memory.

* * * *

Barbara Bealowski was not like any of the other twelve-year-old girls who lived in or around Baddeck, Nova Scotia, where Daniel and Colin grew up. She was different—in a good way.

Baddeck was a small town with no industry and little to do—the kind of town people moved from rather than to. But one day, in the middle of their sixth-grade year, Barbara Bealowski joined Colin and Daniel's class.

That she was their age made her only that much more remarkable.

Standing before the class in pigtails, she told her new classmates that she had moved from Prince Edward Island with her family because her father had been offered the chance to open the first Clicker Chainsaw dealership in Nova Scotia.

"My father told us that Nova Scotia means prosperity," she explained. Everyone in the class looked at each other.

While that statement may have been true, the dealership lasted only eight months before the Bealowski family moved back to Prince Edward Island. Word around town was that Mr. Bealowski sold only two chainsaws during this period.

But in her short time in Baddeck, Barbara Bealowski set the standard for all members of the opposite sex in the eyes of all the boys in the sixth grade, Daniel and Colin included. To them, she was drop-dead gorgeous, with long, straight, blond hair, eyes that were bluer than Bras d'Or Lake on a summer day, soft, pinkish skin and painted fingernails. The fact she took great care of her nails created a bit of a tiff between Barbara and the other girls, who said she "looked like a harlot."

Colin and Daniel figured they were just jealous because their mothers would not allow them to paint their nails.

But there was something else about Barbara Bealowski that Colin and Daniel discovered: she was a fantastic kisser. It wasn't as though either boy had not been kissed by a girl before—after all, what civilized twelve-year-old Nova Scotian boy hasn't been kissed? But no girl in Baddeck kissed like Barbara Bealowski.

"Making out with Barbara Bealowski is like making out with a vacuum cleaner—it takes your breath away," the two boys agreed. Colin became so dizzy after one Barbara Bealowski make-out session that he actually fell down a flight of stairs afterwards.

He didn't mind.

Barbara genuinely cared for both Colin and Daniel. And even though she knew the boys were best friends, she never played them against each other—something that could not be said for other girls in the sixth grade. While Colin and Daniel appreciated this, it did not prevent them from doing their best to try to impress her in hopes of gaining an advantage over the other.

And so it was on a spring day that Colin and Daniel decided to show off their athletic ability while walking Barbara home from school.

Though nearly twenty years had passed, Colin remembered that afternoon with such clarity that he could almost feel the warm spring sun against his face. He could also see how green the grass and trees were following four days of heavy rains that had left many parts of Baddeck flooded.

But there was one image that would be forever burned into his mind. It was that of a fifteen-foot-wide whirlpool that had formed along the side of the road—a whirlpool created by a stream swollen by floodwaters around a culvert that ran below the almost-flooded road that he, Daniel, and Barbara walked along that day.

As the older of the boys, it was Colin's responsibility to keep Daniel out of trouble. He tried.

Daniel had found an old piece of wood from a barn that was floating in the water at the edge of the whirlpool. It was about four feet wide and five feet long—long enough to climb upon, which Daniel did.

"I don't think that's a good idea," Colin remembered telling his friend as he and Barbara watched Daniel from the shoreline. Daniel didn't listen. He just paddled with his hands along the edge of the whirlpool.

"You'd better not get too close to that thing," Colin said, pointing at the center of the whirlpool.

"This is fun!" Daniel called back. "You should try it!"

And then, without warning, Daniel screamed. "Help! I can't get away!"

"Hang on!" Colin responded. He tried to stay calm.

Before Colin could act, the sheet of lumber flipped when it reached the center of the vortex. And then Daniel was gone. He had been sucked down into the black hell of the whirlpool.

"Colin, do something!" Barbara yelled. "Help him!"

What can I do? I'm at least a mile from the nearest house. There's no one near.

Just then Colin had a terrible realization: *What if the culvert under the road was blocked? Normally it's tall enough to stand up in, but if the whirlpool had such force that it could capture someone of Daniel's size and strength, it could easily suck in tree branches and large rocks. If debris blocked any part of the culvert, Daniel would drown.*

"Colin, help Daniel!" Barbara screamed.

What should I do? Colin remembered thinking. *It would be stupid to dive in after him. What would that solve? I would be sucked in by the whirlpool and then what? Two bodies?*

Colin did the only thing he could think of—he prayed. *Please, God, don't let my friend die.*

As Colin began running up the embankment—the piece of wood still swirling in the water—Barbara cried out, "Aren't you going to help him? Colin, you can't just leave him!"

Colin ignored her. He was thinking about how he would break the news to Daniel's parents. How would he explain that their only son was dead?

"Please, God, don't let him die in there," Colin kept repeating as he ran across the road to the other side.

Reaching the other side, he looked down from the embankment into the water.

Nothing. Just the roar of water gurgling as it escaped the culvert. "Oh God no!" Colin cried. "Please don't let him be dead."

Colin heard Barbara, who had followed him across the road, sobbing, and put his arm around her shoulder.

And then, suddenly, could it be? A mop of hair. A face. Shoulders. It was Daniel!

He had made it out the other side.

"*Whooo hoo, that was fun!*" Daniel screamed as he bobbed

around in the current. He looked toward his friends, gave a thumbs-up sign with his hand and started swimming toward the shore.

Colin was not sure what he said after seeing Daniel alive. He hoped he remembered to thank God.

Once Daniel was on shore, the three of them walked the twenty minutes or so to Barbara's house in silence. After saying good-bye, they went to Daniel's house, vowing not to speak a word of the incident to either of their parents. Ever.

It was before Daniel's mother had died and, as expected, she was at the stove, preparing that evening's dinner.

"My goodness, Daniel," she said, putting down the knife she'd been using to slice vegetables. "What happened to you?"

Colin wanted to tell her. But he couldn't. He didn't dare. Daniel said, "Just slipped and fell in the stream is all."

Mrs. Masters looked at her son, then turned her gaze to Colin. "Really?" she said.

"Really," Colin said.

* * * *

"Really what?" asked Daniel.

"Wha…" said Colin, as a bright explosion of flame in the sky was followed by a muffled "poof" seconds later—the result of a British flak gun hitting a Luftwaffe bomber.

Daniel forgot his question. Instead he looked to the sky and said, "God, I wish I were up there. I'd love to get a couple of those bastards right now."

He glanced at Colin and added, "Hell, you should have me flying protection for you over the Atlantic. Even though I'm not a navy guy like you."

"Trust me, I would love to have air cover out there."

"So why don't you tell them?" Daniel demanded, thrusting a finger into Colin's chest. Colin could tell his friend was drunk. "And make them listen."

"Way ahead of you," Colin said, adding more whiskey to each of their cups. He told Daniel about the work the group had done and its recommendation to have an aircraft carrier sent to The Pit.

"All we need are a few aircraft carriers and we'd turn the tide in a hurry," Colin said. "Get some planes out there with some anti-submarine torpedoes. The Krauts wouldn't have a chance."

"You don't need a bloody aircraft carrier," Daniel said. "I'll tell you what you do. You take an iceberg and you saw off the top. Voila, instant floating airfield."

"That's the craziest thing I've ever heard," Colin said. "Man, are you bombed."

He laughed so hard that tears filled his eyes. Daniel leaned forward. He was not laughing.

"What? Wait, Daniel, you aren't serious—are you?"

Before they could continue, an explosion ten or twelve blocks away threw up a wall of flame.

"Think someone's trying to tell us something?" Colin asked. "Like maybe we should go downstairs until the all clear whistle sounds?"

Daniel ignored the question. Instead, he said, "You just remember my idea, arsehole. I'm telling you it'll work."

Another bomb exploded, this time only about two blocks away. The force of the shockwave was so strong that it knocked both men off their crates and onto the gravel rooftop.

Daniel got up first. In his right hand he held only the handle of his coffee cup. He held it up to show Colin. "Time to get below. Show's over."

"Or maybe it's just beginning," Colin replied, as they made their way to the hatch.

THE *PENTICTON*
....

November 1940
Halifax, Nova Scotia

"NOT THAT."

Those were the words the pilot of the launch heard Colin say as they rounded Georges Island in Halifax Harbour and he saw his new ship for the first time, the newly renamed HMCS *Penticton*.

"Yes, sir," the pilot of the launch said. "*Penticton*. Towed here three days ago."

"Can't be," Colin said. He had returned by ship from London just that morning.

Perhaps he was still dreaming.

The pilot of the launch checked the clipboard next to the tiller. "Sir, it is the *Penticton*."

"We're doomed," Colin whispered, turning so there was no chance the sailor could hear him.

Anchored five hundred feet away was the ugliest hulk Colin had ever seen. It had once been gray—or was the color white?—but now long, reddish-brown streaks of rust dominated the surface of the ship's side that was visible from the launch. Even the window glass had a rusty tint. Chain was missing from the rails along the deck, one of the gun barrels of the front turret was gone, and every cowl vent that Colin could see leaned this way and that.

"She's starting to look good," said the seaman, slowing the launch to come alongside a floating stairway that led to the *Penticton's* main deck.

Colin could not believe what he'd just heard. "Say that again, sailor."

"I said, 'she's starting to look good.' Like a real fighting ship. You should have seen her that first day. What a wreck. They've been working day and night to get her ready."

The seaman pointed to a group of workers on deck. They were welding something.

Starting to look good? Colin said to himself. *I'm surprised she floats.*

He knew little about the ship, other than what was in the report given to him by Captain Andrews before he came over from England. This much he had learned: she was laid down in October 1914 and launched the following summer by Bath Iron Works of Bath, Maine, and first saw service in the English Channel toward the end of World War I as the USS *Arnold Caldwell*. The *Penticton* was a Wickes-class destroyer, one of one hundred eleven built for the U.S. government for service in World War I.

Designed to carry one hundred men (sailors and officers), the ship was three hundred fourteen feet in length with armament consisting of four four-inch, fifty-caliber guns; one three-inch, twenty-three-caliber anti-aircraft gun; and twelve twenty-one-inch torpedo tubes. She had two steam turbines capable of producing thirty-five knots—a fast speed for a ship of that era. Most notable were her four vertical smokestacks.

The Americans had a nickname for all Wickes-class destroyers: Four Pipers.

As the seaman brought the launch alongside the *Penticton,*

he cut the engine and jumped off to tie up onto the dock. When he was finished, he stood straight and saluted.

Colin returned the salute and said, "You may take my things to my cabin."

Colin climbed the steps and started toward the bridge. There were workers everywhere. They were cleaning, painting, scrubbing, scraping, and replacing broken parts.

A young man in a blue uniform, who had run from the bridge, approached and saluted. He spoke in a French accent.

"Sir, Ensign Sebastian Ouellet."

Colin saluted and said, "Ah yes, I read your dossier. You're a Quebecer?"

"*Oui*...I mean yes, sir. Born and raised in Montreal."

"Love that city," Colin said, motioning Ouellet to take him to the bridge.

"Is the captain with you?" Ouellet said.

"No, he's not coming until early January now. At the last minute he got a temporary assignment with the Fifth Destroyer Flotilla. I understand Lord Mountbatten asked for him personally."

It was widely known throughout the British and Canadian navies that Lord Louis Mountbatten was Winston Churchill's favorite naval commander. To be asked by Mountbatten to be part of his staff was a great honor.

Colin changed the subject.

"How's progress?" he said. "Are we going to get this tub ready for sea by January 15?"

That was less than seventy-five days away.

"Oh, she'll be ready, sir," Ouellet said. "Even if I have to push her out into the ocean myself, she'll be ready."

Colin liked what he heard. As they chatted, he discovered he had a lot in common with the twenty-three-year-old. They both loved hockey—the Montreal Canadiens were each man's favorite team. They'd both attended the Royal Military College of Canada; Ouellet entered the year after Colin graduated. And they both had a fondness for traditional Eastern Canadian foods, such as back bacon, fried cod tongues, pemmican, and jellied moose nose.

After a tour of the ship, Colin found himself thinking that maybe the old rust bucket wouldn't be so bad—that is, once it had a new coat of paint and its weaponry updated. He knew he should be grateful for the chance to have any command. Serving aboard her beat a desk job. He was eager to get in the fight again.

"About that, sir," said Ouellet when Colin brought up the subject of weapons. "We've got an American coming aboard at ten hundred hours tomorrow to aid us with our weaponry systems."

Colin was not sure he heard the ensign correctly. Despite the best attempts by the British and the French, the Americans continued to remain neutral in the war.

"Ey? An American?" he asked. "Exactly what is this American supposed to be doing?"

"Giving technical support. He was here yesterday but said he had to be out and about today and would return tomorrow. You'll like him, sir. His name is Lieutenant Lee."

At ten o'clock the next morning, Colin was waiting at the top of the stairs leading to the boat launch when the launch arrived with a tall, skinny man in a dark U.S. Navy uniform. The figure bounded up the stairway two stairs at a time and asked for permission to come aboard upon reaching the top.

"Lieutenant Charles Lee," he said. He saluted.

"Lieutenant Colin Williams," Colin said, returning the gesture.

Lee was a tall man—at least six feet six inches. He had black hair and green eyes, a pencil-thin mustache and a bright smile with the straightest teeth Colin had ever seen. Except for the fact that he was much thinner, he could have been mistaken for Clark Gable, as his right eyebrow seemed to be permanently cocked in a frankly-Scarlett-I-don't-give-a-damn position. And he had an accent, though Colin could not place what part of the United States he might be from. He later learned Lee was "just a good ol' a farm boy from French Lick, Indiana."

Though Colin was initially skeptical, Ouellet turned out to be correct: Colin did end up liking the lieutenant. Lee's knowledge of the *Penticton*, which he referred to as "Old 71" (the numeral painted on its bow), was impeccable. Colin learned more about the ship that first day than he did after almost a week of reading manuals on Wickes-class destroyers.

Lee explained that each ship acquired through the Destroyers for Bases program included technical support from an American officer until crew officers were confident they could outfit and operate their vessel adequately.

Colin was most impressed by Lee's frankness. He assured Colin that the Americans—at least those he served with in the navy—were itching to join the battle against the Nazis. He called President Roosevelt and those elected to Congress "nothing but a bunch of chicken shits who don't have a clue what the American people really want." Hitler was "the Antichrist," Lee said, and the quicker the Americans entered the war, "the quicker we'll hang that little prick by his balls."

For the next sixty-six days Colin, Ouellet, and Lee worked fourteen-to eighteen-hour days alongside a hundred other men to get the *Penticton* in battle-ready shape. Over that period, the three formed a deep friendship. They would go to the officer's club in Dartmouth across the harbor after getting off duty four or five nights a week.

By January 6, 1941, the *Penticton* was ready for sea duty. Or so Colin thought. When he arrived for duty at eight o'clock that morning, he discovered that Lieutenant Lee had been aboard for two hours to supervise a crane crew loading fifty-five-gallon barrels onto the deck of the ship.

"What's this?" Colin asked, coming alongside Lee.

"Consider it a gift. Compliments of the United States Navy." He grinned.

"What is it?"

"It's called FS Smoke."

"What's FS Smoke?"

"Not sure exactly what's in it, other than sulfur trioxide. But I've seen the stuff at work. I got it from our lab in Greenwich, Connecticut. It'll create a helluva smoke screen for you and buy you some time to sink a few of those Nazi subs if they come lookin' for you. Come here, let me show you something."

The two men walked to an area at the stern of the ship containing a dozen black barrels with the markings USN-FS.

"Next attack, load two of these into either side of your depth charge catapults and jettison them."

Lee asked Colin to come closer to the barrel beside him.

"You see this gelatin seal?" he said, tapping on a circle about the size of a dinner plate atop the barrel. "Once the barrel hits the water this'll immediately dissolve, and the chemical reaction will cause a smoke screen you will not believe. It's beautiful. I reckon it'll throw the Krauts into confusion something terrible. They won't be able to see you, or anything else two to three hundred feet away. That'll give you time to employ defensive measures."

"I.e., depth charges," Colin said.

"Correct," Lee said.

At that he stuck out his hand to shake Colin's.

"I would really like to see how this works but my work here is done. I'm flying to Norfolk, Virginia, tomorrow. I've got orders to report to the USS *Wasp*, our newest carrier. She's a beauty."

Colin accepted Lee's hand.

"You be safe out there," Lee said. "And sink a Nazi sub for me."

And then he was gone.

BACK TO SEA
....

January 15, 1941
Atlantic Ocean

THE *PENTICTON* STEAMED out of Halifax Harbour at six o'clock on a Wednesday morning. There was a light mist in the air but the water was calm and the air not too cold. Colin watched from the platform atop the bridge as the lights of McNabs Island at the mouth of the harbor flickered, and the ship made for the open sea, smoke billowing from the stacks behind him.

It wasn't long before Captain Andrews and Ensign Ouellet joined him. "Mr. Ouellet, signal the *Achates* to increase speed to thirty knots," Andrews ordered.

Running just ahead of the *Penticton* was HMS *Achates*, an A-class British Royal Navy destroyer similar in shape and size to their vessel. She was one of two warships that had arrived the week before with another convoy. The other, the HMS *Danberry*, had gone north to Sydney, at the northern tip of Nova Scotia, and would be joining the *Achates* and *Penticton*, along with twenty-two merchant ships, around one o'clock that afternoon. The convoy, codenamed HXF-689, would be the fourth to leave Halifax this year. The men aboard the *Achates* and the *Penticton* knew the odds of making it to England without being fired upon were against them. Only one of the previous eight convoys had made it without being attacked.

Unbuttoning the top button of his jacket, Andrews turned to Colin and asked if he had a cigarette. Colin offered him an Old Gold from a carton that Lieutenant Lee had left behind, and held the pack out for Ensign Ouellet before taking one himself. The eastern sky was just beginning to get light.

"Gentlemen, I can think of no finer place to be at this time of day than on the sea," Andrews said, before turning to face Ouellet.

"This is your first time out, isn't it Ensign?"

"Yes, sir."

"Then savor this moment. Capture it in your mind and hold onto it like a photograph. Drink in the sea air. Focus on your surroundings. You'll never want to forget today. It will be with you always."

The cigarette between his teeth, Andrews leaned forward on the rail and clasped his hands.

"Gentlemen, this June marks my thirtieth year in the navy. I still think about my first voyage. One thing has not changed. Going to sea is as exhilarating now as it was the first time."

Ouellet was surprised. "Why do you suppose that is, sir?"

Andrews looked up as if seeking divine help for a proper way to answer.

"A very good question, Mr. Ouellet. To me, each new voyage represents a blank canvas. We begin with nothing—nothing but possibilities—and as we progress through the voyage we find details to form a complete picture. You'll soon discover that no two voyages are alike. Just like, for a painter, no two paintings are ever alike. Does that make sense?"

The young ensign nodded. In truth, he had no idea what the captain meant but the way Andrews said it made him comfortable.

"Think we'll see any U-boats?" Ouellet asked after a moment of silence.

Andrews flicked his cigarette over the railing and said, "I expect we will. But we'll be ready. The *Penticton's* a fine ship with a fine crew. A fine crew indeed."

* * * *

Fifty-four hours later, Captain Wolfgang Eicher watched convoy HXF-689 through the periscope of the UX-1. Another U-boat on reconnaissance patrol just outside the Gulf of St. Lawrence first spotted the convoy and radioed its position two days before. Eicher and his wolf pack planned an attack just inside the eastern portion of The Pit—he called the position "The Door" because it was just beyond the range of the Allied planes operating from North America—but rough seas forced him to cancel his plans and attempt an attack about a hundred miles east of his original point. He knew he was taking a chance. The Allies had stepped up their air patrols of the Atlantic from England over the past few months, meaning an attack on any sub in the region was possible. But Eicher was pleased with his position. The British still lacked planes; he knew it would be a few years before they possessed enough air power to conduct extensive patrols. By all accounts, the captain figured he was in the right place at the right time.

"I count twenty-two freighters and three warships," Eicher told his first officer. "Two British—a destroyer and a cruiser—and another destroyer. It appears to be American but it's flying a Canadian flag."

"This has to be the one U-484 radioed us about," Lieutenant Schopter said. "Shall I have the men load torpedo bays?"

Eicher nodded. He wished he had additional U-boats for this attack; two of the six subs in his wolf pack were in need of repairs and had to return to Germany. While he figured he still had the advantage—after all, they had the element of surprise and the technical advantage of the UX-1—something about this particular convoy made Eicher uneasy. He could not explain why, but decided to be cautious just the same. He understood very well that U-boat captains who did not exercise proper judgment usually ended up dead—and so did their crews.

"Adjust to thirty-four degrees aft," Eicher said. "I'm targeting the tanker."

A thin smile formed across Schopter's lips. He knew that the resulting explosion and fireball would throw the convoy into confusion for a few minutes—all the time the Type VII subs in the pack needed to surface and attack. With luck, the U-boats could pick off a third of the convoy before the warships could deploy their defenses.

"Fire!" Eicher commanded.

* * * *

Colin was in his cabin writing a letter when he heard the explosion, and the alarm signaling battle stations went off. Grabbing his life vest, helmet, and binoculars, he ran to the bridge.

"Hard starboard!" Captain Andrews ordered the helmsman, his voice slightly elevated but still its usual calm. "Hard! Hard! Hard!"

About two hundred yards ahead of the *Penticton* was the burning hulk of the just-struck oil tanker. Colin pulled a helmet and life vest off the hook and handed it to Andrews.

"Mr. Ouellet, do you see any signs of survivors in the water?" Colin asked.

"No, sir."

"The crew didn't have a chance," Andrews said, running the palm of his hand across his bald head before putting on his helmet. "It was a direct hit."

Ouellet yelled: "Two U-boats surfacing! Correction, make that three surfacing off the port bow. Eight hundred yards!"

The *Achates* and *Danberry* began to fire their guns.

Colin scanned the sea with his binoculars. He saw a small speck in the distance.

What's that? he asked himself. *Could it be a periscope?*

Colin lowered his binoculars, blinked a few times, and raised the glasses again.

By now the *Penticton* was also firing on the three subs, one of which managed to fire two more torpedoes on another ship.

Colin made another sweep. And then he stopped. "Captain, periscope sighted!" he shouted.

"Where, Lieutenant?"

He pointed to an area that was about three o'clock to their position. "There!" he said. "Amidships. Approximately one thousand yards."

Andrews looked where Colin was pointing. "I see it. You're right, it's a periscope. Helmsman, bring us to eighteen knots and turn hard to port. Now!"

An idea flashed across Colin's mind. "Sir, request permission to deploy FS Smoke before she fires on us," he asked.

"Do it!" the captain said.

The *Penticton* continued to fire on the U-boats as it listed heavily to the left while making a sharp turn to avoid torpedoes, almost causing Colin to lose his balance as he ran toward the launching unit for depth charges at the rear of the ship. Motioning to the men at their stations, he helped load two barrels onto the catapult and brought his hand down quickly to signal launch. As the barrels struck the water, a thick smokescreen instantly formed around them.

Aboard the UX-1, Eicher had the *Penticton* squarely in his sights. "Torpedoes ready, my captain," he heard Lieutenant Schopter say.

"What the...?" Eicher said, as he watched the enemy ship disappear into the cloud of thick, gray smoke forming over the surface of the water.

They have a new defensive weapon.

"Should I fire, sir?" Schopter asked. His voice was anxious.

Eicher thought for a moment. "No. Signal the others to break off the attack and prepare to dive to two hundred meters. We must hurry."

Eicher could tell by Schopter's expression that he did not approve. It did not matter. Time was running out. "You heard me, Lieutenant," he shouted. "*Now!*"

DINNER WITH THE CAPTAIN

THE TALLY OF losses from the attack on Convoy HXF-689 was one Canadian oil tanker, the *Matilda*, with a loss of forty-two crewman, and two Nazi U-boats, casualty numbers unknown. The *Danberry* was credited with both U-boat sinkings, though the official report of the battle noted the ship could not have fired without the additional time given to it by the *Penticon's* deployment of FS Smoke.

That evening, over dinner in the officer's mess, Captain Andrews had his orderly open two bottles of Bordeaux from a case he had brought with him from England. The orderly poured glasses for the captain and his five officers, Ouellet and Colin among them, then had everyone stand as he offered a toast to King George VI. He then kept his officers standing as he offered another toast, this time to Colin.

"Lieutenant, had it not been for your idea to deploy the smoke shield, I am not sure we would be here right now. Good show."

"Here, here," Ouellet said. "Maybe those Jerries will think twice before trying to jump us again."

"I certainly doubt that will happen," Andrews said as he sat and helped himself to meat and potatoes from a platter held by the orderly.

"Me either," Colin said. "We were lucky."

"Oh, I don't know," Ouellet said. "I think if we equipped all our warships with FS Smoke we would begin to turn the tide out here."

Colin shook his head no. "FS Smoke is just one tool in our toolbox. What we really need is air cover. Then the Germans might not be so bold."

The orderly refilled all the men's wine glasses.

"That would be nice, Lieutenant," Andrews said between bites of his dinner, "but it will be years before we get enough aircraft carriers built for that to happen. In the meantime, we'll have to come up with something a bit more creative—and less expensive, I might add."

Colin's mind went to his conversation with Daniel during the air raid. It made him laugh.

The captain asked what Colin found so funny about his comment.

"It's not what you said, Captain. I was thinking about an idea a friend of mine had when I saw him back in London a few months ago."

Andrews swallowed, put his knife and fork down and said, "Please, share it."

Colin laughed again, but this time it was a nervous laugh. The rest of the officers stopped eating.

Me and my big mouth. Do I tell them?

Colin had no choice. In as much detail as he could remember, he shared Daniel's idea for building airfields from icebergs. A few of the men laughed. Captain Andrews did not.

Following a few minutes of awkward silence, Andrews spoke.

"Lieutenant Williams," he said, as he resumed cutting the meat on his plate, "one day when the opportunity arises, I need to have you meet someone I know."

THE MEETING
....

October 31, 1941
Portsmouth, England

IT TOOK NEARLY eleven months for the captain's so-called opportunity to arise.

Colin had not pursued the matter because he still thought that Daniel's idea was ridiculous. Besides, he had other things to keep him busy.

Between mid-January and late October 1941, the *Penticton* made nineteen convoy crossings, all without incident—a remarkable achievement considering that the Allied losses continued to increase in the Atlantic. The Pit was especially deadly. The Nazi U-boats had sunk nearly six hundred Allied merchant ships since the war began. Casualties were in the thousands. For Great Britain, the Battle of the Atlantic had become a war of attrition—one that it was losing. The British Commonwealth needed a miracle.

Captain Andrews, Colin, and even Convoy Command were at a loss to explain why the *Penticton* and the convoys it was involved in were spared. The crew had not seen one German submarine following the ship's first crossing of that year—not even a periscope. But no one was about to argue with good fortune. Every man aboard the *Penticton* knew the situation could change at any time.

The *Penticton* was on day one of a four-day layover for maintenance in Portsmouth Harbour when Andrews announced that he and Colin would be traveling to London for two days of meetings with none other than Lord Louis Mountbatten.

Mountbatten was a dashing and flamboyant British naval hero who had been serving as captain of the aircraft carrier HMS *Illustrious* until, just days earlier, Winston Churchill promoted him to chief of Combined Allied Operations. In his new role, Mountbatten was to seek out and develop new technologies, no matter how fantastic they appeared, for use against the Germans and Italians. Mountbatten's promotion promoted Andrews to send Mountbatten a coded message about the idea for airfields built from icebergs. The message obviously caught Mountbatten's attention.

Colin did not know any of this, nor did he know about the purpose of the meeting, until the morning of the thirty-first, when the captain stopped by his cabin to give him the news.

"You want me to go with you?" he said. "To talk about iceberg airfields? Begging your pardon, Captain, but you must be joking."

Andrews stared at him for what seemed an eternity before holding up an index finger.

"Lieutenant, I assure you this is no joke. I would advise you to pack your dress uniform."

It wasn't until the two were on the train to London that the reality of the meeting began to sink in. Colin couldn't believe his nervousness.

"Relax, Lieutenant," Andrews said, sensing his first officer's uneasiness. "I assure you it will be fine."

Fine? Colin thought. *Fine? Mountbatten happens to be one of the most powerful men in the world today. He's going to laugh me right out of the navy when he hears about this crazy idea—which is not even mine! If I'm lucky I'll end up transferred to a garbage scow in the South China Sea.*

While Colin was aware that Andrews had been assigned to Mountbatten's Fifth Destroyer Flotilla before taking command of the *Penticton*, he didn't realize that Andrews had known the man for some time—not until Andrews shared his history with Mountbatten on the train into London. Their initial meeting occurred during an exchange program with the Royal Canadian Navy in 1920-21. In March 1921, then-Junior Lieutenant Andrews served on the battle cruiser HMS *Repulse* along with Mountbatten, who was assigned to accompany Edward, the Prince of Wales, on a royal tour of Japan and India. Years later, Andrews and Mountbatten studied electronics together at the Royal Navy College in Greenwich.

"He's quite a charming fellow, actually," Andrews offered. And he was.

That afternoon at five o'clock they met in a small, private room at the Savoy, a short walk on the Strand from Trafalgar Square. Mountbatten's orderly came to the door of what turned out to be two rooms—a small waiting room with four comfortable-looking brown leather chairs, and a larger room beyond that—showed them inside, and asked them to wait.

So this is how the other half lives, Colin thought, as he studied the centuries-old paintings on the wall. He followed that with a quick prayer: *God, I have no idea why I'm doing this but please, please, please don't let me muck it up.*

Moments later the inside door opened and a large frame filled the doorway.

Colin immediately realized why Mountbatten, with his genuine smile and impeccable manners, had such a gigantic reputation. His mere presence seemed to dominate everything around him.

In two strides, he was alongside Andrews. His voice boomed and echoed off the walls.

"Noah, you blaggard!" he said. He hugged his friend, stepped back, then reached out and put his arm around the captain's neck, rubbing the top of his head with his free hand.

"Nineteen crossings thus far this year and not even a scratch! I need some luck off this shiny head of yours."

He straightened and, still smiling, saluted Colin.

"Commodore Louis Mountbatten, at your service," he said. "You must be Lieutenant Williams, the creative one."

Creative one? Oh God.

Colin fought back his nervousness by concentrating on standing as straight as he could, but he wobbled because of his toe.

"Yes, sir!" he said.

"Please Lieutenant, at ease." Mountbatten motioned to both men to chairs. The orderly returned as Mountbatten was taking his seat.

This orderly must have ESP, Colin thought. *He's instinctively in the right place at the right time.*

"Three single malt scotches," Mountbatten said. "Make them neat."

Without thinking, Colin blurted out, "I'll have mine on the rocks, please." He was warm in his dress uniform and thought something cold would make him feel better.

"One with ice," Mountbatten said, smiling.

Colin listened as Mountbatten and the captain talked about Mountbatten's latest assignment.

"Lieutenant, you've been very much silent," Mountbatten finally said. "Noah has told me about your interesting proposal on convoy defense."

Colin took a sip from his glass and cleared his throat. "Sir, I believe our greatest weakness currently is air protection, or more precisely lack of air protection. If each convoy could have fighter escorts, you would see a dramatic decrease in our losses."

Mountbatten leaned back in his chair. He glanced at Andrews, then back at Colin before speaking.

"So, you would have me pull our carriers out of the Mediterranean and the Pacific and place them all in the Atlantic? You do realize that would jeopardize Africa, India, Australia...shall I go on?"

Andrews rose from his chair and said, "Lieutenant, let's not waste the commodore's time. Outline your idea with the same detail you used last January."

My idea? Colin thought. How did this get to be my idea?

There was a firmness to Andrews's voice that told Colin his "idea" had better sound convincing.

Colin began with an explanation about the typical formation of convoys, specifically where warships were placed. Even though Mountbatten was likely familiar with the makeup, it set an important baseline. He then launched into the wolf pack tactics the U-boat commanders were employing, and from there segued into an explanation about how he was cognizant of how precious the Allies' aircraft carrier resources were at the time and how a "radical new way of looking at deploying air power" needed to be considered as an alternative. He finished by sharing Daniel's idea of creating airstrips made from icebergs.

"And where would you deploy these iceberg airfields?" Mountbatten asked.

"Primarily in The Pit," Andrews interrupted. "That's where the Jerries seem to be concentrating their attacks."

"And how would they be deployed?"

Before Colin could tell him that they would be towed to strategic locations by ship, the door swung open and Winston Churchill, clutching his trademark cigar, entered.

"Dickie!" he said.

* * * *

It turned out that a staff member had asked Churchill, who had finished a meeting with the U.S. ambassador at the hotel, if he would be joining Commodore Mountbatten and his guests at his private dinner. Not wanting to waste a chance to see his friend—only Mountbatten's closest friends called him "Dickie"—Churchill decided to stop by unannounced.

"And who am I to pass up a free dinner?" Churchill asked.

Mountbatten said he was delighted that Churchill could join them. Captain Andrews said he was deeply honored. Colin was silent because he was shocked; he feared he would pass out.

Wait until Daniel hears this one. I got to meet the bloody prime minister!

The sensation eventually departed, though it took some time. As with Mountbatten, it was easy to tell that there was something special about Churchill. He exuded energy yet, at the same time, a calming influence. As he talked, Colin began to understand why the man had the loyalty and respect of everyone in England—and anyone convinced that the Axis cause was an evil cause.

"It is I who am honored," Churchill said when he was introduced to Captain Andrews and Colin, "to be alongside two true heroes of the Commonwealth and the hope of all who yearn to be free from tyranny."

Over a dinner of oysters on the half shell, salad, duck breast, potatoes and mushrooms, and crème brulee, Churchill asked question after question—about the morale of their fellow sailors, about the mood in Canada, about life aboard a warship, and, of course, about the battle against the U-boats in the Atlantic.

Mountbatten was largely silent throughout the conversation. It was Andrews who answered most of the prime minister's questions. Churchill was fascinated with the captain's story of their first convoy crossing and the sinking of the *Hancock*. It was at that point that the conversation shifted to Colin, who told Churchill about his encounter with the UX-1 and its captain.

"Incredible!" said Churchill, finishing his third glass of wine.

"If you think that is incredible," Mountbatten said, interrupting his friend, "wait until you hear this young man's idea for winning the war in the Atlantic."

The words snapped Colin back to reality—and near-panic-like nervousness.

Oh God, no. Oh, please don't make me tell him. Not Churchill!

Everyone at the table was silent. Churchill reached into his suit coat pocket, removed a cigar, clipped the end and lit it, and focused his eyes on Colin.

Colin felt he had no other option. He told Churchill everything he had told Mountbatten.

When he was finished there was again silence. Churchill set his cigar in the ashtray, rose, and walked to the other side of the table where Mountbatten was seated. Rocking back on his heels, the thumbs of both hands in his vest pockets, he asked in a hushed voice, "What do you think, Dickie? Will it work?"

Mountbatten considered the question. Before he answered, however, he lit a cigarette, exhaled, and took a sip of wine.

Colin felt a bead of sweat run down the side of his face and used his napkin to wipe it away.

Mountbatten smiled and said, "Hell yes, it'll work, Winnie. It's the last thing the Germans would expect."

Churchill walked back to his seat and sat down. He picked up his cigar, put it in his mouth, and began puffing so intensely that a blue cloud soon filled the room.

"Well then, I shall call a meeting of the Admiralty Board for one o'clock tomorrow." He turned to Colin. "You shall make a presentation then, Lieutenant."

Colin looked at the prime minister but did not say anything. He thought he was going to be sick. He took a gulp from his glass of wine—a very big gulp—before excusing himself to go outside, where he drank in the cool night air.

PROJECT HABAKKUK

COLIN SLEPT POORLY all night and woke up at his usual time of five-thirty. He had a headache. He knew it was partly due to his sinuses, which had been affected by the chilly, damp London weather. But mixing scotch and wine before and during dinner had not helped either.

After some headache powder, two cups of hot tea and a shower, he felt better. At seven o'clock there was a knock on his door. It was Captain Andrews.

The captain wore his dress uniform. Colin was still in his bathrobe.

"I thought it might be a good idea if we spent some time preparing for this afternoon," Andrews said. "You'll want to be on point. It is, after all, the Admiralty."

"I can't believe this is happening," Colin said. "Lord Mountbatten. Prime Minister Churchill. The Admiralty Board. It's surreal."

Andrews smiled and nodded. "It is that."

"Captain, I'll be honest with you. I'm not sure whether I should be jumping for joy or crying. I mean, this isn't even my idea!"

"I understand, Lieutenant. But consider the prospect that perhaps—just perhaps—the reason you're here is because you are meant to be here."

"Are you saying this is my destiny?"

Andrews folded his arms and said, "If you are so inclined to think that way, yes. Yes, I do. Many people live their lives without a clue as to why they exist, and many never take the time to explore the possibility. You have a wonderful opportunity before you today. As your commanding officer—and I hope I can add, as your friend—I want you to succeed, and I want to do anything in my power to help you succeed. Because, quite frankly, everything we cherish as citizens of a free world is at stake right now. These are dark days."

Colin let the words sink in.

Andrews said, "As Commodore Mountbatten indicated last night, this idea may give us a strategic advantage, and heaven knows we could use all the help we can get."

"That's true," Colin sighed. "Yes, Captain, I'd appreciate your help. Give me ten minutes to get dressed. Then we can outline what I need to say and I can practice."

* * * *

Colin was calm during his presentation to the Admiralty Board. Surprisingly so, he thought, considering the number of people in the room—thirty or so. He did not care for speaking in front of groups. That this group contained an assortment of admirals, captains, one Cabinet minister and, oh yes, the prime minister—not to mention at least a dozen aides and assistants—was reason for more anxiety. But he managed to get through what he had rehearsed that morning with Captain Andrews with poise and confidence.

When Colin completed his presentation he asked for questions. An admiral rose from his chair and looked around the room.

"Gentlemen, this is an intriguing proposal. Intriguing indeed." Then, turning to Colin, he added, "But tell me, Lieutenant. You've failed to cover one detail: Wouldn't these floating ice airfields of yours eventually sink? After all, they would be constructed of... ice! And we all know that eventually ice melts."

There it is again, Colin thought. *"My" airfields.* But the truth was that now—today—he was much more comfortable with taking ownership of the idea, particularly following the positive reception from Mountbatten and Churchill. Perhaps it wasn't as farfetched as he'd first thought, he concluded.

Rather than give a direct answer to the admiral, he chose to detail one of the jobs his father had while working as a handyman at Alexander Graham Bell's estate in Nova Scotia. When winter arrived and the many ponds around the estate overlooking Bras d'Or Lakes froze, Colin's father and the other men would saw the pond ice into blocks and coat them with a thin mixture of pulp, water, and sawdust. This layer would freeze, creating a coating over the ice that served as a protective cover for the blocks, which were stored beneath the ground and covered with a thick layer of sawdust.

"It was not unusual," said Colin, "for some of these blocks of ice to last as long as two years."

He went on to say that visitors to Bell's estate could always count on a cold drink or ice cream on even the hottest of summer days. "And mind you, this was decades before the invention of refrigeration units," he pointed out.

"Admiral, creating panels out of a similar substance and attaching them to the sides and tops of the ice airfields would give these objects the added protection to withstand several weeks' deployment in the open sea," Colin said. "Afterwards, the fields could be towed northwards to the arctic waters to refreeze. Then a new protective coating could be added before the fields could be deployed again. The more ice fields that are built, the more inventory we'd have for deployment. As soon as the older ones start losing their integrity, new ones could be brought in and the older ones refurbished."

The admiral seemed satisfied with the answer and sat back down.

"I believe it would be possible to get a year or two out of each airfield," Colin said. "That is all we would need. Again, having adequate air protection would reduce convoy losses dramatically. And this would be much quicker and less expensive than building aircraft carriers."

After seeing that there were no further questions, Mountbatten glanced at the prime minister, stood and said, "Thank you, Lieutenant. That will be all. You're dismissed."

Colin stood, saluted and said, "Yes, sir. Thank you, Commodore."

As he was leaving, Churchill rose and said, "Lieutenant, we'll be in touch. In the meantime, do not leave London."

Colin nodded and saluted one final time as an aide opened the door to an outer room where Captain Andrews was waiting.

"How did it go?" the captain asked, rising from his chair.

"Very well, sir."

"Good show. I had a feeling it would. Let's have a drink to celebrate, shall we?"

"I was told not to leave London, though. I know we're scheduled to leave Portsmouth in less than forty-eight hours."

"Actually, while you were in the meeting, the *Penticton* received new orders. We're to remain in port another day, so I am to stay here with you and then..."

"And then what, sir?"

"And then we're to sail—without you."

* * * *

Captain Andrews took Colin to a small pub not far from the hotel where Colin stayed on his first visit to London. It was three-thirty in the afternoon, and Colin had not eaten since the previous night, so he and the captain ordered bangers and mash and two pints of beer.

Colin had consumed his meal, along with half a loaf of fresh bread, and was on his second beer when two men in tan trench coats arrived. Colin was facing the door and saw them go to the bar but did not give them a second thought until, moments later, they were standing next to the booth he shared with the captain.

"I say, which of you might be Lieutenant Williams?" said the taller of the two men. His words were crisp and authoritative.

Colin stood and faced the man at eye level. "That would be me. Is there something I can help you with?"

"You're to accompany us to 10 Downing Street," the man answered. "Immediately."

Ten Downing Street was the prime minister's address.

"Well, Lieutenant," said Andrews, rising. "It appears destiny awaits you."

He held out his hand to shake and, when Colin did so, gripped the younger man's hand firmly.

"Captain, it has been a privilege to serve with you," Colin said. "Thank you for everything."

Andrews smiled and let go of Colin's hand. "Success," he said.

* * * *

Churchill was seated in a leather chair, a book in his lap, beside a crackling fireplace in his study when the aide showed Colin into the room. The prime minister was wearing a tie but not his suit coat; his vest was unbuttoned. In one hand he held his ever-present cigar. Lying next to the chair was a gray cat, which Colin recognized from the newspapers as Nelson. The cat raised its head as Colin entered the room, looked at him for a moment, then closed its eyes and set its head back down on the carpet.

Churchill motioned for Colin to sit in the chair facing him.

"Would you like a brandy, Commander Williams?" Churchill asked, lifting a crystal decanter at the table by his side.

Colin corrected the prime minister. "It's lieutenant, sir."

"It was lieutenant," said Churchill, who poured two brandies. "It is now commander."

Churchill handed one of the glasses to Colin. "God save the king," he said as he got up. He took a sip and sat down.

Colin did the same. As he did so, he noticed that he was trembling. In a matter of seconds he had jumped two ranks—something that normally took years for a career officer—but he did not know why.

He did not have to wait long for his answer.

"Commander, you handled yourself with a great deal of confidence today," Churchill said. "I was most impressed at the lack of—you must excuse my crassness, but I know of no other way to say it—*pissing dogs.*"

"I don't understand, Mr. Prime Minister."

Churchill took a long draw on his cigar and, as he exhaled, said, "I cannot tell you how many meetings I have attended throughout my career where the participants feel they must comment on each and every jot and tittle. It's not unlike when you take a dog for a walk in the park. The dog must stop at each and every bush and lamp post to leave its mark. People are the same way."

Colin laughed. *How true*, he thought.

"But your idea today left the door open to very little of that," Churchill continued, "which reinforces Commodore Lord Mountbatten's conclusion—and mine as well—that this is the way we must proceed."

He stopped to have another puff on his cigar.

"Commander, today I am entrusting you with Project Habakkuk."

"Project *Habakkuk*?"

"Are you familiar with the Old Testament prophet Habakkuk, son?"

"No, sir."

"Habakkuk was a prophet in Israel years before the Babylonian invasion of 600 BC. In his writings, God gives the prophet a message." Churchill opened the book in his lap—a Bible—and began reading. "Behold ye among the heathen, and regard, and wonder marvelously: for I will work a wonder in your days which ye will not believe, though it be told you."

He closed the book and leaned forward.

"Commander Williams, it is *you* who are going to work a wonder that no one is going to believe, even though it be told to them. I consider the mission I am giving you to be among the Commonwealth's top priorities. *You* are going to make this concept of floating ice airfields of yours a reality. You shall have all the resources of the Commonwealth at your disposal. Money, men, machinery, the latest research. Nothing shall be spared."

Colin looked at the prime minister and drained his glass of brandy. "Commander Williams, I do not have to tell you about the times in which we are living. They are dark and full of evil. As I have said before, Hitler is a monster whose wickedness has no bounds. He will not rest until the entire world is under his heel. But this I know: a monster like Hitler has no place in a civilized world. Humanity cannot allow it, and it will be men like you who stop him."

Colin's stomach growled. Nelson woke up, walked to Colin, jumped into his lap and purred.

"I hope I don't let you down, sir," Colin said, stroking Nelson's ears.

Churchill smiled. "I am confident you will not. The challenge is great, but do not be weary. We need you to succeed. England needs you to succeed, as does the world. So don't give up—even when you want to. Never, never, never give up. And have faith. Faith in what you are doing. Faith in our cause against tyranny and the defeat of Hitler. And faith in the one above. For I promise you, we *shall* defeat him."

Churchill handed Colin the Bible that had been on his lap. "I want you to have this," he said. "Now get to it."

RECRUITMENT
....

A LITTLE MORE than a month after Colin's meeting with Churchill, the Japanese bombed Pearl Harbor and the United States declared war on Japan, Germany, and its Axis allies. Colin viewed the event as further evidence that he needed to deliver results—and quickly. He felt an almost personal responsibility to do all he could to buy the Allies time, reasoning that now that the Americans were in the fight, it would likely turn the tide of the war—but not immediately. Adding to this pressure was the realization that US-flagged ships were now fair game in the Atlantic for the U-boats.

Colin assembled a small team of experts in England to assist in developing a strategy for making Project Habakkuk a reality. They included military personnel, university professors, engineers, and one of the most fascinating men Colin would ever meet—a British-born journalist turned inventor named Geoffrey Pyke.

The forty-eight-year-old Pyke came to the team at the "suggestion of Lord Mountbatten," Colin was told, though *insistence* was a more accurate statement.

While Colin would never know the complete story of how Mountbatten knew Pyke, what he did know was this: Pyke had a brilliant imagination. He had come up with the idea of using radio signals to triangulate the position of objects, which the

Allies believed held great potential and were adapting for military purposes. Pyke had also conceived of a screw-propelled vehicle to transport soldiers in fighting conditions where snow made transport impossible.

It was his third invention, however, that caught Mountbatten's attention. Pyke was working to develop a wood composite material surprisingly similar to the material Colin's father and others had used when storing ice on the Bell estate. He called his creation Pykrete.

"It needs a bit of work," Pyke told Colin, "but when I'm finished it will be a product that revolutionizes mankind. You can be sure of that."

Colin soon realized that Pyke fancied himself as a twentieth century Leonardo da Vinci, viewing himself an authority on a myriad of topics. Politics. Weaponry. Engineering. And, of course, ice.

"The reason ice sinks as it melts," Pyke said during one of his first conversations with Colin, "is because the ice becomes warmer and more dense than the water above it. When it is perfected, Pykrete will slow the natural melting process due to its six-to-one weight ratio."

Colin had no idea what Pyke meant, but acknowledged that Pyke seemed to know more about ice than he. And if Pyke could perfect his substance to ensure Project Habakkuk's success, so much the better. He was in no position to turn down anyone's help.

So, with Mountbatten's and Churchill's blessing, it was agreed that Pyke would become the key scientific adviser for the project, and that Colin and a small team would be in charge of developing a prototype to test whether the idea would actually work.

In short, Pyke would be the brains and Colin, the brawn.

By mid-January 1942, the team had worked out the

technical details for creating panels of the pulp-sawdust composite that Colin knew the formula for; Pyke would remain in Great Britain to work on his "infinitely better" Pykrete material. The plan was to build a prototype airfield of ice and test whether a plane could land on it without damaging either the airfield or the plane.

"How big does the airfield need to be?" one of the engineers asked. Colin was not sure. But he knew someone who would know the answer.

After seeking permission from Mountbatten—under the Secrecy Act, he was not permitted to discuss his work unless he had permission—Colin drove to the RAF fighter-bomber base at Bradwell Bay on England's eastern coast on January 22, 1942. Daniel was stationed there.

By now, Daniel's collarbone had healed and he was flying again. Daniel was at Bradwell Bay in the role of assistant commander of a squadron assigned to provide fighter escort to Canadian and British Lancaster bombers sent to bomb Germany.

Colin, who had not seen his friend since London, wondered what Daniel's reaction would be after learning the true meaning of his visit.

"You want me to do *what*?" Daniel said when Colin told him he wanted him to join the project team.

"I want you to be in charge of the aviation component of Project Habakkuk. I need someone who knows about airplanes. How am I supposed to create something when I don't even know the length a plane needs to take off or land?"

"Three hundred and twenty yards for takeoff and two hundred eighty-five for landing," Daniel said, "for an Mk1 Spitfire. Use that. Job done."

"No, you don't understand," Colin pleaded. "I need someone who knows what they're talking about and can actually try a landing."

"Colin, there are other pilots available. In case you hadn't noticed, there's a war on. I'm a fighter pilot. That's what I do. I wasn't meant to spend the war behind a desk working on some crazy idea. My squadron needs me."

Colin slammed his fist on the table.

"Damn it, this was *your* idea in the first place!"

The statement startled Daniel. "Yeah, I suppose it was," he said in a voice that was barely audible.

"Daniel, you said your squadron needs you. Well, the truth is, *I* need you. Buddy, I *need* you. You're right, I can probably ask another pilot. But you're the only one I know I can trust. This is a huge project. Please say you'll help."

Daniel lit a cigarette and rubbed his eyes with his free hand. "I wish I could, Colin, but I was meant to be up there."

"I could order you."

"*Order me?*" Daniel said. "*Order me?* How is someone in the navy going to order someone in the air force?"

"Oh, I could. Trust me, I could."

Daniel was defiant. "Ha," he said, taking another puff.

Arsehole, Colin thought. *Maybe I should order him to show him how serious I really am. That's exactly what I'll do!*

He opened his mouth to speak but thought better of it at the last moment. No, their friendship meant too much. He would have to find another pilot.

"Okay, Daniel, have it your way," Colin said, as he picked up his cap and coat from the table separating them. "I'm not going to make you do something you aren't committed to. I have to get back to London. I trust that you will keep what I discussed with you today confidential. And take care of yourself up there. I don't want to lose my best friend."

Colin turned his back to Daniel and walked toward the door. As he was about to leave Daniel said, "Six months."

Colin turned and said, "What did you say?"

"Six months."

"Six months?"

"You heard me, Colin. I'll give you six months. Then I come back. Otherwise I'll get rusty, and those Nazi bastards will try to shoot me out of the sky again. And I do not like being shot down."

Colin did not argue. Instead, he smiled and gave Daniel a thumbs-up sign.

COVER STORY
....

January 29, 1942
Royal Navy Headquarters, London

WITH HIS TEAM in place, Colin decided the time had come to make Project Habakkuk a reality. It was decided the first step would be to create a prototype. But that presented a problem. Where could they work on it without arousing suspicion?

A number of remote locations in northern Scotland were recommended before Colin raised his hands and said, "No, no. Too close. We'd be idiots to think that the Germans don't have at least a few spies in the UK. Hell, for all we know they're still flying spy missions over Britain. No, we don't know who can be trusted. It will have to be someplace very remote, and I know just the place. Not too many people. It'll be perfect."

"Where?" someone asked.

"It's called Patricia Lake. It's in western Canada—the Rocky Mountains."

"He's right, it's a perfect location," Daniel said. "But..."

"But what, Daniel?" Colin asked.

"That part of Canada is not totally desolate. Even with the war, there are bound to be tourists. Plus, the locals might get suspicious."

"I seriously doubt the Nazis have spies in western Alberta." Daniel shook his head. "No, that's not what I mean. What I'm saying is we'll need some sort of cover story to keep folks from snooping if we want to maintain secrecy and give the perception that our work is routine. We're going to need supplies and material and all sorts of things. The first thing people are going to wonder is why guys like me and you aren't off fighting the Germans."

"Good point," Colin said. He turned to his team members and said, "Anyone have any suggestions? It has to be credible."

"Can't we just say that we're pacifists who don't believe in war?" someone said.

"Hey, I've got it," said Daniel, snapping his fingers. "I've got the perfect alibi. We say we're Hutterites."

Alan Simpson, a team member, said, "*Hutterites*? What are Hutterites?"

Colin provided the answer: "That's brilliant, Daniel. Hutterites are a religious sect. They mostly live a communal lifestyle, either farming or providing goods or labor. They don't totally shun modern ways—unlike the Amish and the Mennonites, they'll drive cars rather than horses and buggies—but they tend to dress conservatively and live simply. And they're pacifists. There are sects of them all over western Canada. They believe it's wrong to wield the sword."

"Even to Nazis?" Simpson said.

"Yeah, even to Nazis," said Daniel.

Colin said, "We'll need to grow beards. Hutterite men don't shave. You can all grow beards, can't you?"

Everyone nodded.

"Hmm," said Daniel when Colin had finished. "There's just one small detail we need to nail down."

"And that would be what?" Colin said.

"How are we going to explain what a group of Hutterites—

I figure it'll take at least five of us to build the prototype—would be doing in a national park?"

Colin considered the question. As he did so, he loosened his tie.

"I think I have a plausible story," he said. "Daniel will pose as a representative of the Canadian government. The story will be that you hired the four of us, who will dress and act like Hutterites, to supply lumber for the government. It's no secret materials are as scarce back home as they are in England. The Hutterites may be pacifists, but there's nothing that would prevent them from a little commercial activity."

Daniel and the others nodded.

"We'll likely need to hire some locals when we get there," said Simpson, whose background was in ship design, "to produce enough of the pulp mixture to get the model built in time before all the ice melts."

"And I'll need to requisition an airplane beforehand," Daniel said. "Something pedestrian, that doesn't draw attention."

Colin said, "Should not be a problem. We'll leave the day after tomorrow, which will put us in Jasper by mid-February. The ice should be on the lake until well into May, maybe even June. That should give us enough time to build the model and test whether building an airfield is feasible."

"Sounds like a plan, Colin," Daniel said.

"Make that *Brother* Colin."

THE PHONE CALL

February 9, 1942
Montreal, Quebec

THE PHONE RANG at Rudy Hoff's apartment a little after six in the morning. He didn't want to get out of his warm bed and answer it because he knew the bedroom would be frigid—it had been minus ten or colder all week, unusual for Montreal even in early February. But whoever was on the other end of the line was persistent. After the nineteenth ring he rose, put on his bathrobe, and walked across the cold wooden floor to the parlor-kitchen. He swore in German with each step, but did so silently so he would not wake his sister in the other bedroom.

"Hello?" he said, pulling his robe tight.

"Rudolph?" the caller asked.

Rudy immediately recognized the voice. "Yes," he whispered.

"Have you shoveled your sidewalk today?"

That was the code phrase, Rudy knew. He had to give the reply. "The sidewalks are very slippery this time of year."

"Good," the voice said. "Is it safe to talk?"

"Yes."

Rudy knew the man on the other end of the line only as Peter. He was a senior Nazi Party leader, an *oberführer*, who became a member of the SS in the 1930s and later infiltrated the Canadian government as an undercover agent. Rudy was an *unterführer*—a non-commissioned SS officer. While he had never met Peter, he'd had numerous conversations with him since he and Elaina, his twin sister, had come back to Canada from Germany five years ago. The SS made sure that there were many layers to the network of secrecy so that no one person could compromise an agent's identity. As it was, the only other thing Rudy knew about Peter was his telephone number.

"We have intelligence that the British are working on a project that may have grave implications for our Atlantic offense," Peter said.

"What kind of implications?"

"Unknown. We have few details. Very few. We know the project is called Habakkuk. But our source is extremely reliable."

"*Habakkuk?*"

"Yes. It is being developed in western Canada."

Rudy brought a finger to his mouth and chewed a fingernail. It was a nervous habit, one he was aware of and had tried to break many times. It was not unusual for him to bite his nails to the quick until they bled.

"What do you need me to do?" Rudy asked.

"You are to go to Jasper, Alberta, and determine the threat of this Project Habakkuk. There is to be no delay."

"You are not giving me much to work with." There was no response.

The cold room made Rudy shiver. He thought about his sister, asleep in the other bedroom. How was he to explain this to her?

"Is this really necessary?" Rudy asked.

"May I remind you of your present *situation*?"

Rudy did not like it when Peter used that word. He was

making a point. Peter was one of a few people who knew that Rudy and Elaina's parents were Jews—and that Rudy had kept that fact hidden from Nazi officials to protect his family. He had no other choice but to help Peter. Even if it put his life, and the life of his sister, in jeopardy.

"I understand. Of course, I will do anything I can to help."

"Good. You must not in any way arouse suspicion. Be discreet. But learn what you can and, if the opportunity presents itself, ensure that this Habakkuk project, whatever it is, fails. Am I making myself clear?"

"Understood."

"Good-bye."

Rudy placed the receiver of the phone back into its cradle and looked out the window. It was dark, but every once in a while he would catch sight of snowflakes blowing in the wind, glinting in the light of the streetlamp below.

He found himself getting dizzy. *Was it from watching the snowflakes? No*, he decided, glancing at the clock on the wall. A diabetic, he often felt dizzy before his morning insulin shot. But that would not happen for another two hours.

He fell asleep in the chair.

SECOND ENCOUNTER
....

February 18, 1942
Jasper, Alberta

FOR SECURITY REASONS members of the Project Habakkuk prototype team traveled to western Canada separately. The plan was for Colin to arrive first by truck—a 1941 Maple Leaf two-ton stake bed he arranged to borrow from the City of Calgary before driving to Jasper. Daniel would join Colin later the same day after flying to Jasper in a plane he had arranged to have waiting for him at the RCAF training base at Edmonton, followed the next day by the remaining three members.

Colin reached town just before noon. He had three hours to kill before Daniel landed so he decided to drive to Patricia Lake to see what the lake looked like when it was frozen—he had never been to Jasper in the dead of winter—and perhaps stake out a place to establish camp.

The snow was at least a foot deep on the road to the lake and it did not take Colin long to realize that he would likely get stuck if he kept going. He had two choices. The most logical was to turn around and go back to town. The other was to make an almost two-and-a-half-mile walk—he could see some of the snowdrifts ahead were quite high—to the lake.

Remembering that had a pair of snowshoes in the back of the truck, Colin decided to walk.

He pulled the truck over to the side of the road, although there was no danger of anyone hitting it; the lack of vehicle tracks signaled that no one had driven to the two lakes—Patricia and, a short distance further, Pyramid—in a while.

Colin put on the snowshoes and his backpack. The pack contained food; survival tools such as a folding camp shovel, matches, knife, small stove, and canteen; his blanket from the German U-boat captain; a handgun (which he decided he would keep in his room after they were checked in); and the Bible that Winston Churchill had given him.

He brought the Bible as a prop, figuring it would support his cover story.

As he adjusted his backpack, Colin glanced at the outside rearview mirror and caught sight of his bearded face. He smiled. Between the beard, the dark blue wool trousers and suspenders, white shirt, black coat, and hat with the wide brim, he did look like a Hutterite.

Pretty convincing if I may say so.

Before proceeding, Colin looked in each direction to make sure that he was truly alone before lighting a cigarette.

If I were a real Hutterite I'd get kicked out of the colony for smoking. I can only do this when no one's around.

He set off in the direction of Patricia Lake. It was sunny but cold, perhaps five degrees, and otherwise beautiful and quiet, except for the occasional sound of a blue jay or a squirrel in the pines that lined the road. The snow was light and fluffy, and Colin made good progress, despite the fact that it was difficult to balance on one snowshoe because of his missing big toe.

Colin walked for nearly an hour when he had the sensation that he was being watched. He stopped, lit another cigarette, and scanned the trees along the road. He did so slowly, the way he'd been taught in his survival class during basic training.

That's when he spotted the wolf.

Colin almost did not see the animal at first because of the way it lay in the snow, its white, brown, and gray fur blending perfectly with the bushes to its side. The wolf was motionless. If not for the occasional faint cloud of steam caused by the wolf's slow exhale, Colin would have sworn it was dead.

His thoughts went back to the last time he'd walked the road and his encounter with a wolf. This time he was glad he had his gun. This wolf was an adult—and big. Perhaps two hundred pounds.

Staring at the wolf, Colin picked up a stick that was half buried in the snow in front of him. He reached into his pocket for his lighter and lit the tip.

Could this be the same wolf? he wondered as he watched the tip catch fire. *Unlikely. The chances are just too great.*

From an early age, Colin had been taught that it is best to not disturb any creature of the wild. Bees. Snakes. And anything with sharp teeth.

If I ignore you, you'll ignore me, Colin told himself as he slowly resumed his journey to the lake.

He had walked about fifty yards when the wolf rose and disappeared deeper into the woods.

"Good," he whispered, throwing the smoldering stick into the snow.

No forest fires this time.

Colin had proceeded about a quarter-mile before coming upon a bend in the road, which led upwards. As he rounded the turn, he saw a shape in the middle of the road, about forty feet away. It was the wolf!

Oh great. He stopped to consider the situation but before

long found himself wishing that he had a camera to record the scene. A narrow band of bright sunlight shone down on the wolf through the gap in the trees, making the animal glow, like an apparition. It was a stunning, almost supernatural, sight.

Colin had no doubt that the wolf knew he was there, yet it seemed disinterested. "Hey, have you been following me, Mr. Wolf?" he called. His made sure his voice was authoritative, as though he were commanding a dog.

One of the wolf's ears twitched. It lowered its head slightly. Colin was startled to see a white mark on its back and shoulders that reminded him of a cross.

Holy shit, it's the same wolf, but now fully grown!

"I get the distinct feeling you and I have met before," said Colin, his voice steady. "You don't mind if I test a theory, do you?"

The wolf tilted its head.

Colin dropped to one knee, removed his backpack, and opened it. The wolf's ear twitched again.

"Look what I have, Mr. Wolf! Your favorite!"

It was a stick of salami that he'd purchased along with his cigarettes yesterday.

After removing his gloves, Colin used his jackknife to slit the salami casing and cut off a piece, which he threw toward the creature.

The meat landed in the snow about fifteen feet ahead of the wolf. In two strides the animal was at the spot. It lowered its nose into the snow, lifted its head in Colin's direction, then lowered it again and ate the piece in one bite.

"A salami-eating wolf," Colin said laughing. "Who would have thought it?"

Colin cut off another piece of meat, this time about two inches thick, and threw it in the wolf's direction. But this time he made sure to throw it closer to his position. The wolf waited for a moment, walked to the spot, found the meat, and swallowed it in one mouthful.

"You have quite the appetite, Mr. Wolf. Well listen, it was good seeing you again but I have to get going. I have work to do."

Colin picked up his backpack and placed it on his back. The wolf watched Colin, its head tilting occasionally. Colin put his gloves back on and looked at the remaining stick of salami.

"Tell you what, Mr. Wolf," Colin said, raising the salami into the air. "I'm going to let you have this on the condition you leave me alone. Should you change your mind, I'm fairly certain you'll regret it. You see, this time I have a gun."

He gently threw the remaining salami to the side of the road, parallel to the wolf's position. The wolf turned, found the salami and picked it up. It looked at Colin, the stick of salami hanging out of its mouth like an oversized, unlit cigar, and trotted into the woods and out of sight.

* * * *

Colin reached Patricia Lake a little after one-thirty. Although the lake and surrounding terrain were covered in snow, he had no trouble recognizing several familiar landmarks and objects, including what remained of his old wooden boat from two and a half years ago, still chained to the tree. It appeared that someone had tried to remove the chain but instead damaged the side so heavily it now had a hole about the size of a fist.

The desolate beauty and quietness made Colin catch his breath. He had never seen so many shades of white and gray, which changed with each step he took in relationship to where the sun's rays struck the snow and ice of the frozen lakebed. It was so peaceful—incomprehensible that a world war raged on the other side of the planet.

Colin removed his snowshoes and immediately slipped and

fell as he began his walk out onto the lakebed. The snow on the lake wasn't more than three or four inches deep. It was so light and fluffy. The way it clung to his boots made him think of powdered sugar.

He became aware of the sound of an airplane overhead. The noise grew louder.

He looked up. Even with his sunglasses on, it was so bright that he had to cover his brow with his hand. The aircraft emerged over a bend in the lake that Colin had difficulty seeing because of the way the sun was positioned. It appeared to be descending. No, it was descending.

Colin rose and watched with interest as the pilot masterfully brought down the single-engine craft, its front wheels replaced with small skis, onto the ice about a quarter-mile from where he was standing. He was amazed how little space the pilot needed to land.

The pilot turned the plane into the sunlight and cut the engine.

As he was the only other human nearby, Colin decided to walk over and say hello.

It was not until he rounded the front of the plane that he saw Daniel. "What are you doing here?" they said in unison.

"I asked first," Daniel said, stepping forward to shake his friend's hand.

Colin said, "I thought you weren't getting into Jasper until three."

"I wasn't supposed to," he said, kicking a wheel block behind the landing ski, "but by luck they had my plane ready early, so I decided to come early and check out the lake. I've never seen it in wintertime."

Daniel explained that he had been able to "fly jump"—that is, secure seats on RCAF planes when space became available—across Canada to the training base in Edmonton.

Once in Edmonton he discovered that the Stinson Voyager he had arranged to be waiting for him had already been prepped and was ready to go.

"So this is what you'll be using for our test?" Colin asked, wrapping a hand around one of the wing struts.

"That's right. It's no Spitfire, but she'll do. Now what about you? Tell me why you're already out here."

"Same thing you are. I've never seen the lake completely frozen over either. Come here; let me show you what I've been thinking about."

The two men walked to an area of the lake not far from the southern shore, where Colin outlined his plans to construct a small sawmill to produce the sawdust needed to make the compressed sawdust and pulp panels. These would be fitted to the tops and sides of a nine-hundred-foot by seventy-five-foot block of ice they would cut from the lake to serve as their floating airfield. If all went according to schedule, the test would be in May or early June. That would allow sufficient time to build the structures and produce the material they needed, and determine whether it was possible to safely conduct a takeoff and landing off a floating block of ice.

"It'll either work or it won't," Colin said.

"Oh, it'll work, all right," Daniel assured him. "You just watch."

RUDY AND ELAINA

....

Montreal, Quebec

AS WAS HER custom, Elaina Hoff had dinner waiting for her brother when he arrived at their tiny four-room apartment after work.

"How was your day today, brother?" she asked as he hung up his coat and made his way to the table.

"Okay, I guess," he said.

Elaina could tell that something troubled her twin brother. Whenever he was nervous or deep in thought, he chewed his fingernails. She studied him for a clue, as his tenseness made her uneasy. It was as though she could feel what was bothering him.

Rudy was small—five foot three inches tall and less than one hundred and thirty pounds—with freckles and red, curly hair like his sister's, but his was slicked down with pomade and parted in the middle. He walked with a limp, the result of being struck by a bullet in the shin when he was a teenager, and one of his front teeth was chipped and stained brown from years of smoking.

Elaina, the older of the two by four minutes, was strikingly beautiful and, at five foot eight, tall and slender. Like her brother, she had green eyes. Unlike her brother, however, Elaina was quiet and reserved; Rudy was excitable, and seemed to have a penchant for finding trouble. A part-time nursing student, Elaina's idea of fun was painting or reading.

They were both twenty years old and mature for their age. They had to be; they had been on their own for nearly four years.

"You can tell me, you know," Elaina said, as she dished a spoonful of mashed potatoes onto Rudy's plate.

"Uh-huh."

"Does whatever's bothering you have something to do with the call this morning?"

Rudy put down his knife and fork and looked up at his sister. "How do you know about that?" he asked.

Elaina sat down in the chair beside him and said, "Rudy, the phone rang and rang and rang until you got up. It got me up, too."

Rudy grunted.

"So, who was it?"

Rudy got up and walked to one of the kitchen cabinets, opened a door and pulled out a bottle of whiskey and a glass. He poured about an inch of liquid and drank it quickly before returning to the table.

Elaina did not like it when her brother drank. Rudy's doctors had warned him that too much alcohol was not good for his health. It made his blood sugar rise, which could cause blurred vision, and sometimes made him pass out. She kept a close eye on his health—it was one of the reasons she decided to become a nurse—because she knew he didn't.

"There's no good way of saying this, Sis, so I'll come right out," Rudy said, taking his seat. "We're going out west day after tomorrow." He patted a piece of paper sticking out of his shirt pocket. "I got us two train tickets."

Elaina furrowed her brow.

"I have classes," she said.

Rudy's expression turned to anger.

"You wanted to know if what's bothering me had to do with the call I took this morning?" he snapped. "Well, it *does*. The call was from Peter."

Elaina straightened upon hearing the name. Though she had never met the man, she hated him because he held great power over her brother—and somehow, her parents. Tears filled her eyes.

"Are Mama and Papa okay?" she asked. "Tell me they're okay."

Elaina and Rudy's parents, Herman and Henrietta Hoffman, were born in Germany. Mr. Hoffman had been a soldier in the Kaiser's army during World War I but emigrated with his wife to Montreal two years after the war ended, during the throes of the German depression, in search of a better life. The following year, Elaina and Rudy were born.

Herman made his living as a tailor and Henrietta cleaned houses, but by 1930 Herman had gone into business with another Jewish immigrant, Howard Stein, to form Hoffman & Stein Clothiers, a high-end Montreal clothing company.

Leaving his partner in charge of the business, the elder Hoffman returned to Germany with his family in June 1932 with the notion of staying for a year and, if it worked out, perhaps even permanently. He marveled at how Germany had changed following the grim days after World War I, when the world looked down on the German people. There was a renewed sense of optimism and a new spirit throughout the country: a spirit of pride in what it meant to be German. Initially, the Hoffmans even embraced the concept of National Socialism.

It was during that yearlong stay that Rudy made connections that his parents and sister would regret. Because he was sickly as a child due to his diabetes, Rudy spent much of his time in the library, reading. There he met a group of boys—his father described them as "galoots"—who introduced Rudy to *Mein Kampf* and the Hitler Youth.

As Adolf Hitler amassed more power, Herman and his wife became uncomfortable with the rhetoric emerging from the Nazi Party. While they loved Germany, it was apparent that the Nazi racial policy toward non-Aryans would not favor families like the Hoffmans. They decided to return to Canada in June 1933.

Rudy was angry about the decision. He had wanted to stay. For the first time, he said, he had a core of friends who valued him.

"But we are Jewish, Rudolph," his father explained. (He always called his son by his formal name.)

"So? We just don't tell anyone our background," Rudy countered. "We'll be fine."

"No, you don't understand," Mr. Hoffman said. "We are *Jewish*. You are Jewish."

Rudy did not understand because he chose not to. He embraced the Nazi movement. He liked the power and the prestige of the Nazi movement and having control over others, and he agreed with his friends' view that the world would need to pay for its humiliation of the German people after World War I.

After returning to Canada, all seemed well until Mr. Hoffman received a telegram from his sister in Munich on November 10, 1938, informing him that she feared arrest and that the German people seemed to be turning on anyone of Jewish heritage.

November 10 became known as *Kristallnacht*—Night of the Broken Glass—for all the broken glass from the windows of Jewish-owned shops that were ransacked throughout Germany that night.

Mr. Hoffman could have stayed in Canada and been an overseas observer of the plight of the Jews in Germany but, along with his wife, he returned to Germany using false Canadian passports bearing the surname "Hoff." He asked his children to use that same surname until he and his wife returned.

"We will be back before you know it," the parents had told

their children at the pier before the ship set sail. "And then everything will be as it was. Mr. Stein will provide whatever financial means you need until we return."

That part was true. Even though their apartment was modest, Elaina and Rudy never lacked for money. On the first Monday of each month a check for three hundred dollars appeared in the mail—more than enough to pay for rent, utilities, food, Elaina's classes at her university, and anything else the pair needed.

Although she could never be certain, Elaina suspected her brother's ties with the people he'd met nearly a decade before had something to do with the fact that they had not heard from their parents for four years. For a time, while he was in his early and mid-teens, Rudy had hung out with pro-Nazi sympathizers in Montreal, but he had assured his sister he did not do so anymore.

He had lied.

"Rudy," Elaina said again, "tell me Mama and Papa are okay."

"I'm told they're okay, but if you don't help me that's sure to change." Rudy then told her about his conversation with Peter. Every detail.

Elaina felt she was going to pass out when he had finished.

"Oh my God, Rudy! They want you to be a spy? A Nazi spy? Oh my God! You'll hang if you get caught."

"You mean, *we'll* hang if we get caught." She could not believe what he was saying. "We?" she asked.

He looked at her with an expression she had not seen before. It was evil, and it made her shiver.

The expression lasted only seconds. Then Rudy smiled.

"I'm kidding," he said. "You know I'm kidding. I'm a kidder. You know that. So don't you worry your pretty head about it. Things will be just fine. You'll have fun. You'll see."

Elaina knew she had no choice but to go, as she was trained to give Rudy his insulin shots—Rudy could not do it himself because he feared needles—once in the morning and once after dinner. She promised her parents she would take care of her brother while they were away, and it was a promise she intended to keep.

Rudy picked up his knife and fork and began to cut the piece of meat on his plate. "Cheer up, Sis. You like to paint. There are mountains where we're going—and lakes and trees. You'll have plenty of things to paint. And it's not like you have to kill someone."

That would be my job, he thought.

ON THE TRAIL
....

Big Mountain Lake Lodge
Jasper, Alberta

RUDY HOFF WAS ecstatic when he came across the first clue of the puzzle he was trying to solve.

It came from the clerk—a portly woman eating a cookie—working the front desk of the lodge where Rudy and Elaina had decided to stay while in Jasper.

"You're the second group in the past two weeks who's asked to rent for a month at a time," said the clerk.

"Really?" Rudy said, sounding nonchalant as he watched a squirrel monkey in a large cage by the front desk pick fruit out of a bowl. He turned to his sister and said, "Isn't that interesting?"

"Things around here have been dead as a doornail," the woman continued. "It wasn't always like that. We used to have train after train bringing rich folks like you from all sorts of places—the east, the States, Europe—to stay for a month or two at a time. Sometimes the whole summer. And a lot of the time for the same reason—their doctors said the mountain air would be good for their health."

"That is exactly what Elaina's physician told us," Rudy said. "I imagine a lot of people suffer from asthma, as she does. We're told this fresh mountain air is supposed to do wonders.

I suppose because it is so dry. By the way, does your monkey have a name?"

"Her name's Clementine. And don't get your fingers too close to her. She'll bite you."

Elaina said, "I don't think the air here smells so fresh."

The clerk laughed, broke off a small piece of the cookie, put it into her mouth and said, "Oh, *that*. That's the animal rendering plant, about thirty miles up the road from us. Sometimes when it's this cold and the wind is blowing from that direction the odor settles over the area. But it won't last long. We have a saying around here about that smell."

"Pray tell," Rudy said, still watching the monkey.

"It's the smell of money," said the clerk.

Laughing, she reached out a pudgy hand and slapped Rudy's arm, then broke off another piece of her cookie and popped it in her mouth.

"Anyways," she continued, "I was telling you what it used to be like around here before the war. How we would get people from all over. Well, with the war on, these last two and a half years have been hard. The tourists stopped coming like they used to. But then out of the blue we have two groups come in and rent for a month at a time. So maybe the economy's starting to pick back up."

"Is it always this cold here this time of year?" Elaina asked.

The woman took another bite of her cookie and glanced down at the guest book Rudy had just signed.

"From Montreal, ey? Seems you'd be used to the cold. It was six below when I got up, but we've had Aprils where it's been thirty below for three weeks straight. And I've seen snow here each of the twelve months."

Rudy turned to the clerk and said, "Even July?"

"Oh sure."

"Oh my," Elaina said.

"Don't mind my sister," Rudy said. "She's not accustomed to the cold like I am. Tell me about this other group. Where are they from?"

The woman smiled and took the last bite of her cookie. "Only know about the guy who's paying the bill," she said.

Rudy glanced down at the guest book at the names above his signature.

Daniel Masters, Halifax, NS. Below that he saw four more names, all written on the same line: *Brother Colin, Brother Alan, Brother Nigel, Brother Paul.* The address column was blank.

The clerk was watching Rudy and answered his question before he could ask it. "Mr. Masters is a government man. The others are Hutterites."

"Hutterites?" Rudy asked. "What in heaven's name are Hutterites?"

"Religious folks. Simple people, really. They shun a lot of modern ways. They don't own cars and don't believe in using electricity. They come through Jasper every now and then. Can't say as I agree with their beliefs. But they're pacifists. Nice and quiet, too. I think the world would be a better place if there were more Hutterites around."

What Rudy learned convinced him he was on the right path.

Religious people and a government man. And Habakkuk is an ancient religious writing. There has to be a connection—but what?

Before leaving Montreal, Rudy stopped by the library to find out the meaning of Habakkuk. He checked out a Bible and read all the passages, but still had no clue what any of it had to do with the war.

"What are the government guy and these Hutterites doing in Jasper?" Rudy asked.

"They're setting up a sawmill. Up at Patricia Lake, I think he said. Guess the government's in need of lumber, because of all the rationing and such. They keep to themselves. Leave real early in the morning—before sunrise—and don't come back until eight most nights. And they always take their meals in their rooms, except on weekends. There's an extra charge for that, by the way. In case you don't want to eat with the rest of the guests."

"I suppose they can do that if the government's paying," said Rudy.

"Yeah, our tax dollars at work. But it's about time we got some of it back, and a lot of folks here in Jasper are grateful they're here. I know one contractor who's getting paid three dollars to plow the road to Patricia Lake each time it snows. And rumor is they're going to need extra people here fairly soon, now that their equipment's arrived."

"Think I could get a job?" Rudy asked.

The clerk raised an eyebrow. "Why would you need a job?"

Rudy had to think fast.

"Oh, don't misunderstand, we have ample resources," he assured her. "We came out here expressly so my sister could get her health back and to paint, and so I could do some big game hunting. But I tend to get bored rather easily. I thought the prospect of a little manual labor might break up the stay."

The answer seemed to satisfy the clerk. "Well, I suppose you could always check."

"That I shall," Rudy said. "Tell me, how does one get to Patricia Lake?"

* * * *

An early March snowstorm back east delayed delivery of the components needed to assemble the Project Habakkuk team's sawmill by nearly a week. But the group was not idle during that time. Colin, Daniel, Nigel McIntosh, Alan Simpson, and Paul Lord, the final members of the team, and several laborers from town constructed a small shed on the lake ice in two days to house the sawmill. Not far from the mill they set up a large tent to cover what would become the prototype airfield, as well as two smaller tents along the shoreline. One of those housed the equipment to form the composite sawdust panels while the other was used for storage.

They chose an ideal location for the camp. It was a mile off the main road and directly over a portion of the lake that Colin knew to be at least sixty feet deep. Once their work was finished and it was warm enough to melt the thirty-five-inch-thick ice, all evidence of their experiments would sink to the bottom of the lake.

Before arriving in Jasper, Colin arranged for the purchase of a McIntosh 48 sawmill kit. He chose this particular model not because of its reputation for endurance under the harshest conditions—though, admittedly, that was important—but because, in the words of the salesman, "any idiot can assemble it."

As it turned out, assembly was a bit more complicated—and a good reminder to all involved that it is important to first read the instructions. *All* the instructions.

The first task in setting up a sawmill, they learned, is to establish a firm foundation. The men used eight-inch by eight-inch posts, which rested on the lake ice.

Because everything had to be level, they used blowtorches to melt a few inches of the ice here and there.

Once the foundation was set, they set iron tracks in place to support the carriage that the logs would ride on. The tracks consisted of a V-track and a flat track. The flat track was placed next to the saw blade—in this case, a forty-eight-inch blade—and used to support the carriage. The V-track would provide directional guidance for the log so the lumber would come out straight.

Perhaps the most important component of the entire setup

was the engine that powered the mill. While some mills ran on electricity, this one was powered by an old Ford Model A gasoline engine Daniel found in the town of Hinton, which was about an hour's drive from Jasper.

Three weeks after their arrival in western Canada, everything was going according to plan. No one—not even the superintendent of Jasper National Park—was the least bit suspicious of the group. Their cover story was credible. The men had access to all the trees they required. And the equipment was finally in place to produce the massive amount of sawdust needed to create the panels. Even the weather was cooperating: the long-term forecast called for a sunny yet colder-than-normal spring.

By all accounts, things could not have gone better for Colin and his group.

That, however, was about to change.

TABLES TURNED

....

March 15, 1942
The Pit

"THIS IS MOST unusual. Most unusual indeed."

Captain Wolfgang Eicher stepped back from the UX-1's periscope's eyepiece to finish the cigarette he'd left burning in the ashtray. Something didn't feel right and, for the first time in a long time, he was hesitant about his next move.

Why would the ships in this particular convoy be running abreast, rather than in a single file or the usual box formation? It didn't make sense.

He checked the eyepiece again. "Most unusual," he muttered.

Eicher's U-boat had picked up the convoy just after it had entered the western side of The Pit. Here, without the threat of enemy air cover, there was ample time to study the best way to bring down the prey. Because each convoy and its defenses were different, an undetected examination beforehand was the most prudent way to ensure success.

Outwardly, this convoy's configuration seemed to be an obvious weak spot. *But what commander would order ships to run abreast?* Eicher wondered. *It simply made no sense—unless it was a trap.*

Eicher had been watching intently through the periscope

the past two hours for a clue—any kind of clue. It was a small convoy. He counted only ten ships; eight merchant vessels flanked on the south side by a Royal Navy light cruiser and on the north side by an old American Wickes-class destroyer flying the flag of the Royal Canadian Navy.

Perhaps I'm getting too conservative. Or perhaps I'm getting too old and losing my edge. But something just doesn't seem right. What if this really is a trap?

After nearly three years of war, the Allies were more adept at protecting their ships, and the Americans joining made things more difficult for the wolf packs. In the early days, it was not unusual for the Nazis to sink two or three ships before an Allied warship had a chance to get into position and fire. But that had changed. The Allies were much better at A) anticipating and B) defending against *rudeltaktik*.

Still, Eicher knew he had a job to do. He could delay no longer. The rest of the pack was waiting for him approximately two hundred and twenty miles east of his present location. It was time to get into position and set the trap, unorthodox convoy deployment or not.

"Helmsman, increase speed to twenty-one knots and proceed to Point Wolf Seven," Eicher commanded. He had already figured out that would give the UX-1 more than enough time to rendezvous with the other three subs in this particular wolf pack and get into position for an attack, but he asked the navigator for verification.

"We will reach the rendezvous point in ten hours, thirteen minutes," the navigator said.

Hmm, seven minutes off in my calculation. Perhaps I am losing my edge.

* * * *

Noah Andrews scanned the dark waves of the Atlantic

Ocean with his binoculars from the captain's chair on the bridge of HMCS *Penticton*. It was a beautiful, cloudless day, a rarity for late March on any part of the Atlantic.

"Anything, sir?" asked newly promoted Lieutenant Ouellet, handing the captain a mug of hot tea.

Andrews lowered his binoculars and took the cup. "Thank you, Mr. Ouellet. No, nothing. Not yet."

"You think they're out there?"

The captain set his mug down and placed the fingers of both hands together in the form of a triangle, which he brought to his lips.

"Yes, Lieutenant," he said. "I *know* they're out there, and I expect they're quite befuddled. It's only a matter of time before we see a response."

* * * *

Captain Eicher had gone to his quarters with instructions to be notified thirty minutes before reaching the rendezvous point. He took the long way, stopping by Battery Room No. 3 to select a stick of smoked sausage—*Nibbled on! When will they get that rat?*—which he sliced immediately upon entering his cabin to enjoy with a small glass of kirsch.

It was Heidi who first introduced him to kirsch. Before meeting her, he preferred peppermint schnapps. But he soon discovered that when he went to sea, the cherry taste settled his stomach.

Though she had been dead for three years, Eicher thought about his wife many times each day. She was strong, kind, and patient. How she put up with him—a career submariner—for so long, he would never know. After she died, he realized that, of the twenty-two years they had been married, they were together only about half the time. But Heidi never complained. She knew what the navy and service to the

Fatherland meant to him, and that the Fuhrer required anyone who dared put on a military uniform to work hard.

Like thousands of his fellow Germans who recalled the dishonor that Germany was submitted to following the First World War—stripped of military might and the economy reduced to shambles, to the point where citizens were forced to eat from garbage cans and beg for bread on the streets—Eicher swore an oath to Hitler that he would do everything in his power to ensure that Germany withstood any threat of foreign tyranny. If that meant months at sea or long nights and weekends away as he worked at the shipyard developing the UX-1, it was a small price to pay in comparison to all the things the Fuhrer had sacrificed to bring Germany back to its rightful glory.

Eicher was remorseful that Heidi died before she could see the fruits of his labor. She would have been so proud.

There was a knock at the door.

"Captain," said the voice on the other side. "Thirty minutes until the rendezvous point."

Eicher opened the door. "Have Mr. Schopter surface and establish radio contact," he said to the sailor standing at attention. "Then await my further orders."

"Heil Hitler," the sailor said, and left.

Eicher saluted, shut the door, put the cap back on the bottle of kirsch, wrapped the sausage back in its casing, and placed both objects in a cupboard. He opened a box on the table, took out his Iron Cross and put it around his neck. As he fastened the hook he remembered what Donitz had said about the medal having divine protection, but a small voice in his head asked, *"Are you sure?"*

* * * *

"Sir, four U-boats surfacing—dead ahead!" came the call

from the *Penticton's* lookout. "Range: approximately one thousand four hundred yards."

Captain Andrews felt his throat tighten as the battle stations alarm sounded, but externally gave no indication that this was anything serious.

"Notify the *Superior* and the *Chelsea* to begin Operation Slapshot," he said in his usual calm tone. "Helmsman, increase speed to twenty-two knots. Bearing zero-three-nine degrees."

The *Penticton* pulled ahead of the convoy line and began a sharp right turn, thick black smoke pouring from the ship's four funnels. At the same time, the British cruiser HMS *Chelsea* pulled away at the same speed and turned left. The rest of the convoy slowed to form a dual triangle—with the exception of one freighter that broke away and positioned itself between and behind the *Penticton* and the *Chelsea*.

Moving the periscope slowly and methodically, Eicher watched the scene unfolding two hundred feet above him. He ordered the UX-1, which was between the *Penticton* and the freighter, to turn, too, so he could get a better view of the freighter. Ashe did so the sides of what he initially thought were the rear cabin walls dropped, revealing four maneuverable torpedo tubes.

It is a trap! Damn it, I must pay more attention to my inner voice.

Aboard the *Penticton*, Captain Andrews gave the command to fire his ship's starboard-side torpedoes. "Unleash the hogs!"

This was his first battle use of the hedgehog, a new anti-submarine weapon developed just weeks before by the British. Unlike the larger, more cumbersome depth charges, the hedgehog consisted of twenty-four small explosive projectiles launched in a salvo by mortar. The projectiles struck the water like a handful of gravel, but unlike gravel, hedgehog projectiles striking an object would explode, which is exactly what happened.

"Good show!" Andrews exclaimed, pumping his fist as he saw the bow of an approaching U-boat catch fire.

Still racing at twenty-two knots, the *Penticton* and the *Chelsea* unleashed additional salvos. Eicher meantime lowered the periscope and ordered the UX-1's helmsman to dive to six hundred feet.

"Quickly!" he ordered.

Meanwhile, the freighter in the center—actually HMS *Superior* in disguise to hide its lethal weaponry—launched additional torpedoes and depth charges.

Eicher knew the enemy above had no way of knowing his location—much less his existence. Still, he was in no position to take a gamble. The first rule of submarining is to protect one's boat, and he knew he was in a much better position to do that with the UX-1 than his colleagues in the Type IX subs the Allies were targeting.

As depth charges from the *Superior* detonated, the sea around the UX-1 was rocked with turbulence, which slowed the sub's dive. One detonation occurred so close that it sent the UX-1 and its crewmembers on their side, causing the lights throughout the boat to go out for several seconds.

And then, as quickly as the turbulence began, it was over.

"Six hundred feet, sir," said the helmsman.

"All stop. Hold position here," Eicher commanded. "We'll just wait this out." He turned to Schopter and whispered, "Give me a damage report."

The captain knew the battle above him would be raging, and that it would probably not be going well for the Germans. While he was curious to find out what was going on, he dared not risk raising the periscope for fear of exposing their location.

Schopter delivered his report twenty minutes later.

"Minimal damage to the forward starboard diving plane. Seven crewmen injured, all minor. And I almost hesitate to add this, but it appears the explosion shook loose the sausages you have curing in Battery Room No. 3. Crewman Eichmann picked up as many as he could and took them to your quarters."

* * * *

Six hundred feet above the UX-1, three more salvos from the warships finished off two additional subs, bringing the day's kill total to three. There was no damage to the convoy. The ruse worked.

"Good show, Captain," Lieutenant Ouellet said as the *Penticton* and the rest of the ships fell back into position. He was smiling.

"I would say a very good show, Lieutenant," Andrews smiled. "We'll exit The Pit in less than two hours, and without a scratch."

"There's something to be said for the element of surprise, sir."

"That is true, Lieutenant. But thankfully we won't always have to keep pulling rabbits out of our hat." He thought about Colin and added, "I predict we'll have the upper hand here before you know it."

INTRODUCTIONS

....

March 18, 1942
Patricia Lake, just outside Jasper, Alberta

"HAVE YOU NOTICED that we have company?"

Daniel pointed to the opposite side of the lake where a tan sedan was parked.

There were two people nearby. Because they were almost a mile away, it was impossible to tell what they had been doing for the hour or so since they had arrived. Daniel wished he had brought field glasses.

Colin acknowledged that he too had been aware of the pair's presence.

"It's the same car that was there yesterday," said Colin, lifting the stump of a pine tree onto the track of the sawmill. "But yesterday they only stayed about ten minutes or so. I just figured they were tourists wanting to look at the mountains."

"Hmm, I didn't even notice," said Daniel. "What do you suppose they're up to?"

"Good question," Colin said. "On the one hand, it's not like we can't make them stop coming. After all, we are in a national park. Still..." He did not finish.

It would be good to get an answer. Seems to me Pyramid Lake offers a better view.

Daniel said, "I think maybe it's time I check things out. What do you say?"

"Suit yourself," said Colin, trying not to sound concerned.

Daniel buttoned the top button of his jacket, pulled his wool cap down around his ears, and started across the frozen lakebed toward the road. Colin continued to work, but every once in a while turned to check on his friend's progress. Just in case.

It took Daniel about twenty-five minutes to reach the other side of the lake. As he drew closer he could see one of the two people, a woman, standing near an easel, holding a palette in one hand and a paintbrush in the other. He could not see her face because the canvas blocked his view.

The other person, a man, had built a small fire by the side of the road and was sitting on a collapsible stool when Daniel approached. He rose and said, "Well, hello there."

"Hello," Daniel said, extending his arm to shake the man's hand. "Rudy Hoff," the man said.

"Daniel. Daniel Masters."

"And this is my sister, Elaina," Rudy said, taking his sister by the elbow.

The figure emerged from behind the canvas and smiled. Daniel's pulse quickened.

She was beautiful. Her green eyes were striking, like the color of an aurora borealis just before dawn on a winter morning.

"How do you do," said Daniel. He smiled and touched the bill of his cap with his index finger.

"A pleasure, Mr. Masters," said Elaina.

It wasn't what she said that made Daniel take a deep breath; it was the way she said it in her French-Canadian accent: "*Miss-ter. Mas-ters.*" It sounded so rhythmic, so poetic.

Regaining his composure, Daniel asked, "Quebecker?"

"*Oui*," Elaina said. "Is my accent that noticeable?"

"I love your accent. I'm originally from Nova Scotia. It's always good to connect with a fellow easterner again."

Elaina, who had not taken her eyes off Daniel since his arrival, smiled. "You're a painter," Daniel said, pointing at the canvas. "May I?"

Elaina nodded and turned the canvas slightly so that Daniel could see. Though the painting was only about twenty-five percent finished, he could tell that it was a panoramic scene of Patricia Lake looking northeast, with Pyramid Mountain in the background and the lake in the foreground.

"Lovely," Daniel said. *And the painting isn't bad either,* he thought.

"You really think so?" Elaina said. "It's my first time painting a mountain."

"Really? You wouldn't know. You're quite good, and I'm not just saying that. It's very realistic. It's as though I could reach out and touch it."

And that's not the only thing I'd like to reach out and touch right now.

Rudy, aware of the obvious chemistry between his sister and this stranger, cleared his throat. "Hope you don't mind, but Elaina's not going to include your camp or whatever it is you have going over there in the finished product."

Daniel had temporarily forgotten there was a third person in his midst. "Excuse me?" he said.

"What is it you're building, anyway?" Rudy asked. "Sounds like you've got a big saw." He reached into his coat pocket and held out a pack of cigarettes. "Care for a smoke?"

Daniel's eye was drawn to one of Rudy's fingernails, which was bleeding slightly.

While he had been almost instantly smitten with Elaina, he was not so sure about Rudy. Something about the man made him uncomfortable. Still, he accepted the cigarette, then proceed to tell the two his cover story.

"That explains it," Rudy said.

"Explains what?" Daniel asked.

"Why you're not off fighting the war."

"God, I wish I was," Daniel said convincingly. "It's just the government has other ways of using people like me. And how about you?"

"Unfit for duty. Medical condition with my knee."

"And your diabetes," Elaina offered. "Rudy tried to get in but he needs to have someone administer his insulin shots. Apparently nurses are in short supply."

"Sorry to hear that," said Daniel.

"Don't be," snapped Rudy. "I don't need anyone's sympathy."

There were a few moments of nervous silence before Rudy smiled and said, "Say, could you use some extra help? It can get awfully boring watching my sister paint."

"I can't think anything involving your sister could be boring," Daniel said, glancing at Elaina. She giggled.

"Have you ever worked in a sawmill?" Daniel asked.

"No, but how hard can it be? I'm a quick learner. And I'm real good with my hands."

Daniel said, "Sounds like you're hired. That is, if you can start tomorrow."

* * * *

Rudy and Elaina arrived at their usual spot on the east side of the lake about eight-thirty the next morning. After helping his sister set up her painting gear, Rudy walked to the work camp, where he found Daniel.

Rudy was dressed in the same wool pants and jacket he wore the day before but had added galoshes and earmuffs to the ensemble.

"Aren't you going to be cold?" Daniel asked. The temperature could not have been more than five degrees.

"I figure once I start working I'll build up a sweat."

"Do you have gloves?"

Rudy looked embarrassed. "Uh... no."

Daniel turned to Colin, who had come from the sawmill to introduce himself. "Brother Colin, this is Rudy Hoff. He'll be working with you and Brothers Alan, Nigel, and Paul for the next little while. Could you find him an extra pair of work gloves from the supply chest and get him started?"

Colin faked a smile. "Yes, Mr. Masters. Come with me, sir."

"Are you a Hutterite?" Rudy asked as they walked to the mill.

"Yes, sir. I'm Brother Colin."

"Okay, just so we're clear," Rudy said, "I don't mind working with you, but I sure as hell don't want you talking to me about God. Understand?"

"I understand, sir."

"Last thing I want is some Bible-babbler trying to convert me."

Had the circumstances been different, Colin would have called Rudy an "arsehole" to his face. Instead he bit the inside of his cheek and said, "Yes, sir."

Once the two reached the mill, Colin introduced Rudy to Simpson, Lord, and McIntosh.

"Brother Nigel?" Rudy said. "That sure as hell don't sound like a Hutterite name. And I didn't know Hutterites had British accents."

"I'm a convert, sir," McIntosh said. "It's been nigh ten years now since I was baptized into the faith. I'm a changed man."

Rudy looked at him suspiciously before Colin walked between the two and, handing Rudy a pair of gloves, said, "Here, you'll need these."

Rudy put the gloves on as Colin directed him to a tree trunk that was about six feet long and eighteen inches in diameter. Colin took one end and motioned with his head for Rudy to pick up the other end, which he did.

Colin explained the parts of the mill and what Rudy would be doing.

"That's called the flat track," he said. "Put your end closest to the blade and I'll show you how to use the V-track to guide the wood to the blade. Brother Nigel will show you how to operate the blade, and how we cut these into boards."

Rudy turned out to be a quick study. Within three tries he not only learned how to place the wood in the correct position and guide it properly, but had also memorized the three blade controls.

"Very good," Colin said. "Once the boards are cut, we stack them over here." He pointed to a shoulder-high pile of lumber just outside the sawmill. "Then every thirty minutes or so we have you sweep up the sawdust into a wheelbarrow and take it to the tent next door."

"What are you doing with it?"

"Mr. Masters is having us make panels out of it."

"Panels? How do you make these panels?"

"We mix water, sawdust and an adhesive to form a pulp. Then we press it into sheets using forms and a vice."

"Sheets? For what?"

"You'll have to talk to Mr. Masters about that," Colin said. "We just do what he instructs us to do."

Rudy brought a finger to his mouth and began chewing one of his nails. "Not a big deal, Hutterite," he said. "Not a big deal."

* * * *

"You're pretty keen on Daniel, aren't you, Sis?" Rudy asked

his sister as he drove back to their bungalow at the lodge after his first day of work.

Elaina's face tingled. She knew she was blushing. But she also knew her brother could not see her, as the sun was fading.

"I...I do think he's nice," she admitted.

Nice was not the right word, she thought. *Handsome. Kind. Wonderful.* But she was not about to admit that to Rudy.

Rudy snorted as he lit a cigarette and unrolled the window to throw away the match. "Nice, yeah right. I know you, Sis. You're already in love with him."

She was surprised but not shocked at Rudy's intuitiveness. She had learned a long time ago that twins have a bond that lets them recognize things others cannot.

"But that's all right because I think—no, I know—he's sweet on you, too," Rudy added.

"What makes you say that?"

Rudy took a long draw on his cigarette. "He stops working and walks a mile to check on you, that's why. How many times did he do that today? I'll tell you. Three."

"He just wanted to make sure I was okay."

Rudy snorted as he exhaled smoke. "Uh-huh. Maybe you should see what he's doing Saturday. The Hutterites say that's the only day they don't work. That's their Sabbath."

Elaina thought for a moment and said, "What are you going to do? Go spy on the others for your Nazi friends?"

At that, Rudy became angry, holding his right fist up against her jaw as he gripped the cigarette between his teeth and steered with his other hand. "Goddammit, you bitch!" he yelled. "Maybe you don't give a damn about your mother and father but I sure as hell do."

It was a lie. Rudy was more concerned about being perceived by Peter and anyone else in the SS as a loyal Nazi, but he knew the reference to their parents would evoke sympathy from

Elaina and guarantee her help. He needed her to get close to Daniel so he could determine whether what was happening at the lake had anything to do with Project Habakkuk.

Elaina began to sob. Rudy lowered his hand, removed the cigarette from his mouth, and took a deep breath to regain his composure.

"Hey, hey, Sis," he said softly. "I'm sorry I yelled at you. Look, I just want to make sure we do all we can to make sure Mother and Father come back to us okay. So don't worry about me and what I need to do. You leave that to me. Trust me, things'll be fine."

Elaina wiped her tears. She did not believe him.

* * * *

"You know she likes you."

Colin directed his comment at Daniel as he drove the truck back to the mountain lodge. It was just the two of them in the cab. The others huddled together in the truck bed with their backs against the cab wall to keep out of the cold wind.

"What makes you think that?" Daniel said.

"I don't think it," Colin said, shifting the truck into second gear as they made their way down Pyramid Lake Road toward Jasper. "Rudy told me."

Daniel was inwardly pleased. He liked Elaina, but had no idea until then what she thought of him. He wanted to know more but did not want to seem overly anxious.

"Really," he said. He offered Colin a cigarette before taking one himself.

"Yes, really," Colin said. He breathed in the cigarette smoke hungrily; it was his first smoke since the morning.

"And it was he who brought it up, not me," he said. "Maybe you should ask her out sometime."

"Maybe I will," Daniel said. He smiled, took a puff off his

cigarette and reached into his jacket pocket for his flask. He took a swig and passed it to Colin. "The theater in town is playing *Gone With the Wind*. I could take her to that." He waited before adding, "Now that you've been introduced, what do you think of her? Give me your honest assessment."

"She's pretty. Very pretty. I think the two of you would make a nice couple. Hard to believe she's related to that creep of a brother, though."

Daniel raised his right leg from the floor and crossed it at the knee. "Yeah, he gives me the willies."

"Hard worker, though. We nearly doubled our output today. If we can keep up this pace we'll have all the panels completed way before our deadline. Simpson and Lord are making excellent progress."

Daniel finished his cigarette and tossed the butt out the window. "We'll be able to cut the airstrip out of the ice after that. I imagine we'll have ice on the lake for another month and a half."

"You still think you'll be able to land that Stinson of yours on it?" Colin asked.

"Piece of cake, my friend. Piece of cake."

UNEXPECTED VISIT
....

March 26, 1942

DANIEL LAY ON his back on the ice inside the sawmill on Patricia Lake to inspect the damaged saw blade. It was missing some of its teeth. There was no way of knowing how many because a chunk of timber had become wedged between the blade and the track.

"It does not look good, Brother Colin," Daniel said.

"No, sir," Colin said, stroking his beard.

"I told the Hutterite not to push that last piece of spruce through so fast," said Rudy, who was leaning against a wall while smoking a cigarette. "I knew that blade was running hot. It's no wonder those teeth snapped off."

Colin clenched his fists. Rudy had lied. It was Colin who had told Rudy to take his time pushing the log carriage toward the blade but Rudy had ignored him. To make matters worse, Colin had advised Rudy at least a dozen times over the past week to not rush the work.

"That's not true," Colin protested.

Rudy straightened and stepped forward. "You calling me a liar?"

In truth, Rudy had sabotaged the blade to buy himself time. After ten days he was no closer to an answer than when he arrived.

"Hey, hey, hey," Daniel said. "Calm down Rudy. It's not a big deal. The timing works in our favor because I have to fly to Edmonton on Friday for supplies anyway. I'll just get a new blade then. We've been running this the past six weeks. I'm surprised more teeth haven't broken off before now."

Rudy said, "Won't that mean you'll miss your date with my sister?"

Daniel rose to his feet. "No, that's not until Saturday. If I leave just when it's starting to get light out I can be in Edmonton by eight and back in Jasper by four or five in the afternoon. I won't have to stay overnight. Plenty of time."

Rudy dropped the butt of his cigarette to the ground and stomped on it with his boot. "Hey, could I go with you?" he asked.

"Sorry," Daniel said, "government regulations prohibit the passage of civilians on government aircraft."

That, too, was a lie, but a necessary one. One of the things the team was required to do was provide Allied Command with a progress report on the last Friday of each month. The only way to do that was via a secure military radio channel at the nearest military base, which was in Edmonton. Having Rudy along would raise too many questions.

"Not a problem," Rudy said. "Just figured I'd ask. I've never been to Edmonton."

Daniel ran his fingers over the blade again. He said, "Brother Colin, can we use this with three missing teeth? Only for one day, I mean."

"I seem to recall the manual says it would be acceptable," Colin said. "It's still got twenty-nine teeth. Normally we run five hundred rpm, but it should be fine if we back it down to three hundred."

Colin looked at Rudy. "Running at nearly half-speed, though, we won't need any extra help until next week."

Daniel grinned and slapped Rudy on the back. "Looks like you get some time off," he said.

Take that, arsehole, Colin thought.

* * * *

Colin drove Daniel to the airfield along the Yellowhead Highway north of Jasper just as the sun was rising on Friday morning. The airfield was exactly that—a field. There were no buildings, no paved runway, not even electricity. Just a windsock and one plane, the borrowed Stinson.

Although it had been above freezing the past two days, the temperature had dropped into the teens, which meant the two to three inches of snow still covering the field would be hard and crusty and, therefore, not difficult to take off on.

Daniel had not started the Stinson for at least three weeks, so it did not surprise him that the battery was dead. Colin pulled the truck close in order to jumpstart the engine and, after a few minutes, the plane's motor started in a cough of blue smoke.

Daniel let the plane idle for a time so the defroster could thaw the ice on the windshield. "What time do you want me back to pick you up?" Colin asked.

Daniel buttoned his leather jacket to his neck. "Let's say five o'clock. If I get back any earlier I'll start to walk back to the lodge."

Colin said good-bye to his friend and started back to the lodge to pick up his colleagues before beginning the day's work. The day at the site was uneventful, though Colin realized as he drove back to the airfield just after four-thirty that it was the first time in over a week he had not been uncomfortable, because Rudy was not there. Being able to smoke without fear of discovery likely lessened his irritability, he decided.

Colin did not have to wait long before he saw the white speck he knew to be Daniel's plane grow larger as it neared his location. The plane made what Colin thought was a perfect landing and taxied to where it had been parked that morning. As Daniel cut power to the motor, Colin drove the truck just alongside the plane, as close to the door as he could without hitting the wing. He knew the new saw blade and other supplies Daniel was bringing would be heavy.

"Hey, buddy, how did it go?" Colin said as the door to the plane opened and Daniel jumped to the ground.

Daniel didn't answer directly. Instead, he said, "I brought a visitor." At that, Captain Andrews appeared in the doorway.

"Hello, Commander," he said.

Colin was ecstatic to see the captain again and, out of habit, straightened and saluted.

"You can dispense with the formalities," Andrews said. "Hutterites generally don't salute."

"Yes, sir," Colin said, stepping forward to shake hands. "But...but I have to ask you: what are you doing here?"

"I asked him the same thing," Daniel said. "I was in the debriefing lounge having a coffee, waiting for the gear to be loaded, when the base commander comes out and introduces me and lo and behold..."

"And lo and behold, here I am," Andrews said. At that his demeanor changed from jovial to serious.

"Look, as I told Captain Masters, I have come on a matter of great importance. Commodore Mountbatten's office has received some rather disturbing news that you need to be aware of. The *Penticton* was being resupplied in Halifax when the vice-admiral contacted me and asked me to personally deliver the message."

"What message?" Colin asked.

"This project may be compromised."

"Compromised?"

Captain Andrews paused and looked at Daniel before turning to Colin. "We have intelligence that the enemy is aware of Habakkuk. I've been sent here to warn you that all your lives may be in danger."

FIRE
....

March 27, 1942
The Pit

AFTER NEARLY THREE years of service, the UX-1 had performed so well that the Fuhrer ordered the navy to begin constructing eight additional electroboats.

The sub was an engineering and technological marvel, years ahead of its time.

The boat's performance far exceeded expectations. By the spring of 1942, Captain Eicher not only had more kills than any other U-boat captain, but the UX-1 led the German Navy—and this included surface ships—in tonnage sunk.

That is not to say that the boat did not have its quirks. Many of the technologies had never been tested in the field before, much less under strenuous wartime battle conditions. There were a number of things the German engineers still needed to know, still needed to understand. They pored over Eicher's logs and reports with a careful eye each and every time the UX-1 came into port in an effort to learn more, to refine, to improve.

The safety of the crew and the boat were paramount to anyone who had anything to do with the design or operation of the UX-1. One of the issues given close attention dealt with how the lead-acid batteries aboard the sub were charged. This was important because engineers wanted to design a failsafe to avoid the two main risks associated with charging such batteries.

The first risk was the buildup of sulfuric acid in the battery fluid. The engineers and sailors knew they had to be careful when working around the batteries. Because sulfuric acid is extremely corrosive—so much so that it can eat a hole right through the steel skin of the sub—it is critical that batteries are checked frequently to make sure they are not leaking.

The second risk involved various byproducts that can result due to charging.

These included oxygen and hydrogen and, to a lesser extent, arsine and stibine, both of which are toxic.

Because of these risks, the designers of the UX-1 were careful to include robust ventilation systems in all the battery rooms.

What they did not anticipate, however, was what might happen if the ventilation ports became blocked for an extended period.

Unbeknownst to anyone aboard the UX-1, when the depth charges fired during the attack on the HMCS *Penticton* caused the UX-1 to roll on its side and the smoked sausages that had hung from the conduit in Battery Room No. 3 fell to the floor, two of the sausages rolled just off to the side of the back ventilation screen. Had they remained there, things would have been fine. But just the day before, on March 26, the rat discovered the sausages and ate past the casings, which fell to the screen and prevented the air from circulating properly.

Over the next nineteen hours, a buildup of hydrogen went undetected until a crewman entered the room to check for leaking batteries and lit a match for his pipe.

Everyone on board heard the explosion. That was followed by two minutes of silence and blackness until a repair crew established emergency power.

It would be years before German naval command learned what happened to the UX-1. All it knew for certain at the time it lost contact was that the U-boat's last known position was in The Pit, approximately one hundred forty-five miles northwest of its position on March 27, 1942.

* * * *

"What are your readings?" Captain Eicher asked the chief engineer, who was seated at his station on the bridge when power was restored following the explosion. Eicher could feel the boat, which was submerged at almost three hundred feet, sinking nose first.

"I...I'm getting no readings," the chief engineer replied. "I need to get down to the engine room to see what's happening."

As the chief engineer left the controls, a crewman in wet clothing scrambled up the ladder and reported that water was pouring through a hole in the bottom of the boat. An attempt was made to brace the hole with a piece of sheet metal but the force of the water had been too great.

Eicher did not like the sound of that. He knew they were running out of time—and out of options.

"Prepare to blow the ballast tanks!" he yelled. "*Now!*"

The crewman at the ballast controls complied. Nothing.

This is not good, Eicher thought, his ears popping as the UX-1's bow dropped even further. *Not good at all.*

He knew that the high-pressure air should have forced the water out of the ballast tanks and caused the sub to rise rapidly. It did not, leading him to conclude that there was a problem with the air lines.

Could the air lines have been severed as a result of the explosion?

If so, that meant the air required to blow the tanks was likely being vented into the ocean—air the crew would need to breathe.

"*Stop!*" Eicher commanded.

Turning to the radioman he said, "Deploy the buoyant antenna."

The radioman moved to his right and began flipping switches at the reeling machine, the controls that let out and took in the cable attached to the antenna. Within seconds, the power went out again. This time it did not come back on for nearly four minutes.

"Sir, I am getting no response," the radioman said as he checked his dials. "I'm not sure we even have an antenna."

Eicher considered his situation. The sub was running on emergency battery power and there was no way to tell how long the power would remain on. It was possible that they had vented a large amount of air during the attempt to blow the ballast tanks. There was no way to communicate with the surface. And, if all that were not bad enough, the sub was continuing to sink—perhaps as fast as twenty-five feet every five minutes.

Unless he could find a way to stop the movement, they would reach a point where the pressure of the sea around them would crush the UX-1 as though it were an egg. Eicher figured they had two to three hours.

A floor hatch opened just outside the bridge and the chief engineer emerged. His pants were wet to his waist and the expression on his face was grim.

He approached Eicher, turned and whispered, "Not good, Captain."

Eicher looked at the faces of his men, which were turned in his direction, and put his arm around the chief engineer. He said, "Explain. I want facts."

The chief engineer took a cigarette from his shirt pocket, lit it and said, "Battery Room No. 3 is gone."

"What do you mean, gone?"

"Just what I said. Gone. And the engine room is flooded. Four crewmen managed to get out and secure the door." The chief engineer took a long inhale and shivered. "The other seven didn't make it. That can only mean one thing: the engines...*kaput!*"

Eicher was sure his bridge crew heard that last word because everyone stopped what he had been doing.

Not moving his arm from his engineer, Eicher turned. He directed the engineer to turn with him. For the next few seconds they studied the faces of the men. Some were frightened. Some resigned. Others perplexed.

The captain knew he had the respect of every man aboard his boat. There was no question about that. Each man, with the exception of two crewmen in the torpedo room, had served with Eicher since the sub's shakedown cruise in 1939. The crew had experienced battle multiple times. This was not the first time it appeared that the sub would not survive. But each time it had, and that bolstered their respect and loyalty to their captain. Each man knew that Eicher had the power over life and death.

Eicher did not let on that, unlike all the other times, this situation seemed hopeless.

Still, he knew the men were counting on him. And he wanted to make sure the chief engineer fully grasped that reality because he was about to ask him to do the impossible.

The captain turned to his first officer, who had been standing next to the periscope.

"Mr. Schopter, are you familiar with the *Hunley*?" The question took the first officer by surprise.

"The *Hunley*, Captain?"

"Yes, the H.L. *Hunley*," Eicher said, letting go of the chief engineer. Eicher took out a cigarette, lit it, and began to pace the floor of the bridge. He walked with purpose. "The *Hunley* was the world's first modern submarine, invented by the Americans to fight in their Civil War," Eicher said. "It was constructed from an old steam boiler. There were no machines on board. Its crew of eight powered everything by hand."

"I don't understand the significance, sir," Schopter said.

Eicher continued: "Everything—everything—was powered by hand. Propulsion. The dive planes. Weaponry. Even the air system. The men aboard operated bellows with their feet to produce the air. And it was that air which they used to pump in to their ballast tank—there was only one aboard the *Hunley*—to surface."

No one said anything.

They're not making the connection, he realized.

"Don't you understand?" he said. "If our machines are inoperable, then we must revert to the way things used to be done. We must remember our roots. That is very important. Our roots."

He turned again to the chief engineer.

"Chief, I want you and Mr. Schopter to choose six strong men and access the emergency manual pumps. We'll remove the water by hand to surface."

Those words were all that was needed to change the mood of those on the bridge. In an instant, the solemnness on each man's face turned to an expression of hope. That is, all but one: the chief engineer. Eicher knew the chief engineer realized that what he was asking was an almost impossible feat; the chief's face told him that he was not buying the captain's story. They were so deep it would take hours of constant pumping, and there were no guarantees they would even get the boat to halt, much less reverse, its downward trajectory.

Eicher put his arm around the man's shoulder again. "Chief," he whispered, "I know you know what I know. That does not matter. What matters now is our service to our Fuhrer and to the Fatherland. It is our duty as German officers to give these men hope and for that, I need your help."

The chief engineer did not move.

"Chief," Eicher said, this time more forcefully, "I need you. *Damn it*—I need you!"

The chief engineer looked the captain in the eyes and said, "I suggest Steiner, Hauptman, Gunter, Locke, and the Schneider twins."

Eicher smiled and gave the chief a slight nod.

"Go to it," Eicher said. "Meanwhile, I'm going to my quarters to study the blueprints, in case we may be overlooking something."

As he made his way through the narrow corridor to his cabin, the UX-1 offered up a loud groan and shuddered as its bow shifted downward, almost knocking Eicher off his feet. The move took the captain by surprise. He had never felt a boat act this way. As he regained his footing, the sub lurched upward for a brief moment before violently rolling on its left side. Eicher was slammed to the wall but before he could get up the lights went out.

They would never come on again.

A WARNING

....

CAPTAIN ANDREWS INFORMED Daniel and Colin that it had taken him three days of almost non-stop travel to reach them.

"If there was a military transport plane or train, I was on it," he said, adding that he was forced to sleep in a cattle car between Swift Current, Saskatchewan, and Calgary, Alberta, because that was all that was available.

"I knew that if I could somehow manage to reach the garrison at Edmonton by this morning that it was likely I'd make contact with someone on your team, given that was the day you were to report in. I barely made it."

Colin said, "Sir, how accurate do you believe this intelligence to be?"

"Very," Andrews replied. "The British within the past few weeks managed to crack the code on the Germans' outgoing communications. Until then it's been nothing but gibberish. The ciphers came across two messages containing references to Habakkuk and to Canada. Interestingly, the messages also contained the words "solution" and "elimination," which led Command to conclude that one, your lives may be in danger, and two, the Nazis have someone, or someones, working in the country, though they'll be first to admit they have no idea whom."

"This sounds like something out of a radio program," Daniel said. "Nazi agents among us. We're not aware of anyone who would be a Nazi."

"Again, there is no solid evidence there is a Nazi agent," Andrews said. "And if there were, it's not as though he'd be walking around with his black boots and swastika arm band on for all to see."

There was silence.

"What do you suggest we do, sir?" Colin said.

"Commodore Mountbatten expressly told me to advise you to continue with your work," Andrews said. "But be prudent and be vigilant. Trust no one. You must, repeat must, exercise extreme caution."

Colin and Daniel looked at each other and nodded. Colin said, "Will you be staying with us for a time?"

Andrews shook his head. "No, too risky. In fact, Captain Masters will be flying me back to Edmonton almost immediately. The *Penticton* is to lead another convoy to England on Wednesday the first, then we come back and turn around and lead another. I'm putting some miles under my belt. That said, the commodore felt it was too sensitive to put in a communiqué, as we have no degree of certainty that the Germans haven't cracked our code as well."

"So let's unload the gear I brought back so I can get back to Edmonton before the sun sets," Daniel said. "I won't come back tonight. I'll spend the night on the base and be back here at eight in the morning. So be here to give me a ride, okay?"

"Okay," Colin said. They unloaded the gear and within a half-hour, Daniel and the captain were gone.

* * * *

"Where's he taking you?" Rudy asked Elaina over breakfast in the dining hall of the main lodge the following morning. He cut a large piece of waffle, dripping with maple syrup, with his fork and stabbed a thick piece of back bacon before inserting the pile into his mouth.

"It's an American film called *Buck Privates* with Abbott and Costello and the Andrews Sisters," she said. "It debuts today."

Rudy motioned with his fork to a table at the other end of the dining room where Alan Simpson, Nigel McIntosh, and Paul Lord, all dressed in dark pants, light blue denim work shirts, and suspenders, were seated.

"Say, where do you suppose Daniel is this morning?" he said, stuffing another forkful of food in his mouth. "He's usually here for breakfast Saturday mornings. I haven't seen him or the one they call Brother Colin."

"Maybe they're sleeping late," Elaina said. She looked down at her half-empty glass of sauerkraut juice. The truth was that she was aware of Daniel's absence too, though she did not want Rudy to know that.

"Hutterites don't sleep late. I don't even think they sleep. They just work and pray and read their Bibles. They're all a bunch of hypocrites, I tell you."

"Why would you say that?"

Rudy picked up the last slice of back bacon on his plate with his fingers, licked off the syrup and began chewing. "I saw one of them smoking, that's why. While you were painting. Through the binoculars."

"Maybe you shouldn't be spying on them," Elaina said, her voice much softer. "They all seem quite harmless to me."

"Maybe you're right, Sis."

No sense in raising her suspicions, he told himself—even though there was something about these men that raised his. Thus, he was determined that today would be the day he learned what it was. Right after she left on her date.

* * * *

As Daniel drove the truck back from the airstrip on Saturday morning with Colin at his side he said, "Sorry you had to miss breakfast, but thanks for picking me up, buddy."

"Not a problem," Colin said, reaching into his pack on the seat between them. He pulled out a stick of salami and cut off a piece with his jackknife, offering it to Daniel.

"Don't mind if I do," Daniel said.

"So today's the big date. What are you and Elaina doing?"

"We're having lunch, then going to the afternoon matinee." He smiled and, taking his eye off the road momentarily to look at his friend, added, "She might be the one, Colin."

Colin was not surprised. He had not seen Daniel so smitten since their days together with Barbara Bealowski.

"I envy you, my friend," said Colin, putting away the salami. "Hey, what do you suppose ever happened to Barbara Bealowski?"

Daniel brought the truck to a halt in the parking lot outside the main building of Big Mountain Lake Lodge and whistled.

"My God," he said, "it's been years since I've heard that name." He thought for a moment, then added, "Being a good Catholic girl and all, I would imagine she's married and has about ten kids by now."

"I wonder if she's as gorgeous today as she was back then?" Colin said.

"Good question," Daniel said, opening the door of the truck. "Hey, I wonder…" He let the words trail off.

"Wonder what?" Colin said.

"I wonder if Elaina Hoff kisses as well as Barbara Bealowski."

Colin smiled. "I guess you're just going to have to find out."

THE DATE
....

AFTER FINISHING BREAKFAST and giving Rudy his insulin injection, Elaina spent the morning at the bungalow getting ready for her date. She put her hair up in rollers to give it extra bounce, something she thought it lacked in the dry mountain air, and spent extra time with her makeup so she looked just right. She selected a green skirt to match her eyes. It was not too dressy, she decided, and it accentuated her figure, which she hoped Daniel would notice. To complete the outfit, she chose a tan blouse and purposefully left the top button undone, which was the style in Montreal, though she had yet to see a woman with an exposed neck in western Canada.

Elaina had agreed to meet Daniel in the lobby of the lodge at twelve-thirty. The sun shone brightly; there was no wind, and the temperature had climbed into the mid-thirties, about normal for the end of March in the mountains, though it felt a lot warmer, as much of March had been well below freezing.

"You look swell, Sis," Rudy said when Elaina stepped out of her bedroom. Elaina felt herself blush.

"Thank you," she said.

Rudy turned back to his newspaper. After a few moments he asked, "What time's he picking you up?" He was trying to be as nonchalant as possible but wanted to have a timetable, as he had his own plans for that afternoon—plans he did not want her to know about.

"We're walking into town."

Rudy lowered the newspaper. "Walking? That's stupid. I could drive you and pick you up later."

"We decided earlier that if the weather was nice that we would walk."

Rudy hoped she would change her mind. This way he could be in control of her coming and going.

"I really don't mind giving the two of you a ride into town. I'll be heading that way anyway."

"No, we'll walk," Elaina insisted. "Do you have plans when I'm gone?"

"I thought I'd do some exploring," Rudy said, holding his newspaper to his face so Elaina would not see him grit his teeth.

* * * *

Daniel and Elaina's walk into town from the lodge took only twenty minutes.

Much of the snow was gone from the sidewalk, which was a good thing because neither person wore boots.

"Oh no!" Elaina said as they came across a puddle in the middle of the sidewalk.

The pool of melted snow was too deep to walk through and she was wearing heels. It would be difficult to walk in the muddy grass and snow on either side of the walk.

Daniel already had a solution for their predicament. "Don't worry, Elaina. I'll get you past that puddle."

"In heaven's name, how?"

"I'll carry you. You can't weigh more than a hundred and ten pounds."

"Carry me? Daniel, you *can't* be serious." Then she giggled and said, "A hundred and five, by the way."

Daniel smiled. "It's either that or we turn back and put our galoshes on. But then we run the risk of having lunch run late and missing the first part of the movie."

"Mr. Masters, I am at your disposal," she said.

Daniel picked up Elaina. She put her arms around his shoulders as he began to walk.

"Has anyone ever told you that you smell nice?" he asked, slowly following a set of footprints around the puddle and through the snow.

She could feel herself blushing again but did not care. Being this close to Daniel made her heart race. She could not remember the last time she had felt this way. It was a mixture of joy, exhilaration, and dizziness.

I wonder if I'm in love? she asked herself. She quickly dismissed the thought.

They had not known each other long. *It's too early to really know. Or is it?*

A car horn sounded. The two turned in time to see a tan sedan, with Rudy behind the wheel, pull out from the entrance to the mountain lodge. The car turned left as it reached the Yellowhead Highway and headed toward the town of Jasper.

"Uh-oh," Daniel said, setting Elaina down after clearing the puddle. "I hope I didn't get you in trouble."

"I don't mind one bit," said Elaina, her arms still around Daniel. "Not one bit."

* * * *

Because he had the day off—Hutterites were not expected to work on the Sabbath—Colin decided to put on his hiking boots and backpack and take a long walk through the woods. Not because he particularly enjoyed hiking or even the woods, but because he wanted the privacy. The privacy to smoke and drink.

After crossing the highway, he followed an animal trail up

the mountain and into the forest. He could hear the occasional car on the highway below, yet he knew no one or nothing could see him—with the exception of an occasional big horn sheep or mountain goat. He pulled out a pack of Old Gold cigarettes that Daniel had brought back from Edmonton, followed by his flask, which he had topped with rye before leaving the lodge.

He took a sip, lit a cigarette, and closed his eyes.

"Ah," he said aloud before resuming his walk up the trail. He was not certain of his whereabouts, but surmised that if he stayed on the trail, which ran west, he would eventually run into Pyramid Lake Road. Which is exactly what happened about forty minutes later.

Colin had just cleared the summit and was making his way down the trail to Pyramid Lake Road when he heard a car engine approaching from the direction of town. As he continued to walk—making sure to cup the cigarette in his hand in case the driver looked up and spotted him—he recognized the vehicle. It was Rudy and Elaina's tan sedan, the one he had seen at Patricia Lake many times.

Colin looked at his watch. It was almost one o'clock. He knew that Daniel would be on his date with Elaina, which meant Rudy was driving.

Wonder what he's up to? He watched the car speed in the direction of the lake. His original intent was not to walk to Patricia Lake, which he guessed was about a mile away, but rather than continue along his current path he changed direction. Something did not seem right.

Colin walked about ten minutes when he looked to his right and, almost accidently, noticed a dark shape in the woods parallel to the road. Whatever it was, it was headed right at him.

RECONNAISSANCE
....

RUDY BROUGHT THE sedan to a halt at the clearing beside Patricia Lake where he usually parked. Reaching under the driver's seat, he retrieved the .38 caliber pistol he brought from Montreal and put it in the right pocket of his overcoat, which he buttoned to the neck. He wrapped his scarf around his throat and head, knowing that it would be cold during the walk across the lakebed.

There was no one around. *Why would there be?* he thought. *Elaina and Daniel are at the movies, and the Hutterites have the day off.*

Rudy had been waiting for an opportunity to investigate the Patricia Lake site alone. He wondered if today would be the day he would find a clue.

Only one way to find out, he told himself as he started his walk toward the sawmill. With luck he could be finished and back at the lodge in a couple of hours—long before Elaina and Daniel returned from their date.

* * * *

Colin soon realized that the shape was a *wolf*—the same wolf he had encountered before. This was the closest he had been to it. The animal was so close he could see details he had not seen before. There was a three-or four-inch line on the wolf's head that appeared to be a scar, and the tip of its left ear was missing, probably due to a fight with another animal.

"Hello, Mr. Wolf!" Colin called out. "Good to see you again!"

The wolf's ears twitched. *Does it recognize my voice?* he wondered. "Oh, I know what you want."

Again, the wolf's ears twitched.

Colin removed his pack. "Look what I brought you." He held up the remaining chunk of salami he and Daniel had not eaten and tossed it in the snow. The animal approached and ate the meat in one bite.

Colin put his pack back on and held his arms out to his side. "That's all I got. There's another half-stick back at the lodge, but you'll have to wait until our next meeting."

The wolf licked the outside of its mouth with its tongue, turned, and disappeared into the woods.

I swear that wolf understands me.

Colin resumed his walk until reaching a clearing that gave him a view of Pyramid Mountain and, before it, Patricia Lake. He saw Rudy's car, but there was no sign of him.

Deciding to remain out of sight, Colin got off the road and made his way through the woods toward the camp on the opposite side of the lake. He tried to stay as close as he could to what he guessed was the shoreline. When he was almost parallel to the worksite, he stopped and crouched beside a boulder, removed his pack, and took out his binoculars.

As he watched, Rudy emerged from the larger of the two tents set up at the campsite. Rudy made sure the front flaps were tied before lighting a cigarette for the walk back to the car. He walked quickly, stopping once along the way to re-light the cigarette. Once he reached the car, he started it and sped off toward Jasper.

Colin remained in his position for a time—enough time to smoke two cigarettes and drain the remaining contents of his flask. The sun felt warm against his face and the woods, except for the occasional chatter of squirrels or the distant pecking of a Pileated woodpecker, were still. After a while he rose, put his pack back on and walked to the camp. He checked the tents—nothing seemed to be out of place or missing—and then began the walk back to the lodge. As he did so he considered what, if anything, he should say to Daniel.

By the time he returned to his bungalow, Colin told himself he would wait before speaking with Daniel or their three colleagues about his suspicions of Rudy. He needed to know more. He needed evidence. Saying something prematurely to Daniel could threaten his friend's relationship with Elaina; he would have a hard time forgiving himself for putting his best friend's love life in jeopardy.

* * * *

Elaina hummed as she and Daniel walked back to the lodge after sharing a malt at the Rexall soda counter following the movie. Daniel recognized the tune: Hoagy Carmichael's "Stardust." He had heard it many times on the radio while in England during the Battle of Britain. The BBC played the song almost every night.

"*Sometimes I wonder why I spend the lonely nights dreaming of a song,*" Daniel sang. Elaina smiled and joined him, and the two sang the next verse in unison: "*The melody haunts my reverie, and I am once again with you.*"

Daniel stopped and said, "You have a beautiful voice." He put a finger to her cheek. "Like a whippoorwill. Did you get that from your mother?"

For just an instant she thought about how much she missed her mother—and her father. *They had been so close, so happy in Montreal. Why had it been so important for them to leave their lives, to return to Germany, to never be heard from* again? Were they alive or dead? And did any of that really matter to Rudy? She did not want to come to Jasper with him, but felt she had no choice. And now she could not imagine being anywhere else, as long as Daniel was there. Why did things have to be so confusing?

"Yes," she finally said, her voice quivering. "I suppose I did." They resumed walking.

"Tell me about your mother," Daniel said.

"There's not much to tell," she said. That was true—to a point. There was little she was willing to tell Daniel about either her mother or her father. Perhaps later, as they learned to know each other.

"Was she beautiful like you?" Daniel asked.

Elaina felt herself blush. *How can he be so kind, so caring? How is it that Daniel always seems to know exactly what to say?*

She changed the subject.

"I quite liked our lunch, Daniel," she said.

Daniel looked confused but smiled and said, "Me too. I would have never imagined that fried potatoes with cheese curds and brown gravy could be so good. What was that you called it again?"

"There's not really a name for it," she said. "I'm sure the proprietor thought I was loony when I told him to mix everything together. But I have to tell you that my recipe is better."

"Will you make it for me sometime?" he asked.

Elaina laughed. "Only if you make me jellied moose nose," she replied.

Over lunch, Daniel had told her about jellied moose nose, which is cooked in a broth of onion, garlic, spices, and vinegar, then boiled and cooled multiple times before being sliced and served.

"You told me at the restaurant that you thought it sounded dreadful," he said.

They reached the puddle on the sidewalk that they had walked around earlier in the afternoon.

"Are you going to carry me again, Mr. Masters?" Elaina said.

Daniel did not answer. Instead he picked her up as he had done previously and began to walk. When he reached the other side he stopped and looked at her intently. Neither spoke. And then Daniel leaned forward and kissed her.

He put Elaina down. She kept one hand on his shoulder because she was dizzy. "That was nice," Daniel said. He smiled.

"That was nice," Elaina said in a voice that was barely audible. She smiled.

"I suppose I could," Daniel said.

"Could what?" Elaina said.

"Make you jellied moose nose."

"Oh, that," she said. They were close enough to see the lodge now.

"How about I make it next weekend?" he said. "That means another date—if you're willing."

"That would be wonderful."

"Of course, that's assuming one small detail."

"What would that be, Mr. Masters?"

"I'll have to shoot a moose."

As soon as the words were out of his mouth, an image flashed across his mind. It was the face of Barbara Bealowski—the last thing he saw before being sucked into the blackness of the whirlpool when he was twelve years old.

The thought made him shiver. Elaina could not help but notice. "Are you cold?" she asked, taking his hand.

Daniel looked at Elaina and smiled. "Not anymore."

BUSINESS AS USUAL
....

WHEN ELAINA RETURNED to the bungalow, Rudy was sitting in the same chair he had been in that morning. There was an open bottle of Johnnie Walker Black Label on the coffee table before him. Next to that was an empty tumbler.

Rudy put down his pencil and the newspaper crossword puzzle he had been working on and said, "Finally. Do you realize it's nearly five-thirty? I thought the movie ended two hours ago."

Elaina knew her brother was irritated but she didn't care.

"Heavens, is it really that late?" she retorted, taking a seat across the coffee table from him.

"Yes, it *really* is," he said. The dining hall in the main lodge began serving supper at five and he was hungry. Now he knew he'd have to wait until at least six because Elaina would insist on changing her outfit.

"I was sure I was going to have to get Sergeant Preston of the Northwest Mounted Police to search for you," he added sarcastically.

Elaina rose, walked to a cabinet along the wall, and filled an empty tumbler about halfway with soda water. She returned to her seat and poured some scotch into her glass.

Rudy did not say anything. He watched her with bemused curiosity. Elaina rarely drank.

"So, how was your date?" he asked. He figured if he had waited this long for dinner, a few more minutes would not matter.

Elaina took a sip from her drink, made a face, and took another sip.

"It was lovely," she said. "Just lovely."

"That's swell," he said. He wanted details—especially anything to do with Daniel's work.

"What did you talk about?" he asked. "How's his project coming along?"

"We didn't talk about that," she said, taking another sip from her drink. "We just had lunch, saw a movie, shared a malted milk and came back here. It seemed we were only gone an hour."

"Hmm," Rudy said. His sister was not telling him what he wanted to hear.

Though he had gone to the worksite, he was no closer to understanding whether it had any connection to the Project Habakkuk that Peter, the undercover SS agent, called him about in Montreal.

Why were they making panels out of compressed sawdust? And why were dozens of the panels laid out under the large tent to form what appeared to be nothing more than a rectangle? Did it have a purpose? It did not look like a weapon, but what was it used for? Whatever it was, Rudy knew there was more to the story he was told about producing lumber for the government.

"And how about you?" Elaina said. "We heard you honk when you drove by. Where did you go?"

"Like I told you earlier," he said. "Just out for a drive."

Elaina put her glass down. "I hope you don't mind, but I invited Daniel to our table for dinner tonight. I told him I would call his bungalow when we decided what time we would go to the main lodge to eat."

Rudy was pleased. The more time he spent with Daniel, the better his chances of learning what was really going on at the lake.

"That would be fine," Rudy said, pouring another drink. "Tell him six-fifteen."

* * * *

When its investors officially opened the Big Mountain Lake Lodge on June 1, 1921, their vision was to create a destination that would appeal to wealthy visitors from around the world who longed to take in the Canadian Rockies for their beauty, bountiful wildlife, and natural attractions. The lodge soon earned a worldwide reputation for fine food and drink, as well as comfortable accommodations "that exuded rustic charm." One requirement that set the lodge apart from other hotels in the Rockies was that patrons were required to dress up for dinner in the main lodge after five o'clock each afternoon. While tuxedos and evening gowns were welcome, at minimum women were required to wear a dress (a skirt and blouse were unacceptable, as were pants) and men, a suit and tie (no sport coats and dress pants).

A small ensemble usually provided soft music during dinner, unexpected during the war years when such things were uncommon even in large Canadian cities. But the lodge's owners had deep pockets and did not want to dilute its well-deserved reputation, regardless of the troubles that were occurring outside Jasper.

The lodge still managed to draw those who fell into the "Average Joe" category, but most visitors had money and could afford to stay there. With the rare exception, guests would take dinner in their bungalows. Colin and the other team members posing as Hutterites knew it would be out of character for them to dine in the main lodge, though Saturday and Sunday breakfasts and lunches were a different matter, offering a nice change from the routine.

Daniel had only eaten dinner in the main lodge once, his first night in Jasper. And while he had enjoyed it—the food was the same as he would have been served in the bungalow, but the opportunity to have it with a glass of wine or a cocktail was welcome—he had not made it a habit.

Rudy and Elaina usually ate dinner in their bungalow as well. The exceptions were Friday and Saturday nights.

Daniel felt butterflies as he shaved and dressed in the only suit he had brought to Jasper. He was just putting on his tie when he heard a knock on the door. It was Colin.

"Mind if I take a few smokes?" he asked, shutting the door. "Mine are all gone."

"Certainly," Daniel said, pointing to his pack of cigarettes on the coffee table.

To ensure their cover story was as credible as possible, the team had agreed that Daniel should get his own bungalow while the other four shared a separate one. Each bungalow had two bedrooms. Colin's group had arranged to bring in two cots so the four would not have to share beds.

"Well, well, well," Colin said. "If I didn't know any better, I'd say someone has another date. Or is it just a continuation of the first?"

"I don't know what you call it, but yes, I'm having dinner in the main lodge with Elaina and her brother."

Daniel's reference to Rudy reminded Colin of what he had seen that afternoon, but he did not say anything.

"Do you think this tie looks okay?" Daniel said. "Or should I wear the one with the stripes?" He held both up against his shirt.

Colin shrugged.

"You're a big help," Daniel said. "I'll go with the blue one."

Colin continued smoking. "I read the extended weather report in the paper."

Daniel lit a cigarette and said, "I thought Hutterites shunned the news. You don't want to blow our cover." He stood before the mirror in the bathroom separating the bedrooms and began tying his necktie.

"You think that's bad?" Colin said. "Then I won't tell you that I stole it from the gift shop in the lobby and stuffed it into my coat when no one was looking."

"Brother Colin, you are going straight to H-E-double hockey sticks."

"Anyway, they're predicting it's going to be warm next week—in the fifties. Maybe even sixties."

"It's about time," Daniel said, emerging from the bathroom. "We're three days away from April. Even here they must have spring."

"The point is, we may start to get a sense of whether the composite panels will hold up and insulate the ice and keep it firm in the warmth," Colin said. "When it comes time for the test, I'd rather not have you land on a pile of mush or, worse yet, have the ice break under the weight of the plane."

"That wouldn't be good," Daniel said. Colin changed the subject.

"When you have dinner with Rudy, you might mention that we won't be needing him after Tuesday," he said.

"You sure?"

"Yeah, I'm sure. I was talking to Alan and Peter, and the four of us will be able to produce the last of the sawdust for the panels within a couple weeks. If we have a couple more of these heat waves, all the ice except for our airfield will be gone by early May."

"Okay," Daniel said, putting on his suit coat. "Hey, how do I look?"

Colin snuffed out his cigarette in the ashtray and walked to the door. "She won't be able to resist you, Romeo."

Daniel hoped Colin was right.

A SLIP OVER CHAMPAGNE
....

RUDY AND ELAINA were five minutes late for dinner, but Daniel did not mind.

Elaina wore a gold evening gown with a low neckline, which exposed her cleavage, and matching jacket. Daniel thought she looked stunning, and told her so as he pulled her chair out.

It was obvious to Rudy that there was a strong mutual attraction between his sister and Daniel. *How could he use that to his advantage?* He ordered a twenty-dollar bottle of champagne in hopes of getting Daniel to reveal details about his work that he had not already divulged.

"Mr. Hoff," Daniel said, raising his glass to Rudy as they finished the bottle, "you're the first person I know who's ever spent that much on a bottle of champagne. I thank you. However, I must tell you that when it comes to the bubbly, I lean more towards the prime minister's position."

"And what's that?" Rudy asked.

"That champagne should be, and I quote, 'cold, dry and free.'" Daniel laughed. Elaina giggled. Rudy forced a thin smile.

Despite the alcohol, he was having no luck coaxing any information of value out of Daniel. He reached into his pocket for a cigarette but saw that he had run out.

"Damn," he said, crumpling the empty package.

"Here, take one of mine," said Daniel, handing his pack to Rudy.

"Old Gold?" Rudy said. "I didn't know you could buy these here. These are American, aren't they?"

"I just got whatever the base had," said Daniel as he poured Elaina more champagne.

"*Base*? What base?"

Daniel realized the slipup.

"I mean *place*—the place where I got the supplies yesterday," he said, turning his attention to Rudy.

"Easy mistake to make," said Rudy. He smiled as if to say it did not matter and that he did not care, but inside he was pleased at this new information. He quickly changed the subject.

"Is there any more of that champagne left?"

Elaina poured as Daniel, almost as an aside, told Rudy that he would not be needed at the sawmill after Tuesday.

Rudy tried to act unconcerned. Biting one of his thumbnails he commented, "Really? Are you and the Hutterites about to wrap things up?"

The color drained from Elaina's face as she set the bottle down. "Does this mean you're leaving?"

Daniel reached out and put his hand on Elaina's.

"Please don't worry. We won't wrap things up here until early June. It's just that we've reached the point in the project where we don't need extra manpower."

Rudy continued to work on his thumbnail. "What point would that be?" he asked.

"Just the point where we don't need additional assistance."

Elaina was relieved. "Oh, good. That's how long we're here, too."

Daniel patted Elaina's hand again and told her, "Which means we have two more months. A lot can happen in two months."

Elaina smiled.

"I simply will not let you leave until you make me jellied moose nose, Mr. Masters," she said. "Remember, you promised!"

Daniel grinned. "Miss Hoff, I can assure you that I am a man of my word, and I would not lie—especially to you. In fact, I plan to bag a beast next weekend. Just for you."

That gave Rudy an idea.

CLUES
....

Tuesday, March 31, 1942
Patricia Lake

WITH THE NEW saw blade, the team cut more lumber on the last day of March than it had on any day since arriving. Colin, Paul Lord, and Rudy loaded logs and offloaded the cut lumber while Daniel operated the saw and Nigel McIntosh and Alan Simpson took turns collecting the sawdust and making the panels.

At eleven-thirty, as was the custom, Colin stopped working so he could drive back to the lodge to pick up box lunches for the workers. Lunchtime was from noon to twelve-thirty, which gave Colin plenty of time, and he liked making the trip because he could sometimes sneak a cigarette on the way to or from the lodge.

"You mind if I go with Brother Colin this time, Daniel?" Rudy asked when he saw Colin signal that it was time to leave.

Please no, Colin thought. *I really want—need—to smoke a cigarette, and I don't want him around.*

"Sure!" Daniel yelled as he started the saw again.

Colin didn't say anything as he and Rudy got into the truck and began the drive to the lodge. After a few moments, Rudy broke the silence.

"What do you find so appealing about this?" he asked,

picking up the Bible that was on the seat between them. Colin usually brought the Bible—the one from Churchill—to the work site.

Colin gritted his back teeth. "God's word gives me comfort."

"His *word*? You mean words."

"In the beginning was the Word. And the Word was with God. And the Word was God," Colin said.

I can't believe I remembered that, Colin thought. It had been at least twenty years since he'd heard it in church.

"Oh," Rudy said, thumbing through the book. He lit a cigarette.

Why is he tormenting me? Colin wondered.

Rudy stopped when he reached the bookmark. It was at the first page of the Book of Habakkuk.

Is this coincidence or luck?

"So what's this book all about?" Rudy said, holding the Bible at eye level toward Colin.

Colin glanced to his right and then back to the road.

Colin saw the bookmark was on the page Churchill had read from during their meeting in London. He was not sure how he would answer until he finally opened his mouth.

"I thought you didn't want me to talk to you about the Lord, Mr. Hoff. Or was I mistaken?"

Rudy yawned as if he didn't care, and started to pick at his teeth with his pinky. "I don't really give a...I mean, I don't really," he stammered. "I was just trying to make conversation. I don't even know how to pronounce this, this Hab... Hab-a-chuck."

He was certain that Colin was avoiding the truth. *Could he be covering up a covert military operation?*

"It's Habakkuk," said Colin, who did not say anything else.

The two rode in silence for the remainder of the trip. Rudy decided he would have to get his answer another way.

* * * *

"Elaina tells me you're planning to do some moose hunting."

Daniel looked at Rudy. The two were alone in the sawmill and it was almost quitting time.

He nodded. "Yup, that's right. I'm thinking Saturday."

"Can I go, too?"

While Daniel didn't really care for Rudy, he thought it might be a good idea if he spent more time getting to know him. After all, if his feelings for Elaina were as genuine as he thought them to be, it was possible Rudy might one day be his brother-in-law.

"That depends on two things," Daniel said. "First, are you a good hunter?"

"Oh yeah," Rudy answered. "One of the reasons we came out here was so that I could do some big game hunting."

Rudy had lied on both counts.

"I see," Daniel said. "Okay, second question: do you have a rifle?"

Rudy shook his head. "I thought I could rent one."

Daniel found it odd that Rudy had come to the mountains to hunt big game and did not bring his own rifle but said, "Hmm… I only have one. Tell you what; I have to go to the park superintendent's office mid-week to get a moose permit. I'm sure he has one we can borrow."

Daniel, too, had lied. The truth was that the team had brought four military issued rifles to Alberta. But that information would raise too many questions.

"Have you ever been moose hunting before?" Daniel asked.

"Oh yeah, lots of times," Rudy said. Again, he lied. He had never even seen a moose before arriving in Alberta. But he had no intention of actually shooting one, so it really didn't matter.

His real purpose was to spend time alone with Daniel to see what more he could learn about his possible connection to the perplexing Project Habakkuk puzzle he was trying to solve.

The two made arrangements to meet at the main lodge at six-thirty Saturday morning. It would just be getting light out. Daniel proposed that they could drive to Pyramid Lake just north of Patricia Lake and begin the hunt there. He pointed out that he and the others had seen at least a half-dozen moose since setting up the sawmill.

"That's just super," said Rudy, grinning. "I do have one request, though."

"What's that?"

"I'd appreciate it if you don't say anything about me going to Elaina. You see, she's rather timid when it comes to hunting and me and guns. I just don't want her to be worried about me."

The comment seemed a bit odd to Daniel. Elaina had not mentioned an aversion to hunting or guns.

He agreed. "I won't mention anything. The last thing I want to do is upset Elaina."

"You're a swell guy," Rudy said, slapping Daniel on the back. "Just swell."

UPDATE
....

Thursday, April 9, 1942
Big Mountain Lake Lodge

RUDY AWOKE AT five o'clock on the morning of the ninth—an hour and a half earlier than usual. On his way to the living room, he carefully opened the door of his sister's bedroom and peered inside. Elaina was asleep. He pulled the door shut until he heard a click, then stopped by the fireplace and placed a log on the glowing embers.

Finding his favorite chair, he picked up the telephone and dialed zero.

"Hello, operator," he said as softly as he could. "Yes, I realize it's early, but I need to call Ottawa and they're two hours ahead. Yes, the number is Kline eight two seven seven nine. Yes, that's right. No, I don't mind holding."

As he waited, Rudy bit his fingernails.

Elaina had been asleep until she heard the door open. She rose and opened it a crack. She could see Rudy, his back to her, in his chair.

"Yes, thank you, operator. Thank you very much. Good night—er, morning," he said. And then: "Hello, Peter. Rudolph. Yes, I know it's early. I wanted to tell you that I think I am getting close."

He took a long draw on his cigarette.

"No, I can't give you details because I don't know them myself, but I will say that I have infiltrated a group that likely does. No, they don't suspect. No. I'm telling you they don't. Look, do you want to hear what I have to say or not?"

From where she stood, Elaina could hear a muffled voice on the other end of the phone. Rudy held the receiver at arm's length until the voice quieted.

"Look, I should have something more for you in about ten days," Rudy said. "That's really all I can say right now."

Elaina could tell by the tone of his voice that Rudy was holding back his anger. "As long as I have you, has there been any word from my parents?" Rudy asked.

"What's that—you're certain they're all right? Gee, Peter, that's swell. Yes, I know I can trust you. I want you to know you can trust me, too. We are men of honor. You'll let your superiors know about my service to the cause, won't you? That's swell. What's that? I can barely hear you. Our connection is bad. You'll give me more details when I give you more details? Not a problem. Expect a call from me in a couple weeks. Good-bye."

Elaina shut the door and tiptoed back to bed, careful to avoid the one floorboard she knew squeaked.

Rudy smoked another cigarette and watched the fire that had reignited in the fireplace before rising and walking to his sister's bedroom again. He opened the door to see Elaina was still asleep. Or so he thought.

Satisfied, he closed the door and returned to bed.

Elaina pulled the blanket over her head and considered what to do next.

SURRENDER

....

Friday, April 10, 1942
The Pit

"LIEUTENANT SCHOPTER, HOW many days?"

"I lost count."

Captain Eicher reached into the pocket of his coat and pulled out his last two cigarettes.

"Here," he said, lighting them both and handing one to his first officer. "My last."

If he was correct—and he wasn't sure he was—today was April 10, fourteen days since the explosion left the UX-1 crippled. Leaning over the conning tower of the sub, Eicher tapped the end of his cigarette and watched as the ashes fell to the deck below. As he did so he thought, as he had done a hundred times before these past few days, how fortunate he was to be alive. He had been so depressed since Heidi died. Now, being so close to death himself, he was grateful for this second chance. It was as though a new chapter of his life had begun.

"Remarkable, isn't it?" Eicher said.

"What is?" Schopter responded.

"This day. The beautiful sunny sky above us. That sea spread before us, and all that is within it. *Life*." He took a long breath of air and added, "It is a good day to be alive."

He was at a loss to explain why he felt so much...peace. It had been so long. Too long.

"Yes, sir," Schopter said softly, though he didn't really believe it. While the UX-1 had managed to surface after its accident, it was now adrift. Powerless. No radio. Dead, its bow angling downward with the deck partly covered by the sea.

"What is on your mind, Lieutenant? I can tell you are bothered by something. There is no joy on your face."

"I'm...I'm okay."

"No, tell me. We have spent nearly three years together. Though I am your captain, I am also your friend. I know there is something on your mind."

Schopter took a draw off his cigarette and twirled the butt between his thumb and forefinger. "Permission to speak freely, Captain?"

"Always."

"We are in a bad way—we have been since the accident."

There could be no denying that fact. The accident had been costly—too costly. Twenty-six had perished that day, and now the UX-1, the pride of Germany's U-boat fleet, was a lifeless hulk. They were almost out of food and water, and the chances of being rescued by anyone other than the enemy, if they were even that lucky, grew dimmer by the day.

"I will not deny that things do seem rather grim," Eicher admitted.

"Sometimes I think it would have been better for us had we not been able to surface," Schopter said. "At least it would have been quicker that way."

"You are talking about death, Lieutenant?"

"Yes, sir."

Eicher took the last draw of his cigarette and flicked the butt into the sea.

"Why do you say this?"

The first office flicked his cigarette away and sighed a heavy sigh. "I don't know. I guess it is because I am tired. I am hungry. I am cold."

"I would think it is something else," Eicher said.

"What?"

"You have lost hope. Tell me, what were you thinking all those days ago when we were dead in the water and sinking?"

"I thought we were going to die."

"Can I tell you something? I did, too."

The captain's admission surprised Schopter, who straightened and looked him in the eye. "You, sir?"

"Yes, Lieutenant. Do you know the odds of getting this boat to the surface using only manual power?"

"I would calculate—"

"Lieutenant, Lieutenant, stop. That is just a figure of speech. I do not actually want you to calculate the odds. Suffice it to say they were not in our favor. I knew that. The chief engineer certainly knew that. But I knew we had to try. Even in the pitch blackness."

"That was the worst," Schopter admitted.

"Yes, like a tomb. When the lights went out in my cabin I literally had to feel my way to the bridge."

"It was an impossible situation. It is a wonder we did not perish."

"Yes, but the men on the pumps did not lose hope. That is what saved us."

"It took nine hours to reach the surface," Schopter said.

"Yes, nine hours to do the impossible. Let that be an example to you—why you must never give up. Once you lose your hope, you lose everything."

For the first time in days, the lieutenant smiled.

* * * *

It was Lieutenant Sebastian Ouellet, first officer aboard HMCS *Penticton*, who saw the enemy sub first, although he was not exactly sure what he was looking at through his binoculars.

"Seaman Datts," he said to a young man standing to his left. "Can you make out the object at eighteen degrees? I'd estimate it to be seven or eight miles away."

Seaman Ed Datts, nicknamed "Eagle" because of his remarkable eyesight, looked through his binoculars. "It's a sub, sir."

"One of ours?"

"Not any design I'm familiar with, sir."

"American?"

"Not sure, sir."

Ouellet thought about what he should do. Normally he preferred to solve his own problems, but he knew the captain would want to know that a sub—any sub—had been sighted. He looked at his watch. Two o'clock. The captain had only gone to bed two hours ago after serving two consecutive watches.

"I will personally inform Captain Andrews," Ouellet said, leaving the bridge.

As he walked, he remembered Captain Andrews' words before the *Penticton*, the lead military vessel on this latest convoy out of Halifax, departed port: "We've been ordered on a more southerly course this time. It will take us an extra day, but the likelihood of meeting up with the enemy in The Pit is greatly diminished."

"Looks like you're wrong, sir," Ouellet whispered to himself as he tapped on the captain's door.

"Yes," came the calm voice. "What is it?"

"Sorry to disturb you, Captain, but we've just sighted a submarine."

"A submarine? Whose—theirs or ours?"

"Not sure, sir."

The door opened and Andrews appeared. "Not sure, Lieutenant? Let's not take chances. Slow to ten knots and sound battle stations."

* * * *

"Captain, Allied destroyer—Wickes-class—approaching off the starboard bow." Lieutenant Schopter delivered the news to Eicher in his cabin.

"It was only a matter of time," said Eicher. "How much time until she reaches us?"

"Estimate is thirty minutes, my Captain."

"Meet me on the conning tower in ten," Eicher said.

When he was alone, he took the photo of his wife from the shelf and removed it from its frame. He also took the Iron Cross from its box and put it around his neck. If ever there was a time he needed divine protection, it was now. As he was about to leave, a thought occurred to him. He opened a drawer and pulled out a grenade, which he placed in his coat pocket.

After reaching Lieutenant Schopter, Eicher handed him a white towel and said, "Here, tie this to a broom handle and wave it for them to see."

* * * *

"Sir!" Seaman Datts called out. "The sub is signaling surrender. Definitely a white flag, sir."

"Stand down from battle stations and signal the rest of the convoy to hold position," Captain Andrews said. "Helmsman, bring us to within one hundred yards and request confirmation that it is their intention to surrender. Lieutenant?"

"Yes, sir?" Ouellet said.

"Prepare to lower a boat. When we are in position I want you to assemble and lead a boarding party. I'm choosing you, as I recall you speak German."

"*Jawohl*," he said, using the German for "Yes, sir."

When the *Penticton* was about a hundred yards from the U-boat the captain ordered "all stop." As the boarding party paddled toward the submarine, Andrews scanned the scene before him with his field glasses. They were close enough for him to realize that he had seen this submarine before—the day the *Hancock* was sunk.

* * * *

"*Was sind Ihre Absichten?*" Lieutenant Ouellet shouted to the men standing atop the conning tower alongside his launch.

"I speak English," Eicher replied. "Who do I have the pleasure of addressing?"

"Lieutenant Ouellet, first officer of His Majesty's Canadian Ship *Penticton*. I will repeat: What are your intentions?"

"It is our intention to surrender," Eicher said. "We are dead in the water. For us, the war is over. But under the articles of the Geneva Convention, I will only surrender to your captain. Is that understood?"

Ouellet looked at him skeptically. "First, I order you and your men to throw your weapons overboard."

Eicher was the first to toss his Luger into the sea. The others followed his lead, throwing what weapons they had over the side of the sub as well.

"Are there others below?" Ouellet asked.

"No," said Eicher. "There are only twenty-three of us left. We are all here."

"Very well. I shall return to the *Penticton* and speak with the captain. Prepare your crew."

* * * *

Captain Andrews, his first officer, and chief engineer stood in a circle on the bridge as the *Penticton* drew even closer to the UX-1.

"Chief, I want you to rig up a device to tow that boat to England," Andrews said as he pointed to the U-boat.

"Tow it?" the chief engineer said. "That's a job for a freighter, not a destroyer. Wouldn't it be better if we just sank it?"

Andrews shook his head and folded his arms across his chest. "Normally, I'd say yes. But look at her, gentlemen. Do you realize what we have here?"

"The Ghost Sub," Ouellet offered.

"Yes, Lieutenant. No, we're not going to sink her. She'll make a fine prize. Our boys'll be able to learn a lot from her—perhaps enough to turn the tide of this damned war."

"It's not going to be easy, sir," the chief engineer said. "But I'm sure me and my men can come up with something."

The *Penticton* slowed to one knot and maneuvered along the starboard side of the UX-1. Captain Andrews stood atop the bridge and took in the U-boat beneath him. It seemed smaller from this spot than it did the day he saw it from the *Hancock's* lifeboat.

"Are you the commander of this vessel?" Andrews called to Eicher.

"Captain Wolfgang Eicher of the *Kriegsmarine* electroboat UX-1," Eicher responded. "My friends call me Wolf."

"Captain Eicher, in the name of His Majesty George VI, you are hereby ordered to surrender. If you do not comply immediately and unconditionally, I shall destroy your vessel."

"Accepted," Eicher said.

"We are lowering two rope ladders," Andrews continued. "I want your men to climb up one at a time and raise their hands over their head once they are aboard. I understand there are twenty-three of you?"

"Twenty-three, Captain."

"Once you are all aboard, you will be confined to the brig. Is that understood, Captain?"

"Understood."

"As you can see, our guns are trained on your deck, so there are to be no surprises. Is that also understood?"

"Understood."

Eicher nodded, and one-by-one his men began to climb the ladders.

"Captain, may I ask your intentions for my vessel?" Eicher called out. "Will you be sinking her?"

"Oh no. I'm taking her with me."

"Not going to happen," Eicher whispered to Schopter.

Once his crew was aboard the *Penticton*, Eicher and Schopter made their way to the closest rope ladder. Eicher grasped his Iron Cross with his right hand, brought it to his lips and kissed it. He motioned for Schopter to go first. Eicher followed, but stopped after the first rung. He reached into his pocket and pulled the pin off the grenade, held out his hand, and tossed it into the open hatch located a few feet below and to his right.

"Hold tight, Lieutenant!" he shouted.

There was a muffled explosion from within the U-boat. A geyser of hissing flame about a foot high erupted from the hatchway.

Andrews saw everything but was unable to stop Eicher from where he stood. He considered shooting the captain as he watched black smoke billow from the sub's open hatch, but thought better of the idea. Perhaps the UX-1's captain could provide details of the sub's workings, he reasoned.

The UX-1's bow began to angle downwards at an even sharper angle as the sub filled with water.

"Helmsman," Andrews barked into the intercom, "prepare to back us away. Quickly."

His ears ringing from the explosion, Eicher glanced

downward as the sea began to wash over the deck of the UX-1. He was about to resume his climb when he noticed a small object emerge from one of the two open hatches. It was the rat!

Fitting end, thought Eicher, as he watched the creature try to escape the water that was inching ever closer.

Seeing that it had no escape, the rat sat on its haunches and looked up at Eicher, its front legs extended as though it were begging.

"I really shouldn't," Eicher finally said, climbing down to the first rung and stretching out his leg until it almost touched the deck. "Well? I haven't got all day."

In one motion the rat leaped onto the captain's leg, ran up his back and latched onto the rung just above Eicher. Without looking down it climbed up the rope along the side and was on the *Penticton's* deck before Eicher reached the third rung. Eicher hung on tightly as the ship began to back away from the UX-1, the ladder swaying.

The *Penticton* steamed about fifty yards before there was another explosion inside the sub and its bow sank even deeper into the ocean—so much so that its stern rose to reveal the sub's massive propeller and rudder.

Eicher, whose hands were tied behind his back by this time, watched as the UX-1 rolled and slipped beneath the waves for what would be its final time.

"Farewell, *Heidi*," he whispered when it was gone.

MOOSE HUNT
....

Saturday, April 11, 1942

AT SIX-FIFTEEN on the morning he and Daniel were to hunt, Rudy, dressed in long underwear, heavy wool pants, a thick flannel shirt and his heaviest jacket, quietly left his bedroom and walked to the coffee table in the living room, where he picked up a pencil and notepad.

Went hunting with Daniel—Rudy, he wrote.

He put on his hat and gloves and left, stopping by his car to retrieve the pistol that he kept under the seat before meeting Daniel at the main lodge.

Rudy was on his second cigarette when Daniel showed up in the main lodge. He was dressed in a red and black hunting jacket. The clock read exactly six-thirty.

Rudy volunteered to drive, but Daniel said no.

"We'd never be able to get the carcass back," Daniel said. "A male moose can weigh up to thirteen hundred pounds. We'll need to use the truck. By the way, you ever gut a moose?"

"Lots of times," Rudy lied.

The drive to Pyramid Lake took less than twenty minutes. The sun was just beginning to break the horizon when Daniel pulled off the road, got out, and removed a tarp in the back of the truck to reveal two 303 Lee-Enfield rifles. He handed one to Rudy.

"I don't know if you've ever hunted with a three-o-three before," he said, "but I prefer these over, say, a thirty-aught-six. They might not have as much oomph as a Springfield or a Winchester, but they're damned accurate. Our boys over in Europe are using a version of these."

"I didn't know that," Rudy admitted. He watched as Daniel loaded the cartridges in his rifle before pulling back the bolt and doing the same.

"Now let's go get us a swamp donkey," Daniel said.

Rudy looked confused. "*Swamp donkey?*"

"A moose, Rudy. A moose." Securing the rifle to his back, he said, "I've never hunted moose in the spring, only in the fall during the rut, so I'm not sure where to start. I'm thinking we might want to find one of last year's scrapes. Not sure if the bulls go back to them, though. Do you know?"

Rudy had no idea what a scrape was. If he'd asked Daniel, he would have discovered that it is a section of ground, usually located in a wooded area, that a bull moose will clear with its hooves and urinate on to attract females, or cows, during the rut, or mating season. While it is difficult to find a scrape when snow covers the ground, tree damage can indicate that one is nearby. When a bull moose is rutting, the shaking of its head and antlers will remove the bark from trees.

Although Rudy knew none of this, it didn't stop him from saying, "That's exactly what I'd do. Find a scrape."

"Good," Daniel said. "Maybe you can find us one. Lead on."

* * * *

Around seven forty-five, Colin heard a knock on the door of his bungalow.

"It's unlocked!" he yelled.

Colin was alone. Alan, Nigel, and Paul had left for the main lodge fifteen minutes before, promising to save room at the table for Colin and Daniel. Colin had forgotten Daniel was hunting. He assumed the knock was Daniel and that the two would walk to breakfast, which was their routine on Saturday mornings.

Another knock. Colin lit a cigarette, placed it in an ashtray and rose. "Are you deaf? I said it was unlocked!"

He swung the door open and was surprised to see Elaina on the other side. She was not wearing a jacket. Worse, she had been crying.

"Miss Hoff!"

In a voice that he barely understood and between sobs, she asked if she could come in.

"Certainly. What can I do for you?"

Elaina looked at the burning cigarette in the ashtray.

Tactical error, Colin thought. "A sin of the flesh," he said.

Elaina ignored the explanation. Trembling, she reached inside the pocket of her sweater and handed Colin Rudy's note.

Of course, he thought. *Now I remember. Daniel's hunting a moose.*

"I need your help," she said.

There was a tone of desperation to her plea that Colin could not figure out. Elaina put her hands to her face.

"I...I think Daniel's in danger," she said.

"Why? What's going on? Tell me everything."

She did. She told him about her parents, about her German-Jewish heritage, about Rudy's involvement in the Nazi party, about listening in on Rudy's call the previous week and their real reason for being in Jasper.

"Rudy's so impetuous," she said. "And he hasn't had his insulin shot yet. He's bound to do something foolish—I just know it."

"Why didn't you say anything to Daniel?" She cried even harder.

"I wanted to. I really did. Oh, please help me. We've got to find them and stop Rudy before it's too late. I would never forgive myself if something happens to Daniel. I love him. Will you help me, Brother Colin—please?"

Colin reached for his coat and headed for the door.

"Yes. But it's not Brother Colin. It's Commander Colin Williams, Royal Canadian Navy."

* * * *

In their first hour of hunting, Daniel and Rudy spotted three big horn sheep, a herd of mountain goats, and two caribou—but no moose. Several times Rudy attempted to engage Daniel in a conversation about the work at the lake, but each time Daniel held his index finger to his mouth to signal there would be no talking.

"We came out here to hunt," he whispered.

It started to snow about an hour after the hunt began. There were a few light flakes at first, but as the morning progressed they became large and heavy, coating the pines and aspens with a thickness that reminded Rudy of powdered sugar.

The snow worked in the men's favor. It was not long before Daniel crouched and pointed to a set of tracks.

"Look. These are fresh—and definitely moose."

They followed the tracks through the forest and came to the edge of a small clearing. About two hundred feet to their left stood a female moose. A calf was fifty or sixty feet to the right.

Daniel did not raise his rifle. There was no way he could shoot the calf's mother. He knew that one in two moose don't survive the first six weeks, as they are easy prey for wolves, bears, and coyotes.

As he was about to motion to Rudy to move back, the other man ran to the center of the clearing and took aim at the female moose.

Daniel was stunned.

"*No!*" he shouted, running after Rudy. He looked to his left, dropping his rifle along the way. The cow was running straight toward them!

* * * *

The snow was coming down so hard by the time Colin parked Rudy's car next to Daniel's truck that the windshield wipers were caked and barely able to move under the weight.

"Where do you suppose they are?" Elaina asked.

"Shouldn't be too hard to find them in this snow," Colin said, retrieving his backpack from the rear seat after pulling out his half stick of salami. He cut off a piece with his knife. "I didn't get breakfast—want some?"

Elaine said no.

"Let's see if we can pick up their tracks," said Colin, stuffing the rest of the salami in his pocket as he took Elaina by the hand. "Stay close."

They wound their way through the trees along an animal trail for about ten minutes before hearing a gunshot. Colin yelled, "This way! I don't think they're too far."

As they drew nearer to where Colin believed the gunshot had originated, they heard voices. The voices grew louder the closer they got.

"You arsehole!" Daniel yelled. "Are you trying to get us killed? You never, *ever* get between a cow moose and her calf! What are you, a nincompoop?"

Rudy was livid. "Who you calling a nincompoop? Look, I thought you wanted us to shoot a moose. Isn't that why we came out here?"

Pushing aside a branch, Colin and Elaina emerged from the woods and found themselves looking down the rock embankment of the mountain overlooking the Yellowhead

Highway that ran to Jasper. On a clear day the view from the shale ridges running along the mountain would have been breathtaking, but this was one of those mornings when the sky seemed to blend into the whitish gray of the ground.

Daniel and Rudy did not see Colin and Elaina approach. They were too busy arguing.

"Listen you little piece of—" said Daniel, who had Rudy by the jacket collar.

Colin shouted, "*Danny, Rudy's a spy!*"

Surprised, Daniel backed away. "*What?*"

"He's a spy!" Colin said, pulling a pistol from his coat pocket as Elaina ran to Daniel's side.

"Drop it, Hutterite!" Rudy called back, "or he's dead."

Colin looked to see Rudy pointing his .38 at Daniel. He glanced at Daniel, shrugged, and tossed the pistol toward Rudy.

"Well, well, well," Rudy said. "This is my lucky day." He motioned for Colin to move closer to Daniel.

As he did so, Colin caught something out of the corner of his eye. Crouched motionless on the rock ledge just above and to the left of Rudy was the wolf!

Elaina stepped forward and said, "Rudy, what are you doing?"

"Helping Mama and Papa," he said.

"Helping Mama and Papa? *How?*"

"By making sure they survive this war, that's how. Don't you know how this world works, Sis—I mean the way it *really* works? You do me a favor and I'll do you a favor. You scratch my back and I'll scratch yours."

Colin interjected, "Who's back are you scratching, Rudy—Hitler's? Goring's? The Devil's? Whose?"

Rudy's eyes were filled with rage. "I knew you weren't a Hutterite the moment I laid eyes on you," he said. "Who the hell are you, and what is Project Habakkuk?"

Colin and Daniel exchanged quick glances.

"Well?" Rudy said. "I'm waiting."

"Go to hell," Daniel said.

"That's too bad," Rudy said to Daniel. "Here's what I'm going to do. First, I'm going to shoot your friend in the arm, like this."

Rudy squeezed the trigger, and Colin felt a burning sensation as the bullet struck just above his left biceps. Dropping to his knees, he looked over to see blood and ripped flesh. Though it hurt like hell, it appeared he was only grazed.

Daniel started to make his way to his friend's side before Rudy motioned him back with his gun.

"As I was saying, Mr. Masters—if that really is your name—first I'm going to shoot your friend in the arm," Rudy said. "Then I'm going to shoot him in the leg. Then I'm going to shoot him in the head. Then I'm going to repeat the process with you. Unless you tell me what I want to know."

Colin had an idea. He glanced up to see if the wolf was watching. It was. "Hey, Rudy!" Colin called out. "Want some salami?"

"*Wha...?*" Rudy said in disbelief, as the salami landed at his feet. Still pointing his gun at Colin, he crouched, picked it up with his free hand and straightened.

"What the hell? What the hell?"

"*Get it!*" called Colin.

Rudy saw the creature just as it lunged. He squeezed the trigger but it was too late. The wolf landed atop Rudy and ripped away his throat before his body even hit the ground.

DEATH ON THE MOUNTAIN

....

THE MOUNTAIN WAS eerily quiet for what seemed an eternity. With great effort, the wolf rose, slowly at first, but then with more assurance, and stood. Colin could see that it was injured. Blood dripped from its chest. But somehow the animal began to move down the rocks in the direction of the highway.

Colin ran to Rudy. His still-open eyes were glazed, and the blood from his throat had begun to congeal.

"Is he..." Elaina gasped. "Is he...?" She did not need to finish.

Colin shut Rudy's eyes and nodded.

Elaina cried uncontrollably, catching her breath between sobs as Daniel held her.

Colin said, "Daniel, you'd better get ahold of the park superintendent." He started down the side of the mountain. The snow had stopped and the sun was breaking through the clouds.

"Where are you going?" Daniel asked.

"To see if I can help the wolf."

"Help the wolf? Why?"

Colin turned and looked at his friend. Tears ran down Colin's cheeks.

"We'll go into Jasper and get the superintendent," Daniel said. "You do what you have to do."

Colin followed the trail of blood through the snow, toward the sound of traffic on the Yellowhead Highway hundreds of feet below. The wolf was about fifty yards ahead.

It walked with difficulty, swaying to the left and to the right. Every now and then it would stop, sit and pant, and look around. Then it would resume.

Where was it going?

Colin, too, was finding it difficult walking because the sun had emerged and most of the clouds dissipated, causing the snow to melt and make his footing slippery. More than once he fell, once landing on the part of his arm that had been shot. He tried to grab the small aspen saplings that grew here and there to keep his balance.

After some time the wolf reached a treeless ridge and laid down next to a clump that Colin couldn't quite make out until he drew closer. As Colin approached, the wolf, its two front legs stretched in front of its body, picked up its head and turned it in his direction.

"Hello, Mr. Wolf," Colin said. The wolf's ears twitched.

Colin did not move. He was overwhelmed by a feeling of helplessness, and tears formed in his eyes. He tried to fight it but could not. He had not cried like this since his father died.

The wolf watched before lowering its head and placing it atop the object that Colin could now see clearly—the bleached skull of another wolf. Behind the skull was a nearly complete skeleton. It looked as though it had been there for years.

Colin came close and kneeled in front of the wolf. He reached out his hand and touched the animal's fur. The wolf closed its eyes.

Colin closed his eyes, too, for how long he did not know. Finally he rose, removed the camp shovel attached to the bottom of his backpack, and began digging a grave. He placed the wolf and the bones in the hole and covered it with gravel.

Exhausted and dizzy from his flesh wound, he kneeled and sobbed, pounding the gravel with his fist.

Looking down from a small ridge containing a clump of pines and aspens, a wolf pup watched in silence—completely hidden from Colin's view.

INVESTIGATION
....

AS THE HIGHEST ranked government official in Jasper National Park, James Butcher, park superintendent, personally conducted the investigation into Rudy Hoff's death. His work took less than thirty minutes. After taking statements from Daniel, Elaina, and Colin—it was agreed beforehand there would be nothing said about Nazis or the Patricia Lake project—he snapped a few photos with his Kodak Brownie camera and put away his notebook.

When he was finished, he approached Daniel and said, "Say, can't help notice whenever I drive out to Pyramid that pile of lumber you have stacked out by your mill. You wouldn't be willing to part with a few of those boards, would you? Lumber's tough to come by now. The war, you know."

Butcher, a large man with bushy gray eyebrows and scraggily gray hair that hung past his ears, took out a pipe and struck a match.

"Funny when you think about it," he said between puffs. "Here we are, surrounded by millions of trees, and finding good lumber is harder than finding a tick on a marmot. I've been wanting to build some bookcases, you see, and I'm willing to pay cash."

Butcher reached into his pants and pulled out a wallet on a chain.

Daniel held up a hand. "Put that away," he said. "Help yourself to whatever you need. No charge."

Butcher's eyes grew wide. "Really?"

"Really," Daniel said. "After all, we're both on Ottawa's payroll. Different departments, same bank."

Butcher smiled, clenched his pipe in his teeth, and said, "That's just dandy." He turned to face Elaina.

"There's really not much I can offer," he sighed, "other than my sincere condolences. It's clear death was the result of fatal wounds sustained during a wolf attack. A big one by the looks of it."

He directed his next question at Daniel, "You say the wolf has been destroyed?"

Daniel said, "Yes."

Next Butcher turned to Colin and pointed at his bandaged arm. "I'd get that looked after as soon as you can," he said.

"I will, sir," Colin said. "But really, it's not that bad. Mr. Masters just grazed me."

"Yes," Daniel said, stepping in. "I was so startled by the wolf I pulled my gun too quickly. I had no idea I would accidentally hit my friend. I will, of course, pay any and all medical charges that might be incurred."

"Fine, fine," Butcher said. "The main thing is that the wolf is gone. That'll save my ranger the trouble of tracking it down and shooting it himself. The last thing we want is a crazy wolf preying on our park visitors."

Elaina began to sob again. Daniel wrapped his arms around her and she buried her face in his coat.

"The closest undertaker is in Hinton, miss," Butcher said. "I'd be happy to give him a call when I get back to town if you'd like. He's good, but I imagine you'll want to have a closed casket ceremony."

Elaina pulled away from Daniel and nodded. "Thank you, Superintendent Butcher," she said. "That would be fine."

Daniel, Colin, and Elaina watched in silence as the park superintendent walked in the direction of the road.

Colin stared at Rudy's bloodied body and said, "Daniel, why don't you take Elaina back to the lodge? Use Rudy's car. I left the keys in it. I'll get the truck and take the body to Hinton."

He motioned for his friend to come closer and whispered, "Look, she's really upset. Why don't you see if the lodge doctor can't give her a sedative. Meantime, go through Rudy's things. Maybe there's a clue—a telephone number, name, address—that will lead to his contact.

"Okay," Daniel said.

When they were gone, Colin dug into his pack for the blanket from the German U-boat captain. He wrapped it around Rudy and carried the body through the woods to where the truck was parked.

The drive to Hinton took a little over an hour.

"What's this?" the undertaker said, after spotting the red swastika on the blanket.

"War souvenir," Colin said.

The undertaker looked at him skeptically. "You want it back?"

"No, burn it," Colin said.

"With pleasure," the undertaker said.

ARREST

....

April 26, 1942
Halifax, Nova Scotia

CAPTAIN NOAH ANDREWS bought two cartons of cigarettes and a copy of that day's *Halifax Record* on his morning walk to the naval base where HMCS *Penticton* was being readied for its next mission. He tucked the cartons under his arm and opened the newspaper, knowing it would be the last he would read for two weeks. He walked as he read, looking up every now and then to make sure he did not run into another person on the sidewalk.

A headline on page two stopped him in his tracks: *Suspected Nazi Spy Arrested In Ottawa*

He began reading:

> OTTAWA—A 32-year-old man was formally charged with espionage in Ontario Superior Court yesterday after a lengthy investigation.
>
> Lawyers for the Crown allege that Peter Krell of 1818 Gilmor Street in Centretown was arrested by Ottawa Police constables without incident and has confessed to being an undercover agent for the German Reich. Sources said Krell had been employed

as an administrative bureaucrat at the Canadian Ministry of National Defence here for the past four years.

"It should be noted that Mr. Krell's position not only allowed him access to sensitive government records but also to important Cabinet officials," said Crown Attorney Gordon Elke, who was called to the Bar in 1934. "I cannot stress the importance of Mr. Krell's apprehension enough, both for the government of Canada as well as for all the countries fighting tyranny around the world."

According to Mr. Elke, the case received a major breakthrough earlier this month due to the involvement of the Royal Canadian Mounted Police in Alberta. Mr. Elke said he was "not at liberty" to reveal details of that investigation, but this newspaper has learned that the RCMP received contact information for Mr. Krell from the Canadian military after a lengthy investigation in western Canada of a man also believed to be a spy for the German government. Military forces killed the man after a fierce gun battle, a reliable source said.

Mr. Elke said that Mr. Krell would be charged under a provision of the Officials Secrets Act of Canada. The Act prohibits the dissemination and disclosure of sensitive government information and the information of Allies, and encompasses all espionage offences.

The suspect's neighbours were surprised when informed of Mr. Krell's arrest. "He was always so quiet and kept to himself," said Mabel Campbell, *who lived across the street from Mr. Krell. "He would wave, say hello when he got his mail. But it's such a surprise. This is so shocking. Imagine, a Nazi living across the street. I hope he hangs."*

The date of Mr. Krell's next court appearance has not yet been set.

Andrews smiled, folded the newspaper and said, "Good show!" so loudly that a man walking by stopped and looked at him and asked, "Where?"

Andrews tucked the paper under his arm with the cartons of cigarettes and began to whistle as he resumed his walk to the *Penticton*, which he reached twenty minutes later.

"What's the matter with you, Lieutenant Ouellet?" he asked as he strode up the gangplank onto the deck. "It's a beautiful day—a glorious day. Why so glum?" Ouellet's facial expression reminded the captain of a man who had been sucking on a lemon.

"You know that package of smoked meat my mum sent in the mail?" Ouellet asked.

"The one you picked up at mail call yesterday?"

"Yes, that's the one, Captain."

"What about it? You were happy to receive it. You kept talking about how it was nice to have something besides navy chow for a change."

"I was happy to get it, Captain. But look."

Ouellet held out a package wrapped in brown paper that was the size of a loaf of bread. One end of the paper was in tatters.

"I don't understand," Andrews said.

"It's that rat, Captain," said Ouellet. "I don't know how it got on board, but that damn rat got into my smoked meat."

THE LANDING
....

Canadian Rockies

APRIL IN WESTERN Alberta began with a warm spell, but it did not last. On April 29, a westward blizzard swept in over the mountains from British Columbia. Temperatures dropped into the single digits, which was not unusual for the time of year, but the amount of snow that fell during an eight-day period—close to nine feet—had locals talking for years.

The snowstorm paralyzed Jasper. Both the Yellowhead Highway and the Icefields Parkway, which runs from Jasper south to Banff, were impassable for nearly two weeks. So was the rail line, meaning no train service (passenger or freight). The staff at the mountain lodge ran so low on food that it offered free beer and wine with every meal so patrons did not complain about the repetition of potatoes and beef. After three days there was no milk. After four, no more eggs and, after the eighth, no more beer, which forced the staff to substitute mixed drinks. If that weren't bad enough for lodgers, the gift shop ran out of cigarettes as well.

For the Project Habakkuk team, these were days of tedium and boredom. There was no way to get out to the work site and even if they could, it would have been impossible to cut down trees to supply the mill. So the five men spent most of their time in Colin's bungalow playing cards. Poker, gin rummy, pinochle—anything to break up the days.

Elaina was fortunate. She managed to get one of the last trains out of Jasper before the storm struck. She arranged to stop in Hinton to pick up her brother's body and return to Montreal for a private funeral. She would then return to Jasper in mid-May so she could spend a few weeks with Daniel before his assignment ended.

While he did not tell her about Project Habakkuk or his work until after the war, he did share with Elaina that he was a pilot with the Royal Canadian Air Force and was in Alberta on a special assignment for the government.

The snow ceased and the sun came out to reveal a gloriously blue Alberta sky on Friday, May 8. Everyone at the mountain lodge was ecstatic.

That same day, a team of British military investigators arrived in Jasper and spent a day interviewing Daniel and Colin at length about Rudy, and about whether Elaina should be treated as a security risk. They also shared what they had learned from the Nazi spy in Ottawa—which was that he knew nothing about their work. Assured that the project had not been compromised, the investigators returned to London to report their findings to Mountbatten.

That same week, the last of the composite sawdust panels was completed and installed on the section of ice that was designated as the airfield. With Victoria Day approaching, they cut the airfield out from the rest of the lake ice.

And then they waited—and waited. And waited.

Even though much of mid- to late May was warm—temperatures had consistently climbed into the fifties and, on one occasion, actually touched seventy degrees—the ice remained firm. It got to the point where the team, which went back to spending much of its time playing cards and reading, only went to the lake every other day.

On the final Monday in May, the twenty-fifth, the team arrived on a sunny morning to find that the ice was breaking up. A series of large ice islands had replaced the smooth lake ice of the previous week. The smaller tent had collapsed around the device used to form the panels out of sawdust, and the sawmill listed at about a fifteen-degree angle. Two days later, both had vanished.

The ice airfield, still covered by the large tent, remained intact, however. As the rest of the lake ice continued to break up into smaller pieces, the decision was made to remove the tent and try for a test landing on June 5.

"Do you still think you're up to it?" Colin asked Daniel the day before the test.

"I wouldn't have come this far if I weren't up to it," Daniel said. "I can do this. You watch. It'll work. Then you can go back to Mountbatten, start building these airfields, and turn the tide in the Atlantic."

* * * *

The next morning, Colin drove Daniel to the grass strip airfield north of Jasper where the Stinson was parked. It was shaping up to be a perfect day, with just the slightest hint of a breeze coming in from the west. Colin attached the jumper cables to the truck battery and gave Daniel, who looked out from the cockpit, the signal to start the engine. The plane coughed blue smoke before catching. Daniel climbed out to let the motor warm and make sure the flaps were in working order.

"Well, this is it," Colin said, as he accepted a cigarette and light from Daniel. "Finally, the end of the tunnel. So that we're on the same page, you want me to do two touch-and-go landings before one final landing, correct?"

"Correct. Simpson and Lord will be in the rowboat at the end of the strip. Once you do your touch-and-go, one of them will get out and mark where you land with red paint so they can test the integrity of the ice in that spot later. We don't want these airfields cracking in two out in the middle of the Atlantic."

"Understood." Daniel put on his flying helmet and goggles.

"After your second touch-and-go they'll give you the signal to land," Colin continued. "Once you're down and the plane is secure, they'll help you jack it up and put the pontoons on so you'll be able to take off from the lake itself."

The two had discussed equipping the plane with pontoons beforehand but decided against the plan because Daniel was not sure how much control he would have.

At that, Daniel gave the thumbs-up sign and climbed into the cockpit. Before he got his body all the way inside, Colin put his hand on Daniel's shoulder and pulled him back. He reached inside the breast pocket of his work shirt and handed his friend a small pink rose.

"Here, this is from Elaina. She knows you're doing something important today and she picked it this morning while you were in the bath to give to you. She said it's a wild rose. They're supposed to bring luck."

* * * *

Daniel waited twenty minutes before taking off, knowing that would give Colin enough time to get to the lake to witness the first touch-and-go landing. It went perfectly, as did the second and, finally, the landing. After all the measurements were taken, Simpson and Lord rowed back to the shore with Daniel to meet Colin and McIntosh, who had taken pictures and given the film to Colin to have developed when he made out his report of the test.

"Beautiful," Colin said, as he helped pull the boat ashore. "How was it from your perspective?" he asked Daniel.

"Smooth as a baby's butt," Daniel said, clenching a cigar in his mouth. He turned to McIntosh and said, "Did you bring it?"

"Indeed I did," McIntosh said, pointing to a bottle of champagne buried in the remnants of a small snow bank in the trees.

"Well, don't just stand there, open it! Let's celebrate. We'll win this damned war yet."

UNDERMINED
....

August 19, 1942
London, England

"I HAVE TO say, Commander Williams, this is one of the most fascinating reports I've read in quite some time. More tea?"

Newly promoted Vice Admiral Lord Louis Mountbatten rose from his chair and motioned to his aide to pour before Colin could say that he'd had enough. What Colin really wanted to do was use the bathroom. *How could Mountbatten, who had had two more cups of tea than he, not want to use the bathroom too,* Colin wondered.

His mind flashed back to the encounter with Rudy on the side of the mountain back in April. He still had dreams about the wolf's violent lunge and ultimate death.

"Fascinating is one way to describe it," Colin said, shifting uncomfortably in his chair.

"What do you think, Geoff?" Mountbatten asked the other man he had called to the morning meeting at his office, Geoffrey Pyke, Project Habakkuk's scientific adviser.

"I am very encouraged by your test, Commander," Pyke answered. "Very encouraged. I just want to make that perfectly clear at the onset. However—and I direct this statement to you, Vice Admiral—I believe it also points to a weakness, should we continue to pursue this course."

A weakness? Colin asked himself. *What does he mean by that?*

Mountbatten, too, did not understand.

"A weakness? What the devil do you mean? The test itself was quite successful. I'm no scientist, but I certainly can see that." He patted Colin on the back as he passed by. "If I were a teacher, I would give it an A—a solid A."

"Yes, yes, yes," Pyke said, holding his hands together. "I did not say the test was not successful. I merely said that it points out a weakness."

"Could you explain, Mr. Pyke?" Colin asked.

"Certainly," Pyke said, rising and opening the binder on the table before him. "Your report says here that the integrity of the composite-clad ice field remained until July 28."

"Yes..."

"At which time it began—to use your words—quote, to get mushy and break apart with pressure, unquote. Now, according to my calculations that would have been a period of eight weeks."

"So?" Mountbatten said.

"So," Pyke continued, his voice much more animated, "imagine a much larger ice field in much harsher conditions after that period. The Atlantic Ocean is not Patricia Lake, gentlemen. Have you ever been in the middle of the ocean during a storm?"

"Mr. Pyke, you're talking to two officers of the Royal Navy," Mountbatten scolded him. "We are not freshmen at our first day of university. Come to your point."

"Yes, yes, yes," Pyke said, removing his glasses. "I'm terribly sorry, Vice Admiral. The point is that this experiment shows to me that a simple airfield built of ice will not work. It will degrade too quickly due to the forces exerted by the ocean. We'll end up losing every plane—and every sailor—on board once the ice begins to weaken. It simply will not be strong enough."

"That's horseshit," Colin blurted before catching himself and adding, "begging your pardon, sir."

Mountbatten lit a cigarette and offered one to Colin and Pyke, both of whom accepted. "I would have phrased it differently, Commander," he said, "but I was thinking the same thing. Explain yourself, Geoff. You haven't steered me wrong yet."

A smile appeared on Pyke's face as he sat down.

"The problem here is that the majority of the substance in the Patricia Lake airfield was ice. And even though the top and, what, about a foot of the sides"—Pyke stopped to thumb back through the report—"yes, about a foot was covered with the composite material, there was no material on the bottom. And that is obviously where the melting and subsequent degradation occurred."

Colin said, "We knew even before arriving that we wouldn't be covering the bottom of our prototype. Much of the work that was done—I'd estimate at least ninety percent—was completed during temperatures well below freezing. We didn't cut out the section we were working on from the rest of the lake ice until well into May. Besides, even if we were able to get to the underside and somehow attach panels to it, there's no way our composite material would have lasted."

"My point exactly, Commander Williams," Pyke said.

"So are you saying all this work and time was for nothing?" Mountbatten wanted to know.

"Not at all, sir," Pyke said. "Commander Williams has done an excellent job in laying the groundwork for the next phase."

"The next phase?" Colin and Mountbatten asked in unison.

"Yes, rather than constructing ice airfields, I've been working on a plan to build actual aircraft carriers out of

Pykrete. These would not be towed to strategic places within The Pit, as Commander Williams initially proposed, but would be actual, self-contained and self-propelled fighting vessels."

"That's *ludicrous!*" said Colin, rising. "Aircraft carriers made of ice?"

"Here, here," Mountbatten said. "I would like to hear Mr. Pyke out. Continue." Another smile appeared on Pyke's face, for he knew he had captured Mountbatten's attention. Now all that was left was closing the sales job, something he had success with many times previously.

"I've done some calculations," Pyke said, producing several pages of graph paper from a file folder near the binder. "I estimate the weight of a completed aircraft carrier built of Pykrete will be approximately one million to two million tons. The vessel will be externally insulated and fitted with a refrigeration plant, thereby ensuring its integrity for many days of service, and, as I mentioned, would be self-propelled."

"One to two million tons," said Mountbatten. "That's not a small vessel."

"No, Vice Admiral," Pyke said. "It would be slightly smaller than a modern-day aircraft carrier. While I don't envision it requiring the same superstructure, it would be big enough to accommodate, say, twenty-five aircraft, which would be stored below decks, an elevator system, steam catapult launch system, etcetera."

"And when could such a vessel be placed into operation, Mr. Pyke?"

It was as though Pyke had rehearsed his answers to each of Mountbatten's questions, for he did not miss a beat.

"I propose that we—*I*—return to Patricia Lake this fall and construct a small, working prototype of my proposal." He looked up at Colin. "Building on Commander Williams' work, of course. Assuming the refrigeration system is adequate to maintain the integrity of the Pykrete, I could see construction of the first Pykrete carrier beginning late next year, which would mean it could be ready for service by the spring of 1946."

"Sir," said Colin, "that's nearly three and a half years. The Nazis will have a field day with our merchant ships, not to mention our navy, between now and then. What I've shown—what my team's shown—is that we could have ice airfields ready for use within six months. We could give our boys out there in The Pit immediate relief. Think of the ships we'll save—the *lives* we'll save."

Mountbatten returned to his seat, put out his cigarette, and consumed the rest of the tea in his cup. He did not say anything at first, but then looked at his watch.

"Gentlemen, I need some time to think about this. I'll let you know how we'll proceed within twenty-four hours. Dismissed."

Colin leaned over the table, picked up his binder and his hat, saluted, and left the room. Although he was disappointed at the prospect of not getting an answer, he was grateful to finally be able to use the bathroom.

* * * *

Colin was made aware of Mountbatten's decision while having dinner alone in the hotel restaurant where he was staying. A British Navy lieutenant carrying a satchel appeared at his table and said, "Commander Williams? I was asked to deliver a message from the Admiralty."

Colin motioned the lieutenant to take a seat.

"I shan't be long," the officer said, handing Colin an envelope. "I was asked to give this to you to read. When you are finished, you are to return the paper to me. Security protocol. You understand."

"Certainly, Lieutenant," said Colin, opening the envelope. It was from Mountbatten. He began reading:

Commander Williams:

After careful consideration, I have decided Mr. Pyke's proposal bears further investigation. That is how we will proceed.

You are to report to the captain, HMS Illustrious at zero eight hundred on the eleventh of the month in Portsmouth for a six-month special assignment to identify operational efficiencies for the Royal Canadian Navy. Following that you will receive command of your own ship. Congratulations.

In the Service of the King,

—Vice Admiral Louis Mountbatten

Colin returned the paper to the lieutenant, who rose, saluted, and left.

When he was alone, Colin took a sip from his whiskey and water and tried to digest what he had just read. Pyke had obviously been more convincing. *But how could the vice admiral not see the necessity to bring immediate relief to the Allied convoys?* he thought. *How could Mountbatten not grasp the fact that untold lives would be lost? Or did Mountbatten have a better understanding of the situation and it was he—Colin—whose logic was flawed?*

He wished he had the answer.

What he did not know—what he would never learn—was that after the meeting that morning, Pyke arranged for a block of his new and improved Pykrete to be brought to headquarters for a demonstration. On one side of a long table he placed a regular block of ice. On the other, a block strengthened with Pykrete.

He fired a pistol at the block of ice. It shattered. He did the same with the ice containing Pykrete. The block remained intact, with the bullet firmly embedded in the substance.

Mountbatten made his decision then and there.

Draining his drink, Colin thought about the second part of the message: that he was to be assigned to the *Illustrious*. As far as he knew, he would be the only Canadian officer aboard the British carrier, one of the most advanced in the Allied fleet. He knew he would be able to learn a lot in his time there—and then to be given command of his own ship, well, that was beyond anything he had ever hoped or imagined.

Still, his mind kept going back to the Habakkuk Project.

Would the team's work bear fruit, or was it all for nothing? Would it help the Allies win the Battle of the Atlantic?

His thoughts were interrupted by the waiter, who appeared from a side room. "Would you care for another drink, sir?" he asked.

"Make it a double," answered Colin.

* * * *

Geoffrey Pyke went to Patricia Lake in early 1943 and successfully built a working model of his creation.

Further work on the project, however, was suspended in November that year after a cost analysis determined that a single Pykrete-constructed aircraft carrier would cost nearly four times more than a conventionally built ship, primarily because of the precious steel required to build the superstructure.

As the months wore on, the Allies, largely due to the military might of the United States and advancements including radar, sonar, and longer-range aircraft, eventually overwhelmed the German U-boats operating in the Atlantic.

To this day, Project Habakkuk remains little more than an interesting historical footnote.

WEDDING DAY
....

September 22, 1945
Canadian Rockies

ELAINA AND DANIEL chose the Big Mountain Lake Lodge as the site of their wedding. When Daniel proposed, in the springtime, no one was sure when the war in Europe would be over, but they knew it would be soon, as the American and Russian armies were at Berlin's door. To be on the safe side, they chose a date in late September.

The couple wanted an outdoor wedding, on the grass overlooking the lake at the lodge where they fell in love. It would be a small affair. The bride and groom, best man, and maid of honor.

Daniel asked Colin to be his best man. Elaina asked her closest friend from Montreal, a beautiful blonde named Glenda, to serve as maid of honor.

Daniel was discharged from the air force in August, a month before the ceremony. Colin, however, still had six months before his command was up; but he had the time, so he took the train from Halifax. He left early so he could enjoy the trip, and it reminded him of all those years ago when he'd made the journey with his father.

Colin arrived on a Friday morning, the day before the

ceremony. Stepping off the train, he was immediately struck by how little the town of Jasper had changed since he had last seen it—with one exception. With the war over, tourism was up dramatically.

Colin had never seen so many people there—and happy people at that.

The mountain lodge had not changed either—with the exception of a new main building that was nearly twice as large as the previous one.

Daniel and Colin rose early on the day of the wedding so they could have breakfast and drive out to Patricia Lake for a few hours of fishing before the two o'clock ceremony.

At breakfast, Daniel handed his friend a long cardboard box.

"Elaina and I wanted to give you the perfect gift for being our best man," Daniel said. "We really racked our brains, but I think we succeeded. Open it."

Inside was a Wright & McGill fly rod in a matching case—nearly identical to the one Colin's father had given him years before. He was speechless.

"Well?" Daniel asked.

"I... I don't know what to say. Other than thank you. I'm absolutely stunned."

"You've always had my back, Colin. You had it the day I was sucked down the whirlpool. You had it the day the boat capsized on Patricia Lake. And you had it that day with Rudy. You're the best kind of friend there is."

Colin felt tears forming and turned his head so Daniel could not see. "You realize what's going to happen now, don't you?" he said.

"No, what?" Daniel said.

"I'm going to out-fish you again, that's what."

As the two men drove to Patricia Lake, Colin could not help

noticing how beautiful the green and the gold of the pines and the aspens were in the sunlight.

September in the Canadian Rockies is anything but predictable. There are years when the snow begins the first week of September and does not stop until the following June. But this particular September was the warmest, sunniest, and driest anyone could remember in the last twenty years. No one was happier than Daniel and Elaina, because it meant that the wedding ceremony would not have to move indoors.

"So what do you think you'll do once you get out of the navy?" asked Daniel, breaking the silence as they drove.

"Damned good question. I thought about re-upping for another four years. But I got a cable from Alan Simpson—you remember him, don't you?—a few weeks ago, wondering if I'd be interested in becoming a part owner in his company. He's come up with a way to make furniture out of compressed sawdust."

"Like those panels for the airfield?"

"Close. What he's done is mixed sawdust with glue, compressed it, and dried it in an oven. Then he puts a wood veneer over the pieces. He sent me plans for bedroom furniture but says we can make other stuff. What's interesting is that he wants to sell the furniture disassembled. Everything would come in a box and you'd screw it together. He thinks there is going to be a huge market in the next few years with all the soldiers coming home. They'll want to get married and start families. They'll be needing cars and houses and..."

"And furniture to put in the houses," said Daniel. "Makes a lot of sense."

"And you?" Colin asked. "Are you giving up flying?"

"Just until the business gets on its feet," he said.

Elaina and Daniel had decided Jasper was the perfect place to settle down and begin a family. They were in the process of renting a building just off the main street and opening an art gallery to cater to the tourists.

"Eventually what I'd like to do is buy a little pontoon plane and fly rich guys like you up to the fishing camps," Daniel said.

They reached the lake. It still looked like Colin remembered. To the north, Pyramid Mountain was as magnificent as it had looked on his first visit. To the south, Whistler's Peak, its top clear of snow, was barely visible. But rising in the west was Cairngorm in all its spectacular glory.

Colin got out of the car and closed his eyes. For an instant it was the winter of 1942 and he could see the sawmill and tents off in the distance. A blanket of white had replaced the calm blue water that was really before him.

Daniel's voice interrupted the daydream. "Let's fish," he said.

* * * *

Colin looked handsome in his dark blue Royal Canadian Navy dress uniform, Elaina whispered as the wedding photographer snapped pictures following the ceremony.

"What do you think of Glenda?" she asked out of the corner of her mouth.

"She's pretty," Colin admitted.

He did not tell Elaina that he did not find himself attracted to Glenda, however. He knew she would be disappointed; Daniel had told him Elaina hoped to play matchmaker.

The wedding ceremony itself was brief. There was the exchange of vows, a reading of the "Love is patient, love is kind" passage from the Bible, and a short message from the minister who had come from town to perform the marriage.

Afterward, as wedding pictures were being taken, Colin watched with amusement as a little girl with pigtails crept close to check out the wedding party. He first saw the girl—he guessed she was about five—as he was about to hand the ring to Daniel. She ran from the main lodge building to a nearby tree and leaned out every now and then to watch.

As the photographer took pictures of Elaina and the maid of honor, a waitress arrived with a platter containing four glasses of champagne.

After giving the toast, Colin told Daniel he was going to walk to the edge of the lake to smoke a cigarette and that he would return shortly. As he did so he became aware that he was being followed. He turned quickly. It was the little girl.

"Hey, are you spying on me?" Colin said, catching the girl by the arm. He was joking.

The child's eyes grew wide and her mouth dropped open in surprise.

"Gee willikers, no, mister," she said. "I promise I wasn't. It's just that I've never, ever seen a wedding before. I asked my mamma—she works here—and she said I could look if I didn't bother anyone. Honest, mister."

Colin let go of the girl's arm and knelt on the grass before her. He thought she was going to cry.

"Hey, it's okay. I was just kidding. Say, what's your name?"

"Heidi," she answered.

Colin smiled. "That's a beautiful name. A beautiful name for a beautiful little girl."

Heidi smiled. "I'm named after a submarine." Colin laughed.

"A submarine? You don't say."

"Gee willikers, mister, it's true. I promise."

"Oh, I have no doubt." *Children have such wonderful imaginations*, he thought.

Colin stuck out his hand. "I'm Commander Williams," he said. "Nice to meet you, Heidi."

They shook hands.

"Were you in the war?" the girl asked.

"I sure was. On a ship. And guess what? I saw a submarine. In fact, one even saved my life."

Heidi's eyes brightened. "Gee willikers, I wonder if you saw the one I was named after."

"You never know, Heidi, I might have."

"My daddy was in the war. He was underground."

Underground? Colin said to himself. *Does she mean he was in the Underground?* Just then he heard a female voice with a European accent. "Heidi, how many times I tell you to not disturb guests?"

Colin stood up and turned to see a slender blonde woman who was about his height, with the most beautiful blue eyes he had ever seen. She wore a tan skirt and a pale blue blouse—the uniform of the mountain lodge staff—on which was pinned a gold nametag that read "Doris." She carried a tray with empty wine glasses.

"Oh, she's not bothering me at all, ma'am," Colin said. "In fact, we were just starting to become friends. She was just starting to tell me about her father. Was he in the underground movement?"

The faint smile that had been on the woman's lips disappeared. "Yes, he was in Polish Underground. He was shot by the Nazis two years ago."

After a moment of awkward silence, Colin held out his hand. "I'm Commander Colin Williams, Royal Canadian Navy."

"Doris," she said, setting down her tray. "Doris Kowalski." They shook hands.

"I wouldn't have guessed Doris, judging by your accent."

"My Christian name is Dorota. I use Doris ever since coming to Canada."

Colin found himself drawn to the woman in a way he could not understand. "Will you have a cigarette with me by the lake?" he asked.

"I not smoke."

"You don't have to."

"Manager discourages staff from, how you say, intermingling with guests?"

"Yes, but I happen to know that the lodge's slogan is 'Your happiness is our goal.' At least that's what it says on the napkins and the matchbook covers. So make me happy. Keep me company for a few minutes."

There was a perplexed look on her face before she answered, "I suppose...for few minutes." Looking at her daughter, she added, "Come, Heidi, take Mama's hand."

Heidi came between her mother and Colin and grasped her mother's hand. She then reached up and took Colin's hand.

"Hey, Mama, maybe you and Commander Williams can get married." Doris and Colin laughed a nervous laugh.

"Children," she said. Hoping to cover her embarrassment, she asked, "Is that your friend who today marries?"

"Yes, my best friend, Daniel. And the woman in white is his wife, Elaina."

"She is beautiful and he, handsome," Doris said.

"Gee willikers, Mama, I think Commander Williams is handsomer," Heidi said, looking up at her mother. "Don't you think so too?"

Doris was silent. Colin could see that she was blushing. "Well, don't you, Mama?" Heidi asked again.

"Yes, dear. Commander Williams is handsome, too."

Colin was so lost in his thoughts that he failed to see the gopher hole before him.

One moment he was standing, the next he was catching himself from falling.

"Ouch!" he cried, once he had regained his balance. He bent down to feel his right ankle, which throbbed with pain. "Ow, I hope I didn't sprain it."

"Heidi, run up to kitchen of lodge," Doris said. "Use back

door. Tell Chef you need bag of ice. Then bring it down to Mama. Hurry, so we get swelling down."

Heidi ran up the hill.

Doris said, "Here, lean on me." She pointed with her chin to one of the log benches at the edge of the lake. "We seat you there."

When they reached the bench, Doris had Colin sit and raise his right leg. She carefully untied his shoe and removed his sock.

"I'm afraid it's already swelling," she said, gently rubbing the side of his foot.

Colin said, "Was that a gopher hole?"

"Yes, there are many gopher holes in lawn. They say it's been this way since wolves leave. Chef says gophers going to take over one day."

They laughed. Heidi returned with a towel that was partly filled with ice.

"Oh, child," Doris said, wrapping the towel around Colin's ankle. "You lost half the ice while you run."

"Gee willikers, Mama, I'm sorry."

Doris kissed her softly on the head and said, "It okay, but go back up and get more. And be more careful."

Doris and Colin watched as Heidi ran back toward the main lodge. "You're quite lucky to have her," Colin said.

"More than you know," she said in a voice that was barely audible. "And how about you, Commander, you have children?"

"Not married. And please, call me Colin."

Doris nodded in the direction of the wedding party. "Oh, so she is girlfriend?" A breeze blew across the lawn, filling the air with dandelion seeds.

"No, she is definitely not girlfriend, although the bride would certainly like to change that."

"But she so pretty." Doris moved the towel of ice lower.

"Yes, but I just don't feel the chemistry," said Colin.

"Chemistry? What is chemistry?"

"You know, the spark—electricity. If there's no spark—"

"Ah, spark," she interrupted. "I understand."

The breeze blew again.

"Oh, Colin, dandelions are all over you now," said Doris, leaning forward to pick a seed off his hair. As she moved, she shocked his ear with a static electric charge.

Neither person spoke. Instead, they looked at each other and smiled.

"You sit back, Commander Colin Williams," Doris said when Heidi returned with more ice, "and I take care of you."

Colin closed his eyes.

"I'd like that, Doris. I'd like it a lot."

As he felt the sun against his face, Colin heard a train whistle off in the distance. A few moments later he heard a wolf howl, and realized the world was finally at peace. And so was he.

᷈

EPILOGUE

....

AFTER HIS SURRENDER, Wolfgang Eicher was interrogated for four weeks in England.

He revealed nothing to the Allies about electroboat technology. In early June 1942 he was transferred to Camp 30, a POW camp in Bowmanville, Ontario, Canada. There, he spent the remainder of the war.

Eicher had it much better than most German prisoners. Of all the German POW camps, Camp 30, which housed officers, had a reputation for being the most luxurious. It had athletic fields, an indoor swimming pool, a stage (Eicher starred as Prospero in the production of William Shakespeare's "The Tempest"), a tennis court and a small zoo.

Best of all, prisoners were allowed to leave the grounds for the day provided they gave their word that they would return. Because honor was so important to a German officer, there was not one instance where a prisoner failed to return for nightly roll call.

Upon his release, Eicher returned to Germany. He found employment at an upstart auto manufacturer as a line worker. The company grew rapidly, and Eicher rose to the rank of managing director/production before retiring in 1965 as a multi-millionaire.

In 1950, about three years after returning to Germany, he fell in love with a woman twenty years his junior and fathered two boys and a girl. A well-respected member of the community, Eicher founded the Lilly Theatre in Tappenbeck, and even performed once before the chancellor of West Germany.

* * * *

Citing his exemplary record as a convoy commander in the Atlantic, the Royal Canadian Navy promoted Captain Noah Andrews to vice admiral on January 12, 1944. Andrews' last major combat mission was at the Battle of Normandy. Afterwards, he rejoined Mountbatten's staff and served the remainder of the war in the Pacific Theater. He played a key role in aiding Mountbatten, who Churchill had appointed as Supreme Allied Commander of South East Asia Command, in the recapture of Burma. Andrews retired from the Navy in 1946 and moved to Prince Edward Island, where he and his wife operated a commercial potato farm.

* * * *

A U.S. Navy research crew charged with mapping the bottom of the Atlantic Ocean came across the wreckage of the UX-1 in July 1991, just south of an area known as the Charlie-Gibbs Fracture Zone. At first the researchers had no idea what they had discovered and, after receiving orders from the command center, photographed the site. Using those photos, taken at a depth of 750 meters, researchers in Annapolis, Maryland, combed through all classified and declassified war files seized from the German Navy and concluded that not only was it the mythical ghost sub referred to in many logs by convoy captains, but that the vessel also served as the prototype for what became the Type XXI U-boat.

The Germans introduced the Type XXI U-boat toward the end of the war, but only four went into active service. None of the boats sank a ship.

The U.S. Navy took possession of two of the subs after the war. The subs formed the foundation of the modern American submarine program.

* * * *

After a short and highly publicized trial, a jury found Peter Krell guilty of espionage and numerous related charges and sentenced him to twenty years of hard labor at Kingston Penitentiary. Krell never finished his term. A fellow prisoner, whose brother was an infantryman killed during the raid on the French port of Dieppe early in the war, strangled Krell while he was sleeping. When asked why he had killed Krell, the prisoner, a convicted murderer, commented, "I was just doing my part to help win the war."

* * * *

History credits Germany's Fritz-Julius Lemp with the first U-boat sinking of World War II. On September 3, 1939, Lemp's U-30, a Type VII submarine, torpedoed the British liner SS *Athenia* with 1,400 passengers aboard while she was on her way from Liverpool to Montreal. One hundred and twelve people, including twenty-eight Americans, died as a result. Lemp told the German naval command he thought the *Athenia* was a warship because she was zigzagging and that the sinking was a mistake.

A malfunctioning radio is at the heart of the reason that there is no record of the *Anka's* sinking, which occurred two days before the *Athenia* was struck. Because the *Anka* was unable to report what had occurred, coupled with the destruction of the Port of Gdynia, Poland's shipping office, by German bombers on September 1, 1939, critical records of the *Anka's* existence were lost to time.

* * * *

Two years after they were married, Daniel and a very pregnant Elaina Masters visited Munich, Germany, to see what they could learn about Elaina's parents. While the German government offered little assistance, they were able to determine from records at the temple where Elaina's parents worshipped that the Hoffmans were shipped to a concentration camp in 1939 and died there of typhoid.

* * * *

Karl Donitz, Wolfgang Eicher's friend and head of the Nazi U-boat program, replaced Grand Admiral Erich Raeder as commander-in-chief of the German Navy in January 1943. He remained loyal to Hitler during the remainder of the war and, in accordance with Hitler's last will and testament, was named the leader of Germany on April 30, 1945, following Hitler's suicide. A week later he ordered the surrender of Germany, ending one of the bloodiest periods in all of human history.

Donitz was among those who stood trial at Nuremberg. He was found guilty of war crimes and sentenced to ten years in prison. Following his release, he led a quiet life near Hamburg, Germany. He died in 1980.

* * * *

Colin Williams and Dorota Kowalski were married on Saturday, September 14, 1946, at the mountain lodge in Jasper where they met. They had planned an outdoor wedding but because it snowed six inches that day the ceremony took place in front of the stone fireplace in the main lodge.

At the time, Colin was vice president of production for Instant Furniture, a new company that had formed that summer, which was based in Toronto. The company grew so quickly that by the summer of 1948 it opened a U.S. operation in Seattle; Colin became president of the American subsidiary. He sold his share in the company for $25 million in 1961 and took early retirement.

In addition to Heidi, the Williams' had twin boys—Danny and Mark. They both attended the U.S. Naval Academy and served as officers aboard nuclear submarines during the Cold War.

ABOUT THE AUTHOR

CHAZ OSBURN IS a dual U.S.-Canadian citizen who spent more than a quarter of a century as an award-winning journalist before starting his own communications consultancy. A native of Detroit and a lifelong student of history, Osburn got the idea for *At the Wolf's Door* after learning of Project Habakkuk, Great Britain's top-secret plan to build a warship made of ice, during a visit to Lake Patricia in the Canadian Rockies in 2008. Osburn has written one other historical fiction novel, *Incident at Jonesborough*. You can contact Chaz at *author@chazosburn.com*.

www.hellgatepress.com

Made in the USA
Lexington, KY
21 March 2019